ELEGY OF A FRAGMENTED VINEYARD

PALADINS OF THE HARVEST: BOOK ONE

KADEN LOVE

SVETLING PRESS

CONTENTS

For my younger brother Myka, the DM who inspired me to write a story
of my own.
You were only 14 years old, and you changed my life.
I hope you enjoy this. I love you, dude.

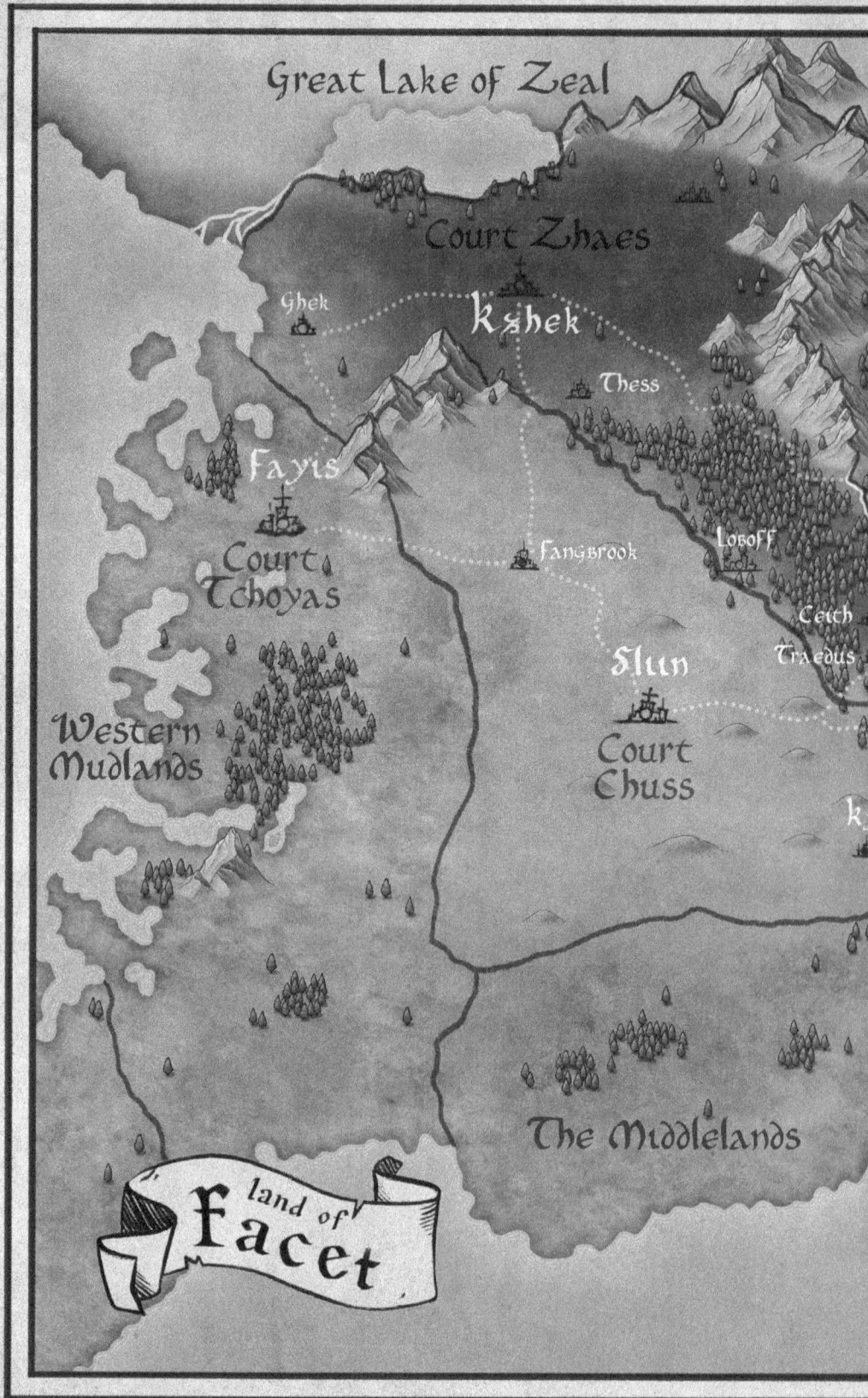

Great Lake of Zeal

Court Zhaes

Ghek

Kshek

Thess

Fayis

Court
Tchoyas

Fangbrook

Loboff

Ceith

Traedus

Slun

Western
Mudlands

Court
Chuss

k

The Middlelands

land of
Facet

GLOSSARY

Beastling: Endowers that can speak with animals.

Canton: A building and institution led by a Thane under their respective responsibility.

Caser: High administrator that serves alongside the Thanes of a Court to serve the Krall and populus. Counted among the nobility.

Cloven Gleff: Center of Facet's mining. Site of export for Zhaes bronze, among other metals. Located near Kzhek.

Court: One of the six fiefdoms that make up the continent of Facet.

- Court Sleff

  ○ Banner: Yellow banner with a black spinerat

  ○ Salute: Place the heels of the palms on the temples and extend the fingers upward

  ○ Ideal: *Pious is the Giver*

  ○ Values: Humility, meekness

  ○ Scripture: The Tome of the Meek

  ○ God: Heitt

- Court Tchoyas

- Banner Blue putle on a light gray banner

- Salute: Interwoven fingers covering the mouth

- Ideal: *Steadfast is the Honor*

- Values: Loyalty, honor

- Scripture: The Tome of Piety

- God: Klen

- Court Zhaes

  - Banner: Bronze Kaesan on a dark gray banner

  - Salute: Steepled fingers over the face, pointing upwards

  - Ideal: *Whole is the Holy*

  - Values: Obedience, perfection

  - Scripture: The Tome of Measure

  - God: Laeih

- Court Gruth

  - Banner: Green leviathan eel on a teal banner

  - Salute: Elbows against the torso, bent at ninety degrees, fists clenched, as if bracing for a strike to the abdomen

  - Ideal: *Firm is the foundation*

  - Values: Endurance, strength

- Scripture: The Tome of Stability

- God: Deilf

- Court Chuss

  - Banner: Crimson ghete on a white banner

  - Salute: Hands creating a circle and placed over the center of the chest

  - Ideal: *Care is the creed*

  - Values: Love, charity

  - Scripture: The Tome of Charity

  - God: Cheric

- Court Priess

  - Banner: White land eel on a maroon banner

  - Salute: Right ear cupped as if trying to hear, left arm raised in a fist

  - Ideal: Mighty is the free

  - Values: Pride, liberation

  - Export: textiles

  - No scripture or god

Currency:

- Base coin: Petiir

- 12 Zhon = 1 Petiir

- 10 Petiir = 1 Jame

- 15 Jame = 1 Maeth

Endower: Children born with an additional intestine, granting them a "god-sent" ability. The cardinal sign is a second umbilical cord at birth. Reports state that many do not survive past their first year of life. Four of the six Courts harvest these organs to be grafted into an adult Endowed.

Endowed: An individual who has received a graft from an Endower in order to gain their congenital ability.

Eurythrin: Endowers that can halt blood flow, regenerate, and help heal.

Facet: Continent composed of six Courts. Its boundaries do not include the Middlelands or nations beyond the northern cliffs.

Feelman: Endower that can read people's emotions by identifying their bodily functions, correctly predict their next move, and almost read their mind.

Foreteller: Endowers that can analyze possibilities to predict the future.

Ghete: Reptilian steeds that share are described as "a large cat with green scales and no ears."

Gorger: Endower increased growth, including of the mind and muscle.

Harmony Allegiant: Coalition of political opposers to harvesting.

Harvest: The medical process of removing an Endowed intestine from an Endower at birth. This intestine will then be grafted into an adult, making them an Endowed.

The Induction: The year in which harvesting was implemented, five years after the Year of Manifest - C.E. 327.

Kaesan: Illusive beasts said to dwell in caves. Their depiction can be seen on the Zhaes banner. They are described as having large, muscular bodies capable of standing on their hind legs. Their abdomen is bare of fur and reaches only to the neck of their ferocious elk-like head topped with large antlers. Myth tells that they are sent to cleanse the plain of humankind from sin through violent purging.

Krall: Monarch of a Court.

The Pact of Province: The agreement upon which harvesting was accepted.

Patriarchy of Scholars: A Scholarly society that is not deterred by Court boundaries. They are said to promote unity and societal growth, though they are very exclusive and do not reveal their works to those outside of their ranks.

Putle: Amphibious creatures, similar to bipedal toads, with large rib cages and sizable nostrils. Their skins are often harvested for water repellent wear.

Seasons:

- Thaust - thawing of ice, second to third month of a year

- Vestning - blooming of buds, fourth to fifth month of a year

- Letur - peak of seasonal heat, sixth to seventh month of a year

- Ousell - death of the leaves, eighth to ninth month of a year

- Holdae - transition from warmth to cold, end of harvest, tenth to eleventh month of a year

- Zeemer - freezing of the land, final month of a year to the first month of the new year

Shiftling: Endower that can manipulate their vocal cords to match any other person's voice, and can shift skin pigments like a chameleon.

Thane: An elect individual that serves over a specific office of a Court. The only office higher than a Thane is that of a Court's Krall. Members of the nobility.

- Offices include the Thanes of:

  - Utilities: Technological advancements, engineering

  - Veneration: Religious practices and law

  - Haleness: Medicinal practice and health promotion

  - Diplomacy: Diplomatic matters with foreign Courts

  - Scholarship: Represent the Patriarchy of Scholars and all scholarly pursuits

  - Agriculture: Livestock, metals, crops, and all other natural materials

  - Progress: Politics, anthropology, and innovation

  - Benefaction: Harvesting and Endowed in Courts that permit the process. Courts who oppose harvesting manage Endower growth, usage, and study.

Year of Manifest: The year credited for the first Endower birth - C.E. 322

Dramatis Personae

Aerhee Kleeh: Caser of Court Zhaes
Bashin: Zhaes Feelman inquisitor

Blenn: Tchoyas Endower Foreteller. Wears a mask with an open mouth and a tongue to each side, tracing up to the outer aspect of each eye hole

Calss Gromm: Zhaes Thane of Scholarship, member of the Patriarchy of Scholars

Coln Tywing: Zhaes Thane of Haleness

Colrig Fesst: Sleffman, founder of the Harmony Allegiant

Crowl: Tchoyas Endower Feelman. Wears a mask of a mink.

Derlik: Aerhee's father.

Dronn: Tchoyas Endower Beastling. Wears a mask of a whistling man.

Faeth: Aerhee's mother.

Felta Zhil: Former Zhaes Caser, Aerhee's predecessor

Fennta Trhet: Tchoyas Thane of Progress, eldest granddaughter of Krall Trhet

Fheo: Scribe to Caser Aerhee Kleeh

Fortik Gett: Gruth Thane of Utilities

Fuih Lettre: Zhaes Thane of Veneration

Garen Renss: Chuss Thane of Haleness

Ghael: Zhaes Shiftling

Golma: Tchoyas Endower Beastling. Wears a mask of a hawk

Gorrhin Vheen: Krall of Court Zhaes

Hir Stolk: Son of Phenmir

Horrah: Alchemical healer that often accompanies Runith's party of Beastlings

Kaela: Tchoyas Endower Shiftling. Wears a mask of a serval.

Kollra Holmn: Tchoyas Thane of Benefaction

Kuid Trhet: Krall of Court Tchoyas

Mehnrin Diphlek: Krall of Court Chuss

Meira Stolk: Phenmir's wife

Phenmir Stolk: Chuss surgeon, proficient in harvesting.

Port Kamen: Sleff scout, close associate of Colrig

Roill Lehket: Tchoyas Thane of Veneration

Royss Belik: Zhaes Thane of Agriculture

Runith: Head of the Zhaes Beastling corp

Semi Ershif: Gruth Shiftling

Shaera: Tchoyas Beastling. Wears a mask of a quail.

Sheath Leisa: Zhaes Thane of Diplomacy

Taeih: Zhaes Gorger, distant relative of Thane Royss Belik.

Voln Zertef: Tchoyas Endower Shiftling. Wears a mask of a wolf.

Yetrik Kloff: Gruth scribe that works close beside Thane Fortik Gett

Zeir Kleeh: Aerhee's husband

"Believe it or not, we all want what's best. The root o' the world's ills is that no one can agree on what it is."

—— **Joe Abercrombie,** A Little Hatred

CHAPTER ONE

CARE IS THE CREED

YEAR 332 IN THE CLERICAL ERA (CL. ER. 332)

Phenmir stood with aching knees, holding an infant's corpse in his bloodied hands.

Cheric forgive me.

His palms shook as he laid the child to rest on the surgeon's table beside the intestinal segment that he harvested from its abdomen. He repeated the mantra that followed each harvest.

I am not at fault. This is the will of the Zhaesmen.

He rinsed his hands alongside his forceps and scalpel, placing them in the polished steel basin. Viscous crimson mixed with water as it ran down his dark hands. Once clean, he brushed his silver dreads back with moistened palms. He had only seen forty-six years, yet his experience had aged him.

Guilt stung him, whispering: *This child would have grown to wield divine powers. Grown to carry a legacy from proud parents. Grown to live.*

Perd those Zhaesmen and their inhumane law. Perd the harvesting Courts that force me to harvest the third bowel of these gifted children. No child could survive a harvest, yet the Zhaesmen justified it in the name of progress.

His eyes wandered to the harvested intestine and the open abdomen.

A second umbilical cord that connected to a third bowel, the cardinal sign of a gifted birth. A blessing for the four Courts who harvested and a death sentence for the youngling. *Thank Cheric, we Chussmen have our allies in Court Tchoyas, the Tchoyasmen, to oppose this brutality.* Two Courts in opposition were not enough to sway the other four towards mercy.

He thought he'd grown desensitized after four years of harvesting. Still, tears rolled down his dry face, complimenting his bloodshot eyes. He did not cry with each harvest, but today was one such occasion. His shoulders convulsed with each sob as he hid watery eyes from the macabre image.

He shivered. The surgical chamber was frigid, causing anyone used to a warm climate to sniff incessantly.

He placed his right hand on the child, bowing his head in reverence. *Lord God Cheric, bless this child as he travels to the realms beyond. Aid those who enforce intestinal thievery to see the wrongs of their ways.*

He felt like a hypocrite for contributing to the very act he abhorred but recognized that he had nowhere else to turn to maintain the peace between his people and the four Courts who chose to harvest. Why couldn't the Zhaesmen train more proficient surgeons? Spending so much to fund the labor of Chuss surgeons should have taught them to divert their attention away from their clerical and philosophical pursuits. While they employed Zhaes surgeons for harvests in villages and hamlets, they always conscripted a Chussman—or even a Priessman—to harvest the organs that would be given to the nobility and others deemed worthy. To whom would this organ be given? Was this all some cruel assignment to force Chussmen to work against their ethics?

Amidst doubts and hatred, he consoled himself through the Chuss Ideal: *Care is the creed*. To avoid bigoted thoughts, he had to accept the Ideals of each of the six Courts. Courts Chuss, Zhaes, Tchoyas, Gruth, Priess, and Sleff made up the continent of Facet. Each one a fiefdom that worshiped their respective god as they saw fit. Phenmir was a devout man of medicine by trade, a Chussman by birth. There was no better manifestation of love for humankind than through service.

He turned to the mirror above the wash bin, hoping he had blinked away the redness in his eyes. The smell of iron stained his nostrils.

A cough from the chamber's entrance caught his attention. A pale, gaunt Zhaesman stood tapping his feet.

"Your report, Chussman?"

"Another successful harvest," replied Phenmir, attempting to bury his frustration. He had grown used to hiding his feelings.

"Yet another small sacrifice for such a gain."

Phenmir avoided eye contact with a conciliatory nod.

"You are dismissed, *med*," the Zhaesman said as he looked down at Phenmir. Compliance was the easiest way to avoid prolonged conversations. Still, he detested the degrading title of "med" that made him seem no greater than a farmhand.

No, he did not believe this sacrifice was worth his effort. No, he did not believe in their view of a *greater good*, nor did he take pride in these tasks. Half of the children born with the additional organ perished before their first year. Some bodies cannot handle the endowed third bowel, while others utilized the additional organ for advanced digestion, turning nutrients into superhuman abilities. The death rate of these children, the Endowers, was no excuse to harvest all those born with the condition.

Phenmir often performed life-saving procedures, but no surgeon of his experience would be exempt from labor in foreign Courts. All Chuss surgeons knew that a period of residency in Kzhek entailed the occasional harvest. He only had three months until the Zhaesmen would grant him home leave. He tensed and wiped his face with an icy hand as he left for his quarters, relieved to exit the dim chamber.

Though Phenmir was no nobleman, the Zhaes Thane of Endowment provided an exquisitely furnished bedchamber. Thane Sorn was one of the more pleasant Zhaes Thanes among the eight who served their monarch, the Krall, but he was still less personable than any Chuss Thane. Phenmir did not seek out the Thanes that made up the Court nobility, but found himself often in their service.

The light that lined the high walls from dozens of long-burning candles left him with time to read and focus on his studies. With the decor in the Chuss colors of crimson and gold, he wondered if they designed it for Chuss surgeons. To his fortune, he saw no Zhaes banner in the room.

He doffed his overcoat and eased his body onto a padded seat to remove his boots, noticing a few stains on the leather tops near the laces that matched the crimson room. *Dismiss it. You have completed your task.* Medical labor required a durable mind, one that could withstand loss and disappointment, like losing a patient after a long war against a festering infection. Though his work did not require the physical demands of a field laborer, it had its price. His mind felt as if he had spent a day studying for exams while attending a funeral.

Despite the hours remaining until dusk, he wilted like a tomato vine in a drought. Though he longed for rest, his mind was fixated on the harvest. He mourned the parents who lost a child to the law of the harvest. He thought of his family and longed for their company.

Seventeen months passed since Phenmir was called to serve in Kzhek, the capital of Court Zhaes, the head of metal mining and distribution. Not only did their prowess cover the most affluent trade, but they had taken the lead in grafting and harvesting. *Seventeen months.* He missed his wife, Meira, and his son, Hir. The light of his family brightened his darkest moments.

Though he resented the assigned harvest, he was passionate about his work as a healer. Joyful moments with recovered patients allowed him to forget the harvests. He was relieved to be assigned other medical procedures besides harvesting while in Kzhek. Nevertheless, harvests came. Perhaps one day, those who enforced harvesting would recognize the errors of their ways.

A prayer seeped past his lips. *Cheric, I need thee.*

❧ ❧

The following day, he dined alone in the feast hall while the Zhaesmen kept to their own circles, but that did not bother him. He had not come to Kzhek to socialize, but to labor.

He looked at his meal, an insipid mixture of oats and dark grains. He longed for the spices of his home. If only he hadn't run out of cardamom and cumin within his first month. Zhaes food was not distasteful in of itself, but it lacked flavor.

Upon finishing, he arose and left towards the open corridor. He turned his head to look out the tall windows and avoid eye contact with the passing Zhaesmen. He did not feel like entertaining a conversation.

Distant, snowy peaks, the northern cliffs, stood beyond the city. The city itself was covered with large rectangular buildings built with little creative freedom, lined with bronze highlights. Large Zhaes banners danced in the stormy winds. The fabric was bronze on dark gray, bearing the sigil of a kaesan, a demonic deer-like beast that represented the punishment of sin.

Despite the tranquil beauty, glares trailed him. *Let them see me as a lost soul for worshiping Cheric. Perd them all.* The Zhaesmen did not hate others for their nationality, only for not worshiping their god, Laeih. In their eyes, all other gods were mere idols.

He did not hate Zhaesmen, did he? He told himself that he simply *disagreed with their way of life.* As a man who lived by the Chuss ideal of charity and love for others, he could not *hate* the Zhaesmen. Distaste was another emotion. One he could live with.

An open room stood at the end of the hall. It was filled with a large, embellished wooden table, fit to be circled by twenty individuals. The room lacked occupants just as it lacked any hint of joy. A touch of natural light or even a rug would do wonders for the too-cold atmosphere. He removed his notes to review the minutiae of his assignment.

Vessel: Male, 4th child of a 30 and 32 year old pair.

Site of incision: Right lower quadrant of the abdomen

Length of harvest: 1.34 units

Time until organ death: 4 days from the time of harvest

Graft recipient: To be determined

The organ's usage was inevitable. He only hoped that the child's life was not a waste. Not to be used by another bureaucrat, but by an advocate for the progression of humankind.

Men and women of godlike strength, sages who could read both minds and the future, and beings who could manipulate their bodies to perform mythical feats were all fruits stemming from the additional organ. Phenmir feared that politics and the concept of a *greater good* were becoming idolatrous figures in the eyes of the public, distracting them from the true gods. When humans abandon the words of the gods, they lose touch with what creates such a *greater good.* It would not be long before more men declared themselves heretics, standing for their Court to adopt the pride of the godless Court Priess.

He glanced at the portraits of the former Proctors of the years' past that adorned the walls, each assisting the Thane of Endowment in overseeing the logistics of harvesting. Three images of graying figures spanned the room, each a melancholic capture of life. Dense brush strokes stuck out like the texture of tree bark.

All Zhaesmen had a distinct pallor, as if their blood had been drained at birth. Their black hair provided a certain melancholy to their appearance. Often stern in their demeanor, they embodied justice over mercy and stood for unwavering virtue, striving to serve Laeih after the Ideal of their Court.

As he averted his eyes from the lattermost painting that depicted the late Proctor, the current Proctor entered, accompanied by nine other individuals. Youthful compared to the past Proctors, this one stood tall, his posture fit to match his sanctimonious personality. He was perhaps the least personable man Phenmir had ever met. This was not a declaration to condemn the man. He merely had the emotional capacity of a corpse and the moral flexibility of a stone, but he served Court Zhaes well. Phenmir could demean the Zhaesmen without end, but he could not doubt the fruits of their labor.

Light banter filled the room, but silence fell as the Proctor called for a start to the meeting.

"Heloath and welcome, fellow councilmen... and Chussman," said the Proctor. "I would like to inform you that we have found an individual worthy of a graft."

Phenmir tensed as the Proctor stared at him.

"The recipient of this graft, this Endowed, will strengthen the union between our Courts. The members of the Canton of Endowment have appointed the Krall of *Court Chuss,* the monarch of one of the anti-harvesting Courts, to be the recipient. This will make him the first of his people to accept an organ graft."

Phenmir stared into the Proctor's sunken eyes. Shock shivered up his spine. *The Krall? Is the ruler of my Court a traitor by embracing the grafting that his people oppose?*

"This is great news for your Court, *med*," said the Proctor. "I can only imagine your *joy*. Your Court will be free from self-imposed restrictions. As a man of medicine, you must have waited for such an event for many years."

Phenmir remained in a silent stupor. *You pretend to know me? You assume my beliefs because of what I am forced to do? What am I to do? What will happen to my home Court? My people? My family? Myself?*

"... and I couldn't be in deeper agreement," he heard one of the council members say as clarity returned. Fear turned to tension. "Med... Phenmir, soon your people will thrive!"

Phenmir tried to offer a response, but words failed him. "Proctor... might you excuse me for a moment?" He hid his shaking hands beneath the table.

"Med, we have only just begun. Surely you can contain your excitement." The man to Phenmir's right placed a hand on his shoulder.

Phenmir brushed the touch away. The chair screeched as he threw himself back, scraping its legs across the polished floor. He stormed out of the room, slamming the door behind him.

Harvesting for the Zhaesmen should have prevented grafts from entering Court Chuss. He served their people so that they would permit the Chussmen to live as they chose, a life free of harvesting. *Has my work been in vain? Did they mistake my compliance as support?* He cursed the Chuss Krall. Progressive Zhaes beliefs triumphed over Chuss morality. The law of Zhaes toppled the love of Chuss.

After a few minutes of pacing and fruitless meditation, he heard footsteps exit the council room. Did they wish to coerce him, pleading for his return? More likely, they sought to ridicule his outburst. He had not behaved with dignity, but it was not often that the laws of one's nation were overturned. He turned away, deciding to avoid the councilmen by returning to the surgical chamber to retrieve his belongings.

His mind turned to his people. *Would the Court answer with riots or cheers? No Chussman would condone this, would they?* He needed to go home, back to Sliin. After gathering his essentials, he would return to his wife and son. *Will rioters sack our property? Would they try to take the lives of Hir and Meira for what I have done?*

He searched for anything that belonged to him, but his efforts were slowed by a bombardment of worries. After deciding that he had all that he possessed, he slung his bag around his shoulder. He tried to leave but was held at the door by the Proctor, whose condescending grimace looked down on him.

"Phenmir, please return to the council room. We are yet to conclude our session," he said, clammy hands clasping Phenmir's shoulders. "I understand your reluctance to accept this change, but you, of all Chussmen, should understand the benefits of harvesting. Just look at the lives made better by the sacrifices of the young. We have helped entire populations because of their donations."

"Do not assume that you understand my beliefs!" He threw the Proctor's hand off of his shoulder. "It is Facet-wide standard that all medical personnel labor on their assigned case without regard to the specific situation. I serve for the benefit of the people, understanding that I will perform *forced* harvests. If our Court's alliance did not force me to harvest, I would have joined the public protests against you *murders* long ago!"

"I trust that having your Krall receive an organ graft to become an Endowed will change your mind on the matter."

Phenmir pointed his finger at the Proctor's face. "You sanctimonious *fiends* are a disgrace to your god and every holy law given to man. I hope you will one day meet the parents of your child-victims as you burn in the depths of the under realms. Go home and read your holy scripts without living the spirit of the law, you *perding* hypocrite."

Phenmir strode off, leaving the Proctor's shouts ignored. He could no longer endure the relentless scorn of the Zhaesmen or their harvesting. His labor in Zhaes only compounded tension as he questioned his career choice. He needed wholesome work that would never contradict the Chuss ideal. Perhaps he could get hired on as a local medic, spending the rest of his days with his family in Sliin. He could teach medical theory to young scholars. He could even pursue writing; he had many thoughts on the ethicality of *certain* modern medical practices.

He entered the borrowed bedroom and gathered the rest of his belongings before his fury caused further complications. When that was done, he made his way to the door and stepped through it, only to be halted by two council members.

"We understand your frustration, med. Plea–"

"I don't want to hear it, Zhaesmen. I am leaving. I have no obligations to your sadistic Court. Find another surgeon."

"We have not come to persuade, only to inform you of the riots in your homeland. If you are determined to return, do so with caution."

Phenmir stopped in his tracks. His hands began to tremble. His wife and son passed through his mind like the afterimage of a bonfire. "What riots?"

"The Proctor thought it fit to inform you that you might wish to reconsider departure," voiced the taller of the two. "Your Krall already came Kzhek to receive his graft. It was placed in him immediately following your harvest yesterday. He committed to the cause some time ago. He informed the Chuss populous of his decision before his journey here. After the surgery, he was given leave to return and is traveling back to Sliin as we speak."

"The Proctor thinks this will inhibit my departure? *Ha!* If anything, I feel more inclined to leave." He suppressed a viper's smile.

"Med Phenmir, the rioting is not all... how should I put this... not all in protest of your Krall. According to our informants, at least half the uproar is to celebrate his decision to receive the organ."

"You mean to tell me—"

"—that it seems as if your Court is divided. Many advocate harvesting. It appears that your people have grown more progressive in the past few years. Political persuasions change. It is natural."

Phenmir assessed their message. Was this true? Had *his* people fallen to persuasive harvesting propaganda? They must have bought into some euphemism, another Zhaes lie to promote egocentrism and selfishness.

"I appreciate your concern, but my decision remains the same. I cannot abandon my family while my Court faces a civil storm." *Breathe and forgive. Leave them on peaceful terms.* "Send the Proctor my apologies for my poor decorum." With that, he departed with his single rucksack into the evening.

Once free from pestering Zhaesmen, worry returned as his thoughts gravitated to his wife and son. Were they safe? Had the riots affected them? Did they support the Krall? No, surely they would not condone his tyranny.

He reached into his satchel for coins and found four jame, five petiir, and twenty zhon. Despite the extortionate Zhaes prices, he surmised it would be sufficient coinage for travel, meals, and at least two nights at an inn. He would have to divide his travel to rest, losing some sleep and skip some meals, but he would survive the journey. It was unfortunate that his medical contract paid him at the end of his stay, but he had prepared an emergency fund beforehand.

Travel routes still bound the Courts. The ghete steeds belonged to all of Facet, making them impossible to monopolize and always available for use. The manner of ghete trade and usage taught a valuable lesson of peaceful cooperation, but personal differences overrode all other matters of life.

He did not look forward to the journey south. The ghete's scales chafed his thighs, not to mention that they smelt like the sea itself had fermented. They were a convenience, not a luxury. Regardless of his opinion, the large reptilian cats could outpace any stallion.

Leaving the city center, he spotted a worn sign hanging from a post. *Kzhek ghete.*

Their fishlike musk grew in strength as he approached the entrance. They placed the stable outside the city for a reason.

Phenmir entered, stomping his feet to clear the rain from the tops of his boots. "Heloath," he said, offering the common greeting. *Act kind or you'll double the price.* "What's the charge today?" A burly Zhaesman rose behind a mound of hay in the stable.

"I'm afraid that the current rate has increased due to high demand. You might have noticed the vacant stables. Where are you traveling?" The man paused as he glanced at Phenmir. "Court Chuss?" Not all the Courts of Facet were so distinct in their characteristics. A Chussman stuck out like obsidian against marble beside the pale Zhaesmen.

"It's no problem. If you need one, you need one," said Phenmir. "Name your price."

"Depends on where you're going." He waved for Phenmir to follow him inside to the front desk. "Are you heading to a village or city? Kyul? Fangbrook?" He tailored his guesses to Phenmir's worn garb.

"Sliin."

"The capital! Haven't been there. Too dry for a Zhaesman. Two jame is the current rate for that distance." The stableman left the ghete to meet Phenmir.

"That is fine. Could you recommend any suitable inns along the way?" Phenmir removed the coins.

"The Putle's Bog in Thess is always my choice when traveling south. I would say that it is just past the first third of your journey, though I do not know if you will make it before morning. I recommend you stay the night in one of our local establishments. Kzhek is more expensive but worth the additional coinage. I advise against Kuith's Comfort. The innkeeper is a conman and they provide the worst sea bread that I have ever eaten."

Phenmir chuckled. "Will do, sir. It was a pleasure to make your acquaintance."

"I hope our services suffice. I treat these steeds like my children, if not better."

Phenmir nodded. "Would it be alright if I take the steed's identification tag now? I can pay now to avoid an early morning disturbance."

"Of course, of course." He took Phenmir's coins and reached into his satchel, removing a small key attached to a leather tag.

"Take number four." He pointed back into the stables behind the desk. She should get you there without a problem. Leave her gate key in the letter slot near our entrance when you leave. *Whole is the holy,* Chussman." he said with the Zhaes salute, placing steepled fingers before his face with a slight bow.

"Care is the creed," replied Phenmir with his Court's Ideal and salute, thumbs and index fingers forming a ring and placing it over the center of his chest. He left the stableman to conclude his responsibilities.

꙳꙳꙳ ꙳꙳꙳

After passing three taverns, each one easily mistakable for a scanty inn, he entered one named *Virtue's Solace,* just before leaving the city.

The building was small, with few occupants in the tavern. He approached a man reading from a tome on an unkempt front counter. The bald man looked up, adjusting his collar and scratched his beard when Phenmir approached.

"What is the lowest price for a room? I'll be out before sunrise."

"One petiir per night, though you seem to be no man of our Court, so it will be an addition petiir for... service charges."

"I see," replied Phenmir with a deep breath. Any desire to haggle or argue fled from him. It was late, and he was preparing for an early departure.

"Very well." He handed the innkeeper two bronze coins.

"Follow me to the second floor." The innkeeper forced a sigh. Phenmir followed.

The innkeeper stopped at the top of the staircase and pointed. "Follow this hallway. Yours will be the third door on the right. Meals are available with an additional charge of five zhon per portion. Keep the sound to a minimum and leave your key on the windowsill upon departure."

Despite the lack of hospitality, the room seemed comfortable and large enough for his liking. Light wooden planks traced the walls with a floor paved with a similar wood of a darker stain.

He undressed and set aside his work clothes on a small table near the bedside. A goblet of water rested there, a proper convenience for such a price. One of the room's three lamps was lit to provide dim light, fueled by oil.

Working as a traveling medic provided many opportunities for a change in surroundings, something he grew to enjoy. A night in a new location was always an appreciated gift in his otherwise routine life.

With stiff leather shoes removed and his belt set beside his baggage on the floor, he slid into bed.

Soon he would stand before his family, who would embrace his return during a time of uncertainty. Or would he meet a family that would reject him for abandoning his position? His home could be a Court in unified protest or facing a civil war. Charic only knew what would come.

CHAPTER TWO

WHOLE IS THE HOLY

The idol of the Zhaes god stood before Aerhee as she prayed.

"Praise be to thee, Laeih, the most high god, the one true deity." The voices of surrounding Zhaesmen repeated the benedictory opening.

Aerhee continued her oration. "Free the Tchoyasmen and Chussmen from their obstinance. Aid them to receive your gift of the harvest. Allow them to permit the progression of Facet and her Courts. Spread thy blessings on the Thanes of our Court and upon the head of the Krall, whom they serve.

"We are grateful for the elect-born younglings, who give their lives for the proliferation of our people. Guide us toward truth. *Whole is the Holy*."

"Whole is the Holy!" echoed from the other worshipers.

She left the bronze idol, allowing room for others to begin their morning worship.

The gifted younglings who give their lives and holy organ for the proliferation of our people. Laeih, among the other gods of Facet, had given these *elect-born* to be utilized, yet Courts Tchoyas and Chuss argued otherwise. With only four of the six Courts participating in the harvest, too many organs would be wasted in stillbirths and in impotent children who were too young to properly wield their power. The organs were much better off in the body of an adult who could make a difference in the world.

She studied the Kzhek cityscape. The day was overcast. The Canton of Diplomacy broke the skyline like an architectural giant of polished stone and corners lined with bronze. She organized the sheets of parchment in her hands to prepare for her upcoming meeting.

She and her husband had left for their day's labors and would thereafter return in the evening for their scheduled reading of The Tome of Virtue, the sacred Zhaes text. While she was the Zhaes Caser, the high secretary to the nobility, her husband was a director of material distribution for the Cloven Gleff, the most fruitful mine in the Court.

With a pull on the Canton's door, she left to pursue the interests of her Court.

"Heloath, Caser," said a guard standing near the entrance.

Though she had been in office for some time, she still admired hearing her title. As the Caser of Court Zhaes she was no Thane but was a close second in their authority under the Krall. A position in the nobility was well worth her efforts to climb the political ranks. She had developed a distinct reputation and was well known by most of the citizens of the Court as one of the most pious members of the Court. Her statuesque figure seemed sculpted and inspired by smoke as it rose from an extinguished candle. Black hair with light streaks flowed down her shoulders.

"To you as well, Zhaesman," she replied.

"Heloath, Caser." Aerhee turned to find her scribe, Fheo, stumbling behind her. The young Zhaesman had not yet reached his second decade but was proving to adapt well to her requests after serving together since she had taken the position of Caser.

"The messengers from four of the Courts have arrived. Chuss, Priess, Gru–"

"Yes, Fheo, I will welcome them."

"But, Caser, the council room is on the second level. Why are you going down this hall?"

She turned to him with an insincerely patient smile. "You think I don't know that? I have things to take care of beforehand."

"Well, *we* should be prompt. Thane Leisa expects to discuss the reports from the other Courts after the meeting." He clenched his notes against his chest, sweat wrinkling the sheets.

"Thane Leisa can be patient. I will not be long," replied Aerhee.

"Yes, yes, Caser. I suppose she can wait."

"Then why do you mention it? If you are so insistent on this meeting, why don't you direct it?"

"Caser? I surely–"

"You must learn to preside, eventually. I will leave you to hear their reports and you can relay them to me once they depart."

"But, Caser–"

"I will wait for you in the study chamber near the council room. Whole is the Holy, Zhaesman."

"Um... yes, Whole... is the Holy... Caser."

※※※※※ ※※※※※

Approaching footsteps thudded across the Canton's hallway, drawing Aerhee's attention. The meeting had concluded quicker than she had expected. Aerhee closed *The Tome of Measure* as Fheo approached with a guest.

"Excuse us, Caser," Fheo motioned to the woman, "but she insisted on speaking with you."

She recognized the Sleff messenger by her garb, though her name escaped her.

"She had little to say," he continued, "but approached me after the others departed and requested to speak with my superior."

Aerhee dismissed Fheo with a sigh and a wave. "I will speak with you after this." He nodded and disappeared.

She invited the timid Sleffwoman to sit beside her. *It must have been a difficult period for Court Sleff. Why else would she be so ashamed to speak before the other Court messengers?* She stared at the Sleffwoman, who smiled with dry, cracked lips. A Sleffman believed that wealth bred pride, which was manifest in Court Priess; therefore, a pious Sleffman would give any more money than is needed for a week's living to their Court. Why give their Court a graft when it could be given to a Zhaesman to enforce justice or maximize labor efforts? What noteworthy accomplishments did the Sleffmen have with their graft-recipient Endowed?

"Forgive me for disturbing you, Caser, but I have a report which my Krall did not desire to be heard by the other messengers."

Aerhee nodded.

"Riots have begun in our Court's capital. This is the third day of public unrest. They increase in aggravation by the moment with acts of arson and even assaults on law enforcement."

"What inspired these riots?"

"They to protest harvesting in Court Sleff."

"But the Sleffmen have been loyal to harvesting since it began five years ago!"

The Sleffwoman gave a timid shrug. "Something has happened to inspire a rebellion."

"What is it? Why now?"

"I only come to deliver this message. I fear we shall all know soon enough what has caused traitors to arise in my Court."

Courts Tchoyas and Chuss have opposed ever since it began? Now some of the Sleffmen have joined them?

❦

"How reliable is your report, Caser? That woman is a *Sleff* messenger. Can we trust their word considering their... financial state?" said Fuih Lettre. As the Zhaes Thane of Veneration, he led and managed the religious dealings of the Court.

"I understand your concern, but how often do *you* interact with the Sleffmen?" replied Aerhee.

"Occasionally."

"In a personal conversation or public matters?"

"More public, I confess, though I know how they are." He was young for a Thane and it showed in his inherent bias against the Sleffmen, though he was two years Aerhee's elder.

"What you have is a bigoted opinion held by too many Zhaesmen. Their economy is far from perfect, but their beliefs are quite beautiful upon study. Honesty and submission are ingrained in their blood. Their entire belief system comprises worshiping god by denying themselves. Suffice to say that the last person to deceive us would be their messenger."

"Yes, yes, I understand, but we should still tread lightly. If people are protesting harvesting, they have fallen into ignorance. They likely bought into Chuss or Tchoyas propaganda. It seems those two anti-harvesting Courts complicate matters more each day. It is difficult for a hungry man to recognize the benefit of a seed when all he desires is the crop. As Zhaesmen, we have a responsibility to correct their misconceptions of harvesting. "

"And what do you propose?"

"Sleffmen will be much easier to placate than the other two Courts. The Chussmen and Tchoyasmen are too set in their ways ... for now." He removed a small pad of bound paper from a drawer in his desk. "Please, Caser, have a seat."

He poured her a cup of deniroot tea. Its lack of steam caused her to pause.

"Tell me," he sipped from his cup, brushing the tips of his midnight hair behind his ears. "How familiar are you with Court Sleff's grafts? Do you know any of their Endowed who received the grafts?"

She shrugged, sipping her tea only to set it back down and push it further away. "I assume it is the same as in our Court."

"Though benefactors tend to grant organ grafts to reputable citizens throughout a given Court, Court Sleff deals more discreetly. For example, here in Zhaes, you have a fair amount of Endowed among the nobility as well as more in trusted offices throughout the land, and so forth."

He took a sip from his tea and frowned. "I sent an envoy to their Court on a matter between Cantons of Veneration, but I could not find an Endowed among their clergy. How odd, I thought, causing me to pry further." He let his cup rest and leaned forward with elbows on the table. "I was unable to find *any* Endowed outside of the bureaucracy. I *know* that the Cantons of Endowment have not deprived them of their share of Endowed. After five years of harvesting, why did they not have as many Endowed as the other Courts? Where were their Endowed law enforcers who can read criminal minds? Where were the Endowed who protected the cities from dangerous beasts?"

Aehree squinted, looking up and biting her lip.

He smiled. "Conspiracy is highly unlikely, but I worry that other Courts have influenced the Sleffmen. In economic matters, they could be easily persuaded to act according to the will of another if offered the proper resources to sustain their decaying infrastructure. I am convinced that these riots must have arisen due to people feeling neglected without a proper abundance of Endowed in their Court. Without Endowed such as the Gorgers, maybe their laborforce is lacking. Perhaps too few Feelmen cause them to feel unprotected when crime runs rampant. What may solve such a mystery? Perhaps their other Endowed have been taken by other Courts. Or maybe they are hidden."

"Have you asked Thane Sorn or their Thane of Endowment about this?"

"How important is this to you, Caser?"

"I was the first to be informed. It is my duty to resolve this. If we allow more rebellions to diminish the power of harvesting, it will not be long before such propaganda reaches our Court. We must stop it before it can grow."

"Are you requesting my cooperation?"

She nodded.

"How coincidental that news of these riots arrived not long after I had discovered their Endowed deficiency. From what I can find, Court Sleff has very few documented Endowed. Far too few to make sense as we strive to balance the power between Courts. I will arrange a meeting with Thane Sorn. As the head of the harvesting in our Court, he may know something of this discrepancy. If we can clear this ordeal related to an Endowed deficiency in Court Sleff, perhaps we can have a solution to stop the riots. If the Sleffmen feel equally treated, we can assume that they will recognize the value of harvesting and we will thereby dissolve the rebellion before it has a chance to truly affect our Court and harvesting itself. I assume you have access to the archives in the city's Athenaeum? I would ask that you read through some Sleff records for me."

She nodded. Despite its proximity, she had only visited the Athenaeum of Kzhek, the largest library in all the Courts, a few times.

"Though I stumbled upon this clerical discrepancy two months ago, there must be some connection with the riots. I know I repeat myself, but it is as obvious as a child's cry for its mother. We have much to discover, Caser. Let's reconvene in three days."

"I will see that it is done." she replied.

"Regarding the city's Athenaeum, find the resident Sleff scholar there. Though you may worry about his discretion, all resident scholars have pledged their life to their Court of residence. He is a born and raised Sleffman, but he is more a Zhaesman than many in Kzhek. The Patriarchy of Scholars ensures that we have only the best in our Athenaeum."

She hid a shudder at the mention of the Patriarchy. Thane Lettre trusted their council, and he was her superior. It was her duty to sustain her elected leaders.

She put on a smile. "I will head there directly."

"Take care, Caser. Whole is the Holy."

"Whole is the Holy." They saluted each other with steepled fingers.

"Should it be necessary"—he removed a small bronze token from his pocket, upon which was inscribed his name below the Zhaes insignia—"show this to the resident Sleff scholar in the Athenaeum if you wish to view any texts that are beyond public access."

Nodding, she took the coin from his open palm and placed it in her pocket.

She exited the Canton and waited on the street for the next carriage to make its round.

Two large ghete pulled an approaching carriage to the curb, splashing the tops of her boots with a puddle. The cabin was lined with bronze, as were all carriages in Zhaes, and conducted by a man in a large cloak of the same material as Aerhee's waterproof overcoat. She stepped up to the coachman and paid him one petiir and tipped him a zhon.

"Athenaeum of Kzhek," she commanded as she entered the cabin. A single occupant sat across from her, a boy of perhaps twenty who dressed in culinary smock with flour residue and red sauce stains. They both offered the Zhaes salute upon making eye contact and followed the action by shifting their gaze to opposing side windows.

"Are you a Thane?" asked the boy, turning away from his window.

"No," she spared him yet a moment before returning to the passing cityscape.

"This is my first time working in this district. You are so regally dressed. I assumed—"

"Assumptions will only cause you harm. Mind your matters, boy." She enunciated her last words with staccato jabs.

"Excuse me. It is just that my overseer assigned me to this part of the city, and I was curious how such a high sector works. I usually work in the lower-eastern territory outside of Kzhek." He scratched his scalp. "I wouldn't be able to afford to travel by ghete if it weren't for the reimbursement from my overseer."

The lower-eastern territory of Zhaes was known for its small share of the border that touched Court Sleff. Some Zhaesmen considered it a region of Sleff, due to its less-than-fortunate state. *Perd him*. The boy had piqued her interest. The more she studied him, the more he looked like a Sleffman.

"Where are you from?"

"Ceith." The Zhaes center of Sleff relations. Meeting him was no coincidence, but a manifestation of Laeih's hand. She expressed a silent prayer of gratitude for being led to such a situation. The Athenaeum was filled with bounties of information, though no text could compare to personal interaction. The boy was not a full Sleffman, but he would serve his purpose.

"Is Ceith as influenced by Court Sleff, as rumors say?" asked Aerhee.

"I suppose so. I've even heard some say that Ceith was once a town in Court Sleff, later transitioning to the Zhaes side of the border after land disputes. Some locals call the border 'the silken curtain,' as if there never was a restriction between the sides. Despite its size, I think the free border has allowed each Court to develop a trusting relationship."

"Do you frequent Sleff?"

"No, but I know many who do. The journey is only an hour by ghete."

"Have you ever... met or... learned of some aspect of their culture that surprised you?" *You've made it this far. Quit dulling your expressions for the boy.* "Anything about the Endowed in their Court?" *Diminish his curiosity.* "I am just a curious scholar. It seems odd that I have never heard of their Endowed placements. Here in Kzhek we make sure that the whole Court honors any new Endowed."

"Rumors circulate. Some say that the nobility are all Endowed. I've met a few Gorgers in our Court, seen their superhuman strength, and even a Feelmen who read my mind. Personally, I think Shiftlings are the most interesting type of Endowed. I still cannot believe that they can change their skin to look like the sky or even like moving water. The Sleffmen are vulnerable, but I know they accept harvesting, so I wondered why Endowed had not yet fixed their weak economic structure with some 'Endowed' method. Just look at all that they have done for us! Zhaes crime rates are much lower and the beauty of Kzhek is evidence enough of what Gorgers can build, not to mention the Foretellers who have saved countless with warnings against future natural disasters."

How much is this boy going to talk?

"So I asked a Sleffman in a tavern, 'Say, what does your Court do with your Endowed?' He said he has seen *one* and only one. 'Well, that's not enough!' I said. He said that no one knows where the Endowed *really* are in his Court, he just assumed they were all nobles and such."

What a blindly trusting population. Are they not the least curious about what their gifted children are used for?

"Interesting," she replied. "The Sleffman was probably some farmer or lowly laborer. It is much more difficult for them to notice the feats accomplished by the Endowed when they are not directly involved in the matters that keep the Court whole and safe."

"You would think so, but he said that he was a medic from their capital."

A medic from the center of their culture should have frequent interactions with Endowed. What are these perding kulfs doing with their grafts? How have I never heard this before? Are we all living of ignorance of so obvious a problem?

The carriage slowed as it approached the gargantuan library. "Thank you for the conversation, Zhaesman. Safe travels homeward, Whole is the Holy." Aerhee descended the two steps from the cabin to walk towards the Athenaeum's entrance.

The Athenaeum of Kzhek was the most imposing building in all of Court Zhaes and arguably in all of Facet. Aerhee had paid the grand collection of literature a few visits, but it impressed her each time. The building was a trapezoidal giant with a slim tower protruding from its center. Like most buildings in Zhaes, a bronze lining traced its edges, while blue-shaded stone fortified the walls around crystalline cubes that allowed for the pale skylight to seep into its inner chambers.

A trio of solemn figures passed her. *Patriarchy Brethren*, she thought as she viewed their white tunics with a platinum-tinted tracing. Unease crept up her arms like an unwelcome caress.

She rarely saw them, as they spent all day in study or council.

She forgot her fears as she entered the embrace of the Athenaeum. Large pillars grew from the floor, making one feel as if the building were a labyrinth. Most of the Athenaeums across the continent of Facet focused on a single Court's works, while the Athenaeum of Kzhek drew the highest scholars due to its vast collection of information. A Zhaes educator could search countless tomes and find as many works on the history of Court Priess as they would for Court Zhaes. Ancient scholars had forged agreements to share knowledge and contribute to the grand library. Likewise, each Court provided a resident scholar who served in the Athenaeum of Kzhek to represent their respective Courts.

The man in the carriage suggested that the citizens were blind to the Endowers in their Court. But what of the young Endowers, the children who were born with that additional organ before the Pact of Province required the harvest to be performed? They are sure to have some surviving children around nine or ten years of age that have manifested powers.

She could not simply ask a rioter why they chose to rebel. If the general Sleff public was blind to how Endowed were used in their Court, a random Sleffman would be of no help. If she could find the answer to this puzzle, they could resolve the confusion and once again win the loyalty of the Sleffmen. *Find the discrepancy, reveal their motive for rioting, restore their loyalty.*

Ten years had passed since the first Endower birth, harvesting only had been enforced through the last five, leaving five years in between for Endowers to freely be born without being harvested. *Endower* was the title given to those who had not been taken for a harvest, the children who would grow to use their gifts of divine birth, while those granted the organ were *Endowed*. An *Endowed* who took an *Endower's* organ would obtain the same ability that the child would develop. Many parents still hid their child's strength, foresight, body shifting, and other abilities out of fear they might be the target of a future harvest. Aerhee scoffed at their ignorance. All people should know by now that the organ can only be harvested immediately after birth.

In the eastern halls of the Athenaeum, she found signs indicating that she was approaching the Sleff collections. Finally, she found the desk to seek counsel with the resident Sleff scholar.

She approached the Sleffman carefully to startle him from his reading. He was bald with most of his skin sagging or in wrinkles and many rings adorned his fingers. He wore Sleff-yellow robes with silver patterns embroidered on the front and along the sleeves. He appeared to be such a cliché scholar that Aerhee wondered if the commonly illustrated depictions were based on his appearance.

He looked up at her and adjusted his spectacles.

"Heloath, Sleffman."

"Caser Kleeh, how may I be of assistance?" A slight smile lifted his wrinkled cheeks.

"I am here on account of the Thane of Veneration and may require access to certain texts. I need to find all the information I can on the Endowed of Court Sleff."

His eyes sparked with interest.

"I have heard that most Sleffmen do not know where their Endowed are."

"You must have heard that from an uneducated lowling." he scoffed.

"I know that they are not placed among the nobles of the Court. I need the truth." *For peace to remain. For rioting to cease. For my dignity to prevail.*

"Denying the commonly held beliefs of Sleff Endowed? Heresy!" he jested.

"I want records," she said.

"I cannot provide any answers, having never found any myself, but I can direct you to a promising start. You are on the Thane's errand?"

She removed the bronze token that was given to her by the Thane and showed it to the scholar.

"I trust he has the best in mind for Facet," he responded after closely examining the token. "Keep this information under discretion outside of trusted circles." He removed a key to unlock a small cabinet at the base of his desk, then removed an additional bronze key from a drawer. "Scholar Brooth is my name. Follow me, Caser."

CHAPTER THREE

FIRM IS THE FOUNDATION

Yetrik's face nearly brushed the page of his book. Unblinking eyes ran across the words with the focus and speed of a ghete.

"Though Court Gruth arose to be the trading capital of Facet in the one-hundred-and-thirtieth year in the Clerical era, Court Chuss remains a center–"

He brushed through the pages to find a promising heading.

"The Middlemen still trade with those of Court Chuss but have severed all other human connections. The last interaction with a Gruth diplomat was recorded at the dawn of the fifth year in the Clerical Era and was described as a 'silent exchange of hand gestures and patterned breathing.' Chuss trading with the Middlemen is conducted with no interaction, only by leaving carts of assorted goods in specified locations. Many attribute the lack of interaction to the cryptic language of the Middlemen; however, no records have noted any linguistic factor in their communication." There seemed to be no information in the library regarding the Middlemen, or more often referred to in bards' tales as the "plant or crop people." The inhabitants of the Middlelands, a land south of Facet's Courts, were said to be plant-like humanoids

Focus on your labors, put childish interest away. He shook his head, closing *Chuss Wisdom: A History for the Scholar.* Though his superiors would disapprove of his search, he was relieved to find at least a mention of their presence after hours of fruitless reading. Perhaps one day he could prove there was value in researching the middlemen. He was sure that they were more than mere oddities of nature. He felt compelled to study them more, but knew not why.

He arose to stretch his back with a catlike arch, then returned to his seat. He took *Writings of Chuss Prophecy: Cl. er. 5* with a limp hand and placed his palms on heavy cheeks to rest. By trade, he was a financial advisor to Fortik Gett, the Gruth Thane of Utilities. When free from responsibility, he spent his time in texts of philosophy, religion, and whatever else struck his fancy.

The sun approached its resting place beyond the horizon and cast a warm orange glow across Yetrik's reading. He closed the tome, gathering his belongings.

Before returning home for the night, Thane Gett requested his presence in his office. Yetrik proceeded down a spiraling stone staircase and departed in brisk stroll towards the Canton of Utilities while daylight remained.

The Canton was a large cylindrical building with few windows, causing one to wonder how much of the Court's accumulated taxes would be spent on candles to light the enclosed structure.

Before approaching the door, he stumbled upon the Thane of Utilities, out for an evening stroll. Yetrik forced an innocent grin.

The Thane was older, yet still appeared younger than Yetrik's grandparents. Yetrik was late into his second decade of life but was often mistaken for a youth of sixteen or seventeen. He kept his dark brown hair up in a modern fashion, with short sides and lengthy curls on his crown. Of average height, he fit well into Gruth with skin slightly lighter than a Chussman's, but nothing like the sickly pallor of a Zhaesman or even a Sleffman.

"Yetrik Kloff, just the Gruthman I have been waiting for."

"Thane Gett, my favorite Endowed." Yetrik slowed his breathing to mask his fatigue, the salty sea air filling his nostrils.

"I doubt that is true," he chuckled. Thane Gett was an amiable mentor, but Yetrik could not hide his interest in the nobleman's grafted ability. As an Endowed, his ability gave him the title of Foreteller, one who could analyze probabilities to accurately predict future events. The ability was the gambler's dream but found better use in a worthy individual. Yetrik had met very few Foretellers. They seemed as rare as a Chuss rainstorm compared to the mighty Gorgers in Court Gruth who could toss a boulder into as if it were a pebble. Perhaps they were useful to some degree, but many dismissed the Foretelling branch of Endowed as a mere parlor trick to win a drink in a tavern.

"Sorry for the delay."

"You know me. I am a Foreteller. Did you think I would expect anything else?"

"I suppose not." Yetrik chuckled, unsuccessfully masking his embarrassment. "You called and now I'm here. What can I do for you, sir?"

"No need to jump right to matters of business. Beyond the Court's needs, I hope we are friends." He turned to Yetrik with a grandfather's smile. "Now, what text kept you occupied today?"

"Gruth trading history and the evolution of our Court's industrial progression in recent years. At a deeper glance, I found some more... questionable information that inspired further study."

"And what might that be?"

"The Middlemen."

"Once again pondering the lives of the crop people, I see," said Thane Gett, as if Yetrik was a child looking into the veracity of fables.

"I know you think it fruitless, sir, but is there anything you can tell me about them?"

"I have already told you all that I know. The people are a society of hermits as far as it concerns Facet."

"Why are they so often mentioned in ancient texts when modern scholars omit their existence?"

"Perhaps it reflects our relations with those of Court Priess or Chuss. Yes, their existence is verified, but their matters are beyond our concern. Relations are safe and we each live our respective lives."

"But, sir, it seems that there is more beyond our ignorance. I read that they were last spoken to by a Gruth diplomat at the dawn of the fifth year of the Clerical Era. Sure, that is over three hundred years ago, but the Chussmen still trade with them."

"Those queries are more fitted to the jurisdiction of a historian or someone from the Canton of Agriculture." He turned to Yetrik with a wink. "You are one curious spirit, my boy. I admire that."

"Thank you, sir," Yetrik replied. "Firm is the Foundation, Thane Gett."

"Firm is the foundation," the Thane repeated the Gruth Ideal. "Now, I would like your opinion regarding some financial matters."

Yetrik faced the Thane with a nod.

"My facility scholars have developed the plans for the production of a certain utility, but the material demand will be cumbersome, especially regarding metal."

"What will you require?"

"We have considered a plethora of options for various metals, but my advisors insist that neither steel nor pewter could replace the durability of Kzhek bronze. It is unmatched by any other alloy known to Facet."

"Yes, they are reliable... but, sir," challenged Yetrik, "exports from the Cloven Gleff are far from... how should I say... the ideal choice of a frugal spender."

"Yes, I recognize that, but I would rather have half the amount of the finished product rather than double the size of materials that would quickly wear within a year."

"True. What do you want to manufacture?"

"Unfortunately, I can not yet tell you that. Those in our coalition will surely debrief you in the coming weeks if all goes as expected. I do not need you to make an immediate purchase, but to lay the foundation with our suppliers. I wished to inform you of the situation before we solidify our production planning. This may not begin before the close of the year."

"Then why ask now?" Yetrik asked.

"Well... this information must be kept confidential, though I trust I make no error in informing you. The Thane of Progress is leading this project and wanted to lay an early foundation. Thane Lekik has been in communication with the Zhaes Thane of Agriculture, who oversees the mining of the Cloven Gleff, and he has agreed to meet with you in two weeks. Would you be willing to visit Kzhek?"

"Y-yes... sir..." stuttered Yetrik as he reassessed their conversation thus far. "Are you sure? I am merely your financial advisor and by no means a diplomat."

"Worry not, Yetrik. All I request is to set our expectations with him and discuss the possibility of large shipments of bronze at a decreased price for our Court. Perhaps such work in means of persuasion could prepare you for your future," Thane Gett often suggested his predictions, but Yetrik wondered how many of these comments were born from visions and how many were generated by creativity or humor. How much faith was the Thane willing to place in him?

"I would require some time to prepare. When do you want me to leave?"

"Acknowledging the distance to Kzhek, we had planned on three days. We would provide a ghete carriage. Have you ever visited their capital?"

"I haven't been to any city in Court Zhaes. My travel outside of Gruth has been limited. I've visited Sleff a few times but that is the extent of it. Is there anything specific that I should expect? I have met very few Zhaesmen."

"Well then," Thane Gett sighed. "They are... quite literal, as I am sure you have heard. For example, let us compare our Ideals. Let us say my brother is ill. How would I help him? As a Gruthman, I would endure every moment with him, seeing his recovery to the end with compassion and diligence. A man of Court Zhaes would spend a moment with his brother, but perhaps his brother was struck ill by a past 'unrighteous act.' The man would abandon his brother at a moment's notice to avoid any unholy contamination. These people follow their law exactly as the angles on their dreary city structures. Their law is the law and there is no exception to it. Now, I might be biased due to some past disagreements in bureaucratic matters, but I am sure you will have no issue."

Yetrik envisioned the Zhaes people to be as inflexible as a statue, but he was a man to form his own opinion.

"Spices."

"What?" He turned to the Thane with a confused squint.

"If you wish to enjoy your meals, bring spices. Dill, turmeric, maybe some honey."

"Is their food truly that bland?"

"Oh yes, to salt your potatoes is very uncultured and adding pepper will 'ruin' a meal."

Yetrik's laugh descended to a nod once he saw Thane Gett's sober mien.

"That should be enough for now." Thane Gett stopped, Yetrik looked surprised to realize that they had circled the entirety of the Canton. "Thank you for your time. I must leave now, a guest awaits me. It has been a pleasure, Yetrik."

"Firm is the Foundation, sir," declared Yetrik, saluting the Thane.

"Firm is the Foundation." Thane Gett copied the Gruth salute with arms against the torso, elbows bent at a square angle, and fists clenched as if bracing himself before a strike to the gut.

Yetrik strode down the cobbled road with thoughts of anticipation accompanying him. His chest seemed to swell with excitement, knowing that he was on the cusp of his own bard's tale. Though traveling to Zhaes would seem a prison sentence for many Gruthmen, he thanked his god for the opportunity to see beyond the seaside.

❧❧❧❧❧ ❧❧❧❧❧

With two days remaining until his departure, Yetrik wanted to ensure that he spent his time effectively. He enforced a strict schedule, never so much as altering his meal times, for doing so would leave his digestion out of routine, therefore disrupting his day. If one were to observe his meticulous compulsions, one might have presumed him a citizen of Court Zhaes. Such criticism only flattered him, increasing his desire to socialize with more Zhaesmen. He had become so occupied with studying their culture that he even read about their religious practices. Doing so did not make him a heretic. He only wished to be informed. Limiting one's knowledge to one's area of expertise keeps the mind from expanding beyond a hatchling's shell.

Thane Gett mapped his course, indicating a brief stay in Court Priess and Sleff on the way. Only a few visits to Court Sleff decorated his past, but he had never been to Court Priess. He longed to see it, but only in brief. Without a god to direct their people by a single Ideal, the Priessmen were unlike any other Court. There was little structure to their society, as they lived by the Ideal, "Might is the Free." One could describe them as a "free people," but their conviction drew closer to anarchy.

Closing his copy of *Zhaes Traditionalists: Fathers of an Unwavering Faith*, he prepared for the day.

Reading was one of Yetrik's passions. He was often mistaken for a scholar based on his frequent visits to the Athenaeum of Thusk. Would he have a chance to visit the Athenaeum of Kzhek while in Zhaes? He laughed at himself for dreaming of a library while Gruthmen dreamed of hunting and drinking. He savored the pride he felt when others regarded him as intelligent and well-versed, but doubted he was near the level of an actual scholar. *Perhaps I could even write a piece of my own one day.* Despite his aspirations, guilt stung him. Another hope of his that would be unfulfilled, another goal with a beginning, yet likely absent an end. He tried to forget the harpsichord that he had purchased on an impulse and soon after neglected.

The memory of his current task fled him like a bemused dove, until he spotted the Zhaes tome once again. *Ah, review the trip with Thane Gett.* He took his travel sack from the floor near his bed and filled it with writing utensils, notepads, and a volume to read if time would allow any spare moments.

A few clouds filled the sky and the sun beamed onto the chilled cobblestones. A brisk pace kept him warmer and allowed him to pass through the streets quicker than those on a morning stroll.

The surrounding booths and shops opened with the sunrise. It was good to see many familiar faces among the shop owners. Living near the marketing district had its benefits. Genuine interest in others was one tenant of the Chuss religion that he admired.

Upon entering the Canton of Utilities, he found the charismatic Thane leaning against a doorway as if awaiting Yetrik's arrival.

"Heloath and good morning," he said as he approached Yetrik. "How have your preparations been thus far?"

"Lots of time in the Athenaeum. I know, I know, quite surprising." Yetrik's response provoked a grin from the Thane. "Aside from Zhaes, I was excited to hear that I will stop in Priess and Sleff. I spent some time reading about their culture and customs. Did you know you can simply ask a Sleff man to pay for your meal and he will pay for dessert as well?"

"Well... yes, but that is a tenant of their holy ideal, 'Pious is the Giver.' You should know that already. Many people wonder why their economy is on its last string, but poverty is written in their doctrine. I suggest you spend more time focusing on their beliefs rather than on means of exploitation."

"I know. I have spent most of my time taking an interest in Court Zhaes."

"And I appreciate your effort, Yetrik. Dedication is a complex virtue to teach. Follow me." He turned his back on Yetrik and proceeded through the doorway and into the east hall. "There is someone I would like you to meet."

"And who might that be?"

"Your travel companion."

Travel companion? Yetrik thought with an aghast sense of confusion. *Does Thane Gett not trust my capabilities so far that he has hired supervision?*

"I do not mean to discount you, Yetrik. I only hope to provide you with a comfortable guide who knows the area well enough to keep you focused on your task. You could use someone with more international experience."

'Keep you focused on your task.' *Ah yes, a taskmaster to strike me when distracted. Thank you for the chain sir, it will fit nicely around my neck. Does he want me to kneel before him as well?*

Yetrik kept silent as they continued toward a room lit by the rising sun. On a seat in the middle of the room sat a young woman, around his age.

"Yetrik, this is Semi, she'll be your guide during your excursion."

"Pleased to meet you, Gruthman," she said as she stood to greet Yetrik. Her light brown hair fell to her jawline and seemed to be unaffected by the humidity. Bangs hung to right above her eyebrows, an unorthodox style for a Gruthwoman, but it looked good on her. Gray eyes glanced into him with an elegant spirit. Tight black pants showed the definition in her lean thighs, complementing her beige tunic with a wide collar and sleeves to her elbows. Her clothing was not that of a courtly woman, but of an experienced traveler.

"You as well," he said, blushing. Though he did not know the girl yet, he was relieved to not be paired with a fifty-year-old soldier with an intimidating name such as "Scartooth" or "Bloodfist." Who knew what names such barbarians adopted, Yetrik avoided their company.

Thane Gett gestured to her. "Semi is quite the journeywoman. One of the few people I know to have been to each Court and even the Middlelands."

Middlelands? Yetrik offered a pleasant grin that reflected polite interest.

"I've only seen the border of the Middlelands," she accused. She turned back to Yetrik. "He likes to embellish my accomplishments, but don't get your hopes up. I've never seen a Middleman."

It disappointed him to hear this but did not diminish his curiosity.

"Yetrik is one of the finest scholars for his age, though that is not his profession." The Thane turned back to Semi. "Not only is she experienced, but Semi is a gifted Gruthwoman."

The girl lifted her shirt to expose her abdomen. *What is she doing?* Yetrik thought as he averted his eyes to respect her modesty.

The Thane let out a small, forced laugh. "No need to be concerned, Yetrik. You can look."

He turned back to the her, hoping he hadn't blushed too much. A long purple scar traced along her upper abdomen. An Endowed? *How serious must this task be if Thane Gett is sending me with an Endowed?*

"Perd!" he yelled before containing his emotions. "Excuse my profanity, but ... by Dielf's might!"

The Thane replied with a chuckle, expecting such a response. "She's a Shiftling. Have you met one before?"

"I haven't met more than one or two Endowed besides you. I have read a little about Shiftlings, but rumors cloud the truth of your capabilities." He shifted to look toward Semi. "Are you a complete shapeshifter?"

"Close, but as you might presume," she replied. "The rumors are exaggerated. Also, Gorgers cannot manifest an extra set of arms."

"Well, I know that," said Yetrik as they shared a laugh.

"We can perform two skills." She changed her voice to match the Thane's tenor. "We can manipulate our vocal cords to strike the tone of any voice with exactness, even animal calls." She reverted to her natural voice, or at least the one she expressed. "And we can manipulate our skin pigment to adjust to a wide spectrum of colors and patterns." She laid on the couch and shifted her skin to match the pattern and texture of the furniture, practically disappearing.

"What a talent," said Yetrik.

"Hence the reason I have invited her on your journey. She is skilled."

"I understand her role as a guide, Thane, but how will her abilities be of use?" He looked at Semi through his peripheral view, hoping that she did not take offense.

Thane Gett considered his words. "She is no spy, but your goal is very crucial. If you were to be rejected by Zhaes authorities, she could use her gift to appear as a Zhaeswoman. She and I have discussed some proposed strategies of avoiding too much questioning by those outside of our targeted members of the Zhaes nobility. Should circumstances require such extents, she will debrief you on them along the way."

Espionage? Spycraft? Though he was anxious, he trusted the Thane, knowing that his intentions were for the benefit of the people. Or at least for Court Gruth.

Semi remained quiet during their discussion. Yetrik could not determine if it was her character or if she felt pressured to silence by Thane Gett's presence.

"How were you able to recruit Semi?" Yetrik asked as he turned toward her.

"First, the request must pass the Krall. Then, if a Thane requires additional assistance, an Endowed may be requested. Semi has aided me in the past. I knew she was capable and expected that you would work well together. I have seen you progress as a fine assistant, Yetrik, and I believe great opportunities lie ahead of you. While you help me in pursuits that will benefit the Court, you will gain experience and will associate with high-ranking officials of other Courts."

"Thank you." Yetrik nodded. He scratched his scalp, tracing his eyes along the floor.

"While I brought you here to meet Semi, that is not the sole reason for this visit." The Thane turned solemn. "The Court nobles did not accept the expenditure of resources necessary to send you to Zhaes. Travel, inn, food, and especially the cost to send an Endowed all may be deemed too much. They denied my first request, but we found a way to send you with all that might be required."

"Fundraising through the tithes?" guessed Yetrik.

"No, but we found success with our Thane of Endowment, who has taken an interest in something related to harvesting in Courts Zhaes and Sleff. Court Zhaes has been looking into the anti-harvesting riots in Court Sleff. They have discovered some anomalies with the power distribution in that Court. Our nobles expressed interest in the situation. We are not as worried as the Sleff nobility, but the Krall felt it wise to send an envoy to Court Zhaes to ensure a strong political tie with them if the riots continue. Knowing this, the Krall agreed to send you to seek counsel with some of their Thanes. You will provide our Court with as much information as you can provide on the state of Court Sleff. This made it quite easy to ensure Semi as your travel companion, seeing that she is an Endowed and is therefore involved with the politics of harvesting."

"Why are riots such a concern? Don't they happen frequently in other Courts?"

"Priess protests religious organizations and Chuss protests harvesting, but this is the first recorded protest against harvesting in a Court that is loyal to the process. Sleff has cooperated with us and with Zhaes since the Pact of Province. We all agreed that the positive aspects outweigh the negatives of harvesting. Now Sleffmen oppose the Pact? I heard a rumor that the rioting even killed members of the Sleff Canton of Endowment, displaying their corpses publicly!"

Yetrik was taken aback. "Sure, crimes occur, but the Courts are usually peaceful, especially within their borders!"

"Exactly my point. I am mostly concerned with my personal motivations for your journey, but we have a part to play in securing the peace between Courts."

"I doubt our Court would ever revolt. Grafts and Endowed have done so much for us! Just look at our economy. Gorgers have given us an unprecedented workforce. We are the agricultural center of Facet!"

"I agree, but it would surprise you to hear what is spoken among the lower-class areas of the Court. Even the criminals and street dwellers live by Gruth doctrine, but they distort words of truth and justify wrongdoings. I would not be so astonished to hear if any of them take inspiration from revolts in other Courts. Sin only requires justification to be permitted in the heart of a man."

Yetrik had spent most of his life among the aristocracy, his parents were both employed in high scholarly positions, providing him with a privileged upbringing in the affluent sectors of Thusk. He had rarely seen the slums of his own Court. Most of his knowledge about the impoverished Gruth lifestyle was based upon rumors and children's offensive humor.

"On with you two then." The Thane lifted his hands in dismissal. "You have little time left to prepare for your 'heroic journey.'"

Semi stood with Yetrik. They took their belongings and departed. Yetrik wondered if he should talk with the girl more or leave the conversations for the road.

"Are you ready for this?" She faced him with a smile.

"I guess so."

"Don't worry, you will enjoy Kzhek, even though many of the Zhaesmen are as stiff as the pride of a Priessman."

"How many times have you been there?"

"A fair amount, enough to experience their culture for what it is."

"Do you recommend taking anything there while on assignment? Any spices, as Thane Gett suggested?"

"I like their cooking. It's tame and basic enough to focus on the core ingredients. Other than that, anything he recommended."

"I don't mind broadening my horizons." The two exited the Canton and walked into the midday sun.

"Well, I will leave you here. We'll see each other soon enough." She gave a friendly wave as she turned and departed to the west.

Hours remained before sunset. His stomach urged him to find some food at a local market or tavern. He deserved it, having pushed off his second meal too long.

Checking inside his small coin pouch, he found two petiir, enough for a decent meal. He was better off financially than most his age, much of it due to the investments that he had made in local establishments as a youth. His financial acumen surprised many, but in truth, his parents had monitored his funds until he reached his twenty-second year.

The poorer sections of the city—not the slums beyond the center—provided some of the finest cuisines at a cheaper price. Eastern Gruth dishes were his favorite, comprising potatoes, carrots, onions, and a liberal amount of seasonings, topped with the most popular fish of the season.

The food sector of southern Thusk was filled with vendors and customers alike, appearing like a swarm of bees in a narrow corridor. The scent of sauteed root vegetables and grilled fish filled the air. Booths lined each side of the street, spanning half as wide as an average Thusk cobblestone way. From above, one could feel the excitement of rich cultural unity, while marks of poverty hid on the streets below. Rodent excrement lay crushed in gutter corners, food waste and other trash remained strewn along the street. Beggars sat curbside, hoping to obtain sustenance to let them live yet another day.

Trying to avert his eyes from the gloom, Yetrik searched for a Zhaes eatery. He found one to his right, advertising "authentic steamed ham." As he approached the door, he saw an empty produce box held by a disheveled man sitting against the building.

Yetrik leaned down, handing him the contents of his coin pouch.

"Why?" the man said as he turned his bearded, dirty face to look at Yetrik.

"Because we are not yet as Sleffmen, my Gruthman," he said with a grin. "You are of more worth than my two coins."

The man smiled and shed a tear as he clutched the coin pouch. Yetrik left without another word.

CHAPTER FOUR

REST AND UNREST

The journey homeward was lonesome, yet peaceful. Phenmir's nights had been spent at affordable inns and were more pleasant than his final night in Zhaes. His stomach growled. It felt like it was digesting itself, though he couldn't tell if the sensation resulted from hunger or the anticipation of seeing his family again.

The Northern city gate looked same as it had the day he left. Had he been overconcerned by the riots? The steed continued through the arched gate, entering the cobblestone streets of the Chuss capitol.

He had returned. He dreamt of this since his arrival in Kzhek. His soul breached the surface of the seas and could finally breathe after months of drowning.

Domed buildings and red rooftops characterized the city. Large palms decorated the streets. Though the climate seemed harsh and desert-like, the land continued to produce life. It was late in the afternoon, though the sun remained on the horizon, providing sufficient light for people to wander the town. Children accompanied their parents, men conversed over spiced tea, and shopkeepers received tips for service. Hints of cumin and cardamom wafted from plates of grilled camel steaks. Red sand filled the cracks of the cobbled streetway. Musicians paddled on large drums to accompany the songs of long-necked lutes. This was Court Chuss. This was home.

After a few minutes of slow riding, a wooden sign hanging from a post came into view. Sliin Ghete. The large panther-like beasts were already visible by the shimmer of their green scales. He dismounted and tied the steed to a post, entering the establishment to retrieve a stablehand to accept the return. His ghete scratched over its hearing holes, trying to pry off the bridle from its earless scalp. He had grown quite proficient at ghete riding under the circumstances. In the past, he often traveled with a slower group, but riding on his own was a freeing experience.

A brawny woman with short black hair in a white blouse and red trousers prepared ghete feed inside the wood-paneled building. Phenmir caught her attention upon entering. He approached her with a smile.

"Heloath," Phenmir said. "I'm returning a ghete from Kzhek."

"Quite the journey," she said with a smile as she placed her held food basin on the floor near the feed trough. "The tag, please?"

He removed the leather tag.

"Thank you. Care is the Creed." She took it and placed it in her left pocket to be sent back to Zhaes to confirm an honest return of the ghete.

"Care is the Creed." He left and continued southward.

He had not yet heard anything related to the Krall or any revolts. Shopkeepers cleaned entryways as they prepared to close their doors and taverns bid farewell to their dining guests while welcoming the nighttime crowd.

Chussmen of all ages filled the city square as he entered the dense center. A large group had aggregated near the grand footsteps at the entrance of the Krall's castle. Curiosity tempted him forward and led him towards the group.

The square's occupants held large sheets of parchment with a variety of words poorly inscribed on them. The banter was loud, but they seemed like a docile mob compared to what he'd been expecting. He estimated it held a minimum of two hundred Chussmen.

"Excuse me Chussman," Phenmir asked a bystander. "What is going on here?"

"Where have you been? We have been here each day from dawn till dusk!" the man snapped at Phenmir as if he was a dullard.

Phenmir paused. "Forgive my confusion, but I have just returned from Kzhek. I rode into the city moments ago."

"Conspiring with the enemy, huh? Are you one of them that supports our sorry excuse of a Krall?" He turned away from Phenmir to leave him without another word.

"We have been protesting the Krall and his graft," said an approaching Chussman. "I recognize protests aren't the most effective form of political activism, but we needed hope that something might change."

"Have you had success?"

"I guess we will see tomorrow during his speech."

"How many of you are there?"

The man forced a laugh. "Today was our largest crowd yet. I have heard rumors of similar groups forming throughout the Court. I even met a traveling Sleffmen who came to protest. You heard they had groups protest harvesting in their Court, right? Can you imagine? Sleff banning harvests and Chuss allowing the crime? What is happening to Facet? Anyway, join us tomorrow. There is strength in numbers."

The spirit of justice burned within Phenmir, yet he focused on his return home and left the central square.

The rest of his way home was spent in quiet contemplation as he took in the familiar sights of shops and homesteads near the city center.

Phenmir slowed his approach to the red wooden door at the top of a staircase. Their home sat above his health clinic, which was in operation whenever he was not on a foreign assignment. Though it was a smaller house, it fit their family of three well. At their age, he and his wife expected no more children. They would need no additional space unless Hir married soon and continued to live with them. The boy was almost nineteen. Still young, but not far from marriage.

He climbed the stairs and knocked on the door. The scratch of wood on wood broke the silence as a chair moved beyond the closed door. Footsteps approached, and the door drew open.

"Phenmir?" Meira embraced him as he dropped his belongings on the doorstep. She was a slender woman with dark Chuss skin. Her platinum hair was voluminous, with tight curls that reached down to her mid-back. This was the woman who won Phenmir over so many years ago and continued to impress him at every glance.

They stood with arms intwined.

"Hir! Come to the door!" Meira shouted, stepping back. The years had not worn them in their marriage, but had bound a relationship stronger than the finest alloy smelted in the Cloven Gleff.

"Father!" Hir shouted. He ran around his mother to take his turn to embrace his father. "It's good to have you back."

"I could not stay in Zhaes any longer after I heard—"

Meira smiled. "It's okay," she said, placing her hand on his shoulder. "I figured. We're fine. Very few have embraced the Krall's choice. Their numbers have diminished to nothing, or so I've been told. Most of the protesting has shifted against the Krall."

"Thank Cheric that you two are safe. Don't worry, I'll keep away from the riots." He saw her worry and winked to diffuse it. "I know it's getting late, but I need food. I've eaten nothing besides a small bowl of oatmeal this morning."

"What about the Krall's speech, mother?" Hir said, catching his mother's attention.

"Yes, Hir," she then turned to face her husband, apprehensive. "Tomorrow the Krall will try to defend his acceptance of the graft, or so we suppose. I feel it would be worth our time to listen before we condemn him further." Her words brought a scowl from him. "I'm not advocating for him, Phenmir, but it is our duty to lend an ear."

"Well then, we'll go. I just pray that we will have nothing like the forging of The Pact of Province," said Phenmir. "When the other Courts tried to bring us into their pact of harvesting, I almost raised a spear myself."

"You mean The Induction? When they decided to implement harvesting?" asked Hir.

"Sorry, I forget that the Zhaes radicals have given that pseudo-war a name." The Induction. No better way to hide an atrocious agreement than by giving it a bureaucratic title.

"That's been the worry." She brushed her palm against his unshaven cheek. "I'm just happy to have you here. We can discuss your career once the Court ensures peace." Regardless of his employment status, leaving Kzhek in the middle of an assignment would result in a significant gap in their funds.

"It's good to have you back." Hir bid his father a good night, returning to his room. Hir seemed the same as always. Phenmir had worried he had missed much of Hir's coming-of-age while on assignments. All a father could hope for was to be present enough in his child's youth to help shape them into a stalwart citizen.

Phenmir placed his hand on the back of Meira's neck. He pulled her in to kiss her forehead. "We'll talk in the morning. Let's enjoy the night as if all is peaceful." She nodded and left for their bedchamber while he went to prepare a small nighttime meal.

A variety of fruit lay on the corner table next to assorted grain and two loaves of bread. He smiled as he caught the scent of cumin and crushed coriander seeds. The stone counter was wiped clean, though Hir's books remained stacked in the corner. Red dust still stained the doorway, but little else remained on the black and white decor. Phenmir ate two cinnamon dusted chunks of bread with a honey drizzle at the pace of a starved predator, eager to return to Meira's side. He wiped the corners of his mouth with the edge of his sleeve, brushed the crumbs into his hand for one last swallow, and took his belongings with him back to his bedchamber.

Warmth filled his chest as they shared a grin. She was folding his clothing, having already taken his bag into the bedchamber. "Please tell me you have left minimal stains on your clothing this time."

Phenmir let out a quiet laugh. "I try my best, but you know what I have to deal with. Let me help."

"No need. I enjoy your husbandly scent."

"You mean my bodily fluids and the putrid odor they carry?"

"It's natural," she replied. They laughed. He had missed her unconditional love. She could take the driest land and produce the finest of roses.

"I have missed you, Phenmir. I hate your absence in the bed. Sleeping without you is not the same."

"I'll be here for a good while now. We will leave any problems for the future." She embraced him again, and he noticed a tear sliding down the side of her nose. "Meira? What is it?" He stroked her hair to console her.

She let herself go, neck jerking with each sobbing gasp. He wiped her tears away with his calloused fingers. "I'm here, Meira. Let it all out."

"I just—" She sniffled. "I didn't know what to do when the Krall announced his support for harvesting. It feels like I am still traumatized by when they introduced the horrendous process and forged the Pact of Province for the harvesting Courts. I have never seen so much hate and I cannot bear to see it repeated. Hir was too young to grasp the magnitude of it. He was only thirteen at the time, so I have been trying to keep myself together and not draw my emotions into it. Perd, it's been five years of harvesting already. I just... I need you here with me."

"And I will be," he said, pulling her tighter. "Nothing will happen to us and we will not allow harvesting here. I promise. I will do anything to ensure it." *Even if it means my death.* "Let's get some rest, Meira. We have a lot to catch up on in the morning."

After crawling under their covers, Meira drew close to Phenmir. She quickly fell asleep as he stared out their window, contemplating his sins.

I am done. I will never take part in or allow a harvest to occur in front of me again.

His guilty conscience warred with his attempt to sleep. *You still allowed it. You took part in a child's death.*

But they had already perished! Killed by the guilty only moments before. I had no choice.

You were their tool, the one to bury the body.

I was forced against my moral law to provide for my family. I will find another way. It is over, never to be continued.

Your past cannot be absolved. You are complicit.

He paused in fear, muffling his own sobs.

You did it. The Zhaesmen told you that the Krall took the organ from your last harvest and returned to Sliin before you. You provided the last graft. You provided your Krall with this organ.

⸻ ❧ ⸻

Phenmir arose from the bed as Meira slept. The sun had warmed their room beyond his comfort. Had he grown too accustomed to the chill of a Zhaes morning?

"Heloath, Phenmir." Her husky morning voice was one of the many qualities that he had missed.

"Heloath, Meira." He returned to the bedside to kiss her cheek. "When is the speech scheduled?"

"Noonday. They will ring the central bells an hour prior." They looked into each other's eyes. They would have each other, no matter how divided Facet would become. "Will you make sure Hir is awake?"

"Of course,"

It felt nice to wear clothing other than those he had in Kzhek. He felt cleaner at home. His spirit was where it belonged.

Hir's door was already open. Stepping around the corner, he saw his son in the depths of a thick text.

He turned to see his entering guest, placing a hand in between his book pages.

"Heloath, Father."

"To you as well, Hir. What are you reading?"

"Medical Advancements in the Age of the Harvest. Don't worry, I am not being indoctrinated. Wasn't it written by a Chuss guild?"

He nodded. "I know the work." Just like his father. The thought brought warmth to his soul. "I read it the year it was published. Was that two years ago?"

"Something like that. I'm enjoying it. Our scholarhood has been focusing on medical philosophy, hence the assigned reading. Maybe later I can get your opinion on our lectures. This reading was educational, but I had some opposing opinions to the progressive ideations of many of the Zhaes scholars."

"Just wait until you read from the Priess philosophers if you want to experience a waste of words."

"Oh, I know," he said with a laugh. "Feuith Gedrhee is the worst excuse for a scholar that I have ever read from. No one can learn anything from his philosophy."

"Your parents raised you well," Phenmir said with a wink. "Ready for the day?"

"I guess so."

"No matter what occurs, it is important we are there."

"Yes, yes, just let me know when you are ready and I will be at the door."

He nodded and left to prepare his morning meal. Three portions of grain were prepared and set on the table, topped with seeds and honey. He took a seat and began to eat, savoring the Chuss honey once again.

He should inform Garen Renss, the Thane of Haleness, about why he left. He and Thane Renss got along well, dancing the line beyond professionalism into friendship. Phenmir was one of the most respected medics in Sliin and worked as his commanding advisor for the Canton of Haleness. The Thane always provided a considerate ear when Phenmir needed to let his emotions run.

He spotted a pile of letter parchment on a desk across the room and found a quill and inkwell in the drawer. Without finishing chewing, he set his spoon down and began to write.

Garen Renss, Chuss Thane of Haleness

I hereby inform you of my temporary resignation from medical practice outside of our Court's boundaries. My stance against harvesting is not unknown to you. My care will be henceforth designated to the benefit of humankind, and no more shall my title be associated with the atrocities that are practiced abroad.

I look forward to seeing you soon,

Phenmir Stolk, your commanding advisor

He sealed the letter in a small package, tucking it into his pocket to be dropped off on their way to the city center.

He pulled his empty bowl to the edge of the table as Hir and Meira sat beside him to break their fast. He told them stories of his time in Court Zhaes.

Likewise, they relayed stories about how they had spent their time. Meira cultivated crops in their sector's shared field, visited her sister and mother, and gave voice in public sessions related to the Chuss faith in the years of harvesting. Hir had continued his studies and was preparing to finish his primary years of schooling. Soon, he would attempt acceptance into the Patriarchy.

Phenmir, like many, was uneasy with the Patriarchy of Scholars, despite the prestige of their membership. Their secretive sect was exclusive and their machinations were reclusive, but they were the most renowned scholars on the continent. Scholars from all the Courts joined their ranks to study the 'unknown tenants that bound humanity' as the nobility proclaimed, whatever that entailed. Hir felt drawn to them as a youth and spent much of his time reading the works of Scholarly brethren. His interest was sparked when a messenger presented him with an invitation to apply for the Patriarchy. Many of his classmates were intelligent, but there was something special about the boy. Beyond his doubts, Phenmir knew that the Patriarchy stood for the benevolence of the Courts. Hir was the embodiment of beneficence.

"Hir was already studying when I woke!" Phenmir said.

"Really?" Meira did not sound surprised.

"Father even knew the book that I was reading."

"Well, what did you learn?" she asked, taking a bite of her oatmeal.

"The recent advances in medicine are remarkable, thanks to the Eurythrins who are, in my opinion, the most remarkable type of Endowed. I had heard that they were responsible for grafting, but never knew the details of their history."

"Yet another gift from Cheric that is abused by the harvest," Phenmir said.

"Well, yes, they can heal, and I understand that they were used in surgical practice, but what do you mean the Eurythrins helped establish harvesting?" asked Meira.

"You tell her," Phenmir said, gesturing to his son. "Let us see how well you recall your facts. Show us you are the scholar you claim to be."

"You really don't know?" Hir asked.

"You know I'm a woman of politics. Medicine is your father's world and harvesting has only been a part of our world for five years. Seeing that we do not harvest in our Court, I might not know as much as you would expect, especially regarding the science of the endowed organ."

"Besides being able to heal themselves from wounds, they have increased blood flow and can clot exposed areas in less than a second. This allows healing and support when part of the body is missing or dead. This was discovered after some of the first Endowers experienced miraculous recoveries. People lived when they should have died. Well, medical information was quite archaic before this, as I am sure Father can tell you. The past ten years since this discovery have been the most remarkable period of medical advancement in history. Does that make sense?"

"Yes, yes." She nodded.

"Once medical professionals began to work with Eurythrins, they attempted to compensate parents for the Endowers to perform tests for medical research."

"They must not have been Chuss parents with such a careless attitude." scoffed Meira, turning to Hir. "I would never give you over to become an object for research, even if you were a born an Endower."

"I believe the parents were Zhaesmen or possibly even Sleffmen," Phenmir replied. He gestured for Hir to continue.

"They opened these subjects so they might study live human anatomy, even discovering how parts of the body function. This provided information for life-saving surgeries and taught them proper ways to close open wounds for effective healing. I cannot bear to think about the pain they endured."

"Eurythrins have a higher pain tolerance." Phenmir added. "Call it a benefit or a curse, as you will."

"We still lack crucial information for repairing many of the complex parts of the body, such as the brain. When the researchers opened an Eurythrin, they found the key to the Endowed abilities. Endowers were born with two umbilical cords, but they found that these children had an additional organs. One connects to the placenta while the other feeds the mother's nutrients directly into this third intestine. They hypothesized that if they were to graft this portion of the organ onto an adult, the adult would manifest similar abilities. Unfortunately, they were correct. No Endowed could survive without that aspect of the intestine. It was as crucial to their body as the heart."

"Yes, that is how I understood it." she said. "Something that I never understood was how they could transplant these organs, but a heart transplant never works."

"Oddly enough, the body practically never rejects the endowed organ, no matter the host. Bodies reject foreign organs, such as hearts and lungs. Perhaps one day we can understand this issue, but the endowed intestine is almost always accepted by the host's body. If the organ would make that person into an Eurythrin, a Gorger, a Feelman, or any type of Endowed, it doesn't matter. The specifics of that are beyond my area of expertise. I'm sure that father could clarify any of my discrepancies."

"You seem to know it as well as I do," he smiled at his son.

"From then on," Hir continued, "children under one year of age were chosen. It went through the courts, The Induction, and henceforth. You know the story, now you have the science behind it."

She smirked.

"But you already knew most of that, didn't you?"

She chuckled. "Have you forgotten who your father is? I just wanted to see how much you have learned. Lets see if you know this. What of the blood flow of those who received the grafts? Surely, that much blood loss during surgery would kill anyone trying to receive it."

"What I've heard," Hir turned to his father searching for confirmation, "is that surviving bloodloss is yet another feat of the Eurythrins." Phenmir nodded. "As Shiftlings can alter parts of their body, Eurythrins can alter bodily functions of others. While the host is opened, a Eurythrin can halt their blood flow long enough for the organ to be added. The blood stops like ice in a frozen tunnel and resumes after. By then, the host is stitched up, and the Eurythrin can cause their heart to pump faster to keep the blood moving. They can also induce sleep, preventing pain during the operation."

"You've raised a wise one, Phen." said Meira.

"You have done just as much as I have, Meira. Well done, Hir," said Phenmir. "I can tell you've spent a lot of time in those tomes. Just never forget the consequences of harvesting. Zhaes scholars often omit undesirable information. They claim that most Endowers die within their first year, but it is actually less than half, according to Chuss research."

Phenmir turned toward the sun casting through the window. Morning had come. The hour of the Krall's speech was nearly upon them. Anxiety filled him.

Following their morning prayer routines, the family took to the cobbled streets. Doors opened and closed around them in a cacophony of excitement as townspeople joined them to walk towards the castle grounds in the city's center.

The crowd moved like honey through a thin tube. Progress was slow, but they had left well before the scheduled start. Unfortunately, it seemed as if half of the city had done the same.

From the corner of his eye, Phenmir recognized the central message station. Drawing his family to the left side of the alleyway, he placed his letter within the collection basket for high priority sending, leaving an additional payment attached to the back side. A letter from a commanding advisor to his Thane would likely be delivered before twilight if the city remained intact after the Krall's speech.

Taverns and shops had closed to allow people to attend, although some remained open to reap the benefits of the high traffic. Phenmir held his wife's hand with his left and placed his right on Hir's shoulder to prevent losing each other.

He had not yet seen the most current Krall, having been so recently inducted, yet he already loathed the monarch.

After a bottleneck into the city square, the castle was visible, high above the crowd. The central square was designed so the balcony of the southern castle wall stood near monumental stone walls that curved outward from the castle's balcony. This feat of engineering projected a speaker's voice, allowing distant viewers to hear what was spoken. The balcony was free of any occupants, as expected so long before the scheduled speech, yet all present Chussmen fixated on it, unsettled.

Most of the crowd remained calm and collected, but some rejectionist extremists stood together to voice their opinion. Hir informed his father that he recognized many of the rioters. Phenmir admired the spirit of the younger generation. Youth often spend their early adulthood trying to overturn tradition, and yet these were fighting to preserve it.

A trumpeter played from the castle balcony. The call silenced the audience but did not quell their anticipation. Seconds passed like hours as each Chussman maintained eye contact with the small crack between the castle doors.

Finally, the doors opened and Krall Mehnrin Diphlek stepped to the railing to face his audience. The crowd erupted in a thunder of shouts, the sound of an ocean amid a hurricane. Phenmir could not hear a positive word or sound of praise only defamations and curses worse than any angry drunkard would dare speak. At least unity could be found somewhere in Facet. In protest, people often meet their closest allies.

The Krall remained silent through the chaos. Minutes passed until another blast from the horn silenced the cries of unrest. Gradually, the audience settled.

"People of my Court!"

"Traitor!" was shouted alongside a variety of other degrading slurs.

"Zhaes pawn!"

"Power-hungry swine!"

"False Krall!"

"Child eater!" was possibly the most derogatory way to refer to an Endowed. While it was not particularly correct, it packed a strike of abhorrence. Endowed did not eat the child's organ, but Phenmir appreciated the grim defamation of the process.

The trumpeter blew again. "Respected Chussmen!" shouted the Krall to gain the audience's attention. It felt as if he was trying to stop the wind from blowing.

"Fear not change, Chussmen, for we are at the dawn of a glorious epoch!"

The doors behind the Krall opened yet again to welcome another individual onto the balcony. Distance obscured the figure, but a yellow robe was visible with a hood that shadowed the face. More followed, but the Krall paid them no notice . They formed a line before the door like guards.

"As many of you have witnessed, riots and protests continue to arise. We will maintain strength through acceptance of divine power, while others fall into false ideals of righteousness. Court Sleff is facing such a crisis. Falling away from the change that we will now accept. Only the sinful fear change. Let us not be as the impoverished Sleffmen."

Upon mentioning Court Sleff for the second time, a figure stepped forward. A flash of silver near their waist caught Phenmir's eye.

"I have—"

Suddenly, the Krall collapsed. His head fell off his shoulders, tumbling past the railing of the balcony and falling into the crowd as the frontmost man in yellow clove it from his haughty neck.

CHAPTER FIVE

CURIOUS BEGINNINGS

S cholar Brooth lit the torches as they descended the Athenaeum
stairwell; Aerhee followed.

"Mind the steps, Caser. Many fall victim to their steep angle."

"Are the texts below limited to Sleff writings?" she asked.

"No, but we will focus on those regarding Court Sleff. Each Court has
an area for its more exclusive writings. I suppose you have not been here
before?"

"Unfortunately not." *How difficult can it be to find a mention of Sleff
Endowed? Surely information is scattered throughout their records from
the past five years.* She would not disappoint Thane Lettre. Finding the
source of the lack of Endowed in Sleff was an important piece to resolving the riots against harvesting. Regardless, it was sure to be a significant
step. She did not fully understand the connection between the missing

Endowed and the riots herself, but she trusted the Thane's insights. He believed that revealing the whereabouts of their Endowed would help dissolve the distress in Court Sleff, thereby preserving the peace in Court Zhaes.

"A 'secretive' section may seem fascinating, but do not lose yourself in the search. This part of the library provides extensive personal information on many living nobles, others within their circles, their ancestors, and the Court as a whole."

Brooth descended the last step and proceeded toward the right wall of the spacious chamber, lighting a torch, which triggered a cascade of lights to line each of the walls.

A long corridor between shelves that reached the ceiling continued onward for what seemed like the length of the entire building. Each section of shelves bore a Court's banner that faced toward the walkway. As she proceeded, she noticed that intricate gates stood at the foot of each of the banners.

Scholar Brooth removed a chain of keys from his robe's inner pocket. Together, they halted at the gate that stood below the yellow Sleff banner that bore an embroidered silver spinerat.

The lock clicked open. Brooth held the gate back to invite Aerhee forward.

"You are unlikely to find any works of fiction within this collection, unless undeniably relevant to the Court's core. Ledgers of past Kralls, statistical reports from past Casers, and historical documents make up most of this area," he said, pointing to the shelves on their left. Turning to the right, he repeated the wave of his hand to display the monument of tomes. "And on this side, you will find that which interests you. Here are the collected works and associated texts related to the past years of Thanes and their respected Cantons. Follow me down a little to reach... which Canton were you inquiring about?"

"Endowment, though I only need records from the year of Manifest onward, nothing before the first Endowers were born."

Nearing the end of the section, Scholar Brooth stopped under a sign written in the scholar's tongue. She was surprised to find the language on this floor of the Athenaeum, but it only clarified that these records were not intended for the public eye. The inscription appeared to be no more than a long line with peaks and depressions, like a child's horizontal drawing of lightning.

"Four volumes cover your requested period. Do you want each one?"

"Yes, though I only need the texts for relevant areas to the Thane's request."

Brooth nodded and removed four large tomes from the shelf. Finely dyed leather and a flattened steel stud on each corner covered each volume of the front cover. Aerhee took each bulky volume, each one from Brooth's trembling hands.

"Any further requests before we return, Caser?"

"This should suffice for now. Thank you for your guidance."

He smiled, though it hinted at pain. Did her inquiries bother him? He passed Aerhee and beckoned her forward as he began to return to the main level, but she remained for another moment. Aerhee spent a few more moments scanning the other titles on the shelf, without discovering further works of worth, before moving to the exit where the scholar waited. He pulled on a lever near the base of the staircase that capped each torch, leaving the room hidden in darkness once again.

"I find it unlikely that any scholar would be disappointed by the absence of these volumes, but I ask that you read them quickly. These tomes are priceless and irreplaceable. You will not find such detailed collections anywhere else in Facet."

She thanked him for his assistance and left him at his desk with the Zhaes salute to bid each other farewell.

Upon exiting, she saw a ghete carriage and made swiftly to the street, catching the coachman's attention. She was relieved to find the carriage vacant. A quiet cabin provided some time for some reading.

Her homestead was in the northeast sector of Kzhek, neighboring the innovatively designed homes of the Court's Thanes and their high officers. Zeir, her husband, awaited her arrival.

"Aerhee!" he exclaimed, while concluding a report on his desk. "I missed you this morning." *I know, you tell me every day.*

"I had matters to attend to. Thane Lettre is keeping me busy."

"Yes, yes, everyone is in need to see the finest Caser throughout Facet." He winked at her, turning away from his work.

"The public would believe so." She replied and went to her bedchamber.

He was a fine companion, but requested too much of her time. They were legally wed, was that not enough for him? She felt he had spent too much time around the influence of Chussmen, based on his excessive desire for expressive affection. She avoided any form of confrontation, but he commented occasionally that she was "too literal a Zhaeswoman." An erroneous claim. One could not be *too* Zhaes, *too* loyal a servant to the almighty Laeih.

Aerhee placed the books on her bedside table. She shut the door to her study, catching a glimpse of Zeir's melancholic eyes.

⚜

Dawn brought the sound of the Stelcrested doves. Aerhee pried her face from her desk, feeling the creases from the book's edge on which she had fallen asleep. Leaving eating for another hour, Aerhee dressed and prepared to find answers. She took the four historical tomes on Court Sleff and left toward Zeir's writing desk. She determined, or justified, that he would not need the space until further into the evening.

Sleff Cultural Observations: Vol. 14. Aerhee pulled the largest volume from the bottom of the stack, surmising that it covered the events around the year of Manifest, which was confirmed upon reading the printed subtitle on the first page inside: *Years 322-324 in the Clerical Era.* Lifting the other covers, she found the volume to address the collected years of 325-326, 327-329, and 330-332, respectively. The binding creaked as it opened, the stiff hinge revealed that the book had not been used for frequent study. The abundance of information was overwhelming. From Zeir's desk drawers, she found a small, unmarked set of bound parchment and located a quill and inkwell.

She flipped past the title page and minutiae within the first pages to find the list of contents:

One: Recapitulation
Two: Proposed theories of endowed origins
Three: The year of Manifest
Four: The First Child
Five: Court Endowers
Six: Analysis of Calibers
Seven: Endowed origins - Zhaes
Eight: Endowed origins - Sleff
Nine: Endowed origins - Gruth

The titles continued, though she didn't know where to begin. Though she could entice herself with Court Sleff's initial reaction to the manifestation of abilities, it would be more fruitful study the Sleff Canton of Endowment during the years of harvesting. She lay aside Volume 14.

Endowment, Endowed, grafting, she thought would be the most efficient keywords for her search. She took the more substantial Volume 16, which observed the Pact of the Province and the following two years.

Hours of reading yielded few results. As suggested by Thane Lettre, there were many Endowed in Sleff during the earlier years of grafting. She could not tell if they had reached a hiatus, for all mentions of additional

Endowed in Sleff were omitted. Furthermore, she could not find any significant mention of Chuss influence, as Thane Lettre proposed. If they had influenced the Sleffmen, their activity was likely more recent. *More than anti-harvesters was influencing Court Sleff.*

The lack of clarity harried her. If she could not find a solution to the Sleff-Endowed dilemma, to whom would she go? Scholar Brooth would be a viable option, though she doubted that his area of expertise would cover such intrigue.

She followed the mentions of "benefaction," as indicated by the index. Near the end of the listed mentions, she happened upon a passage that caught her attention.

Zhaes Caser Felta Zhil served as a messenger to relay information between the Zhaes and Sleff Thanes of Endowment.

Astonished that she had missed this excerpt, she reread the two sentences.

Caser Zhil? She had met the previous Caser on fewer than five occasions and never became acquainted with her work, despite following her in the office of Zhaes Caser. Had the Caser controlled the information that was relayed between the Courts heads of harvesting, the Thanes of Endowment? Was she a pawn to the Zhaes Thane of Endowment? Was that Thane responsible for the missing Endowed in Court Sleff? Was he therefore responsible for the Sleff riots?

Caser Zhil's name was not the answer she was looking for, but the mention of her name provided a promising start to her search for the missing elusive Endowed.

She noted her thoughts in her personal ledger, a small, gray leather volume the size of an open hand with the Zhaes insignia on the cover—a bronze kaesan on a gray banner. *Why did they choose that demonic lion-elk for our sigil?* Most of her reading left her frustrated by wading through a fog of insignificant historical accounts, but relief filled her after finding a beginning through the former Caser Zhil, if she could locate the woman.

Metal on metal rang through their homestead's hall as Zeir prepared their midday meal. Her stomach growled. Politics was her language, while Zaer was better versed in the culinary arts, something she missed while traveling. Saliva flooded her mouth.

Zeir often worried that his wife distanced herself from him emotionally, but she treated others likewise. Her signs of affection matched the default for a Zhaes citizen. He was a true-bred Zhaesman, more Zhaes in blood than she, but he spent his adolescence raised on the southern border of Zhaes in the village Loboff, an hour's walk from the Chuss border. The proximity had etched itself into his character. He seemed to be more personable than any other man in Zhaes. A stern individual herself, she enjoyed his polarized view of the world. They complemented each other well.

A metal pot that hung above a modest flame, emitting the scent of steaming roasting carrots and chicken.

Aerhee joined her husband at the dining table which stood near the fire. It was not particularly cold outside, but Aerhee liked warmth. If she was envious of any Chuss attribute, it was their Court's heat.

Zeir reached across the table to provide Aerhee with a wooden dining plate and utensils. He removed the steaming pot from its hook and placed it on the table above a cooling cloth to prevent tarnishing their furniture. Aerhee spread the vegetable conglomeration on her plate, noticing small amounts of chicken, and took a piece of bread from a platter across the table. Zeir took the rest of the pot's contents and began eating as Aerhee stuffed the first bite into her mouth.

"I noticed you were reading this morning," he said with a mouth half full.

"Thane Lettre asked that I look into the historical basis of Sleff Endowment."

"Is he concerned with the state of their Court? I heard that the rioting has escalated to violence."

"I believe so." She hid the details of their discussion from Zeir. Spreading misinformation was on the same plane as gossip.

"Interesting." He focused on his meal.

Aerhee finished her course and proceeded to the washbasin while Zeir continued to savor each bite.

She returned to the desk, placing Volume 16 in her bag, and left for the city center, hoping to find a source of inspiration, perhaps within one of the Cantons. Zeir likely wanted her to stay and talk, but she had told him too many times how busy the Caser of Zhaes was. She knew he wanted more from her, yet she denied him. She denied it herself. She held back to focus on her work. Court Zhaes demanded as much as it had given her. She held a repressed hope that she could offer more, but recognized that it was unlikely with the demands of her calling as Caser.

Storm clouds of varying gray-blue hues decorated the sky with the somber spirit of Court Zhaes. Petrichor filled her nostrils. The beautiful scent had accompanied her almost every day since her arrival in Kzhek as a girl. Rainfall had ceased for the day, but evidence of precipitation was scattered across the damp road. Weather rarely bothered Zhaesmen. The skies could act as they pleased and it would not change their plans. To change would halt productivity. Maintaining one's composure in all situations was a Zhaes Ideal.

She walked towards the city center along the main road. Each step brought her closer to the center, while most of the citizens seemed to flee from it. Had something happened? She pushed it from her mind as she proceeded towards the city's Cantons.

CHAPTER SIX

A HUMBLE SLEFF EMBRACE

Court Sleff was a beautifully painted masterpiece of a wasteland. Yetrik could not move from the window as he viewed the capital city of Paiell. The architecture contrasted with the poverty he saw. Why did the city maintain its allure while the people appeared to be homeless? White buildings lined the streets The pale palaces stood like guardians without blemish or imperfection, yet they seemed empty of spirit.

Was the Court poor in general or did it have more poor citizens? Perhaps the inner city housed the nobility and scholars, or were they, too, without coin?

"Semi?" Yetrik said, trying to catch her attention as she watched the city through the opposite window.

"Yes?" She turned to look at him. Piercing eyes caught Yetrik, almost causing him to forget his words.

"Have you been among the Sleffman?"

"I've met a few," she said. "But I feel like I know the Court well enough. I have... spent some time here."

"Espionage?" He asked with childish excitement.

"Not quite, but you're not far off. Why do you ask?"

"Are all the people of Sleff poor? Or is there just an overabundance of beggars and homeless citizens that make the Sleff reputation? I just don't understand what 'Sleff poverty' actually means."

"I never took you to be so interested in the economy of other Courts. Most Gruthmen live their lives with their minds stuck in their homeland. Regarding the Sleffmen, the economic struggles span the population. A field laborer is just as likely to have a modest home as a Thane. Are you familiar with their law of humility?"

"Avoid the Priessmen?"

She laughed, "They might as well if they want to abstain from pride, but that is not the *written* law. They 'humble' themselves by giving their income away. It is a divine decree that each Sleffman gives their capital and only keeps enough to sustain themselves for a week."

"That is quite the dedication, but how can that sustain a community?"

Semi shrugged. "I don't know how, but it works."

Humility and submission are pressed so far that one becomes a victim of society.

Although he spent the journey with Semi, he read most of the time, sharing only occasional small talk when he felt prompted. In the coming days, he would be sure to make up for lost time and learn more about her, rather than sustaining empty small talk.

"We should be approaching the city center soon, if my memory serves," said Semi. She tried to look as far forward as she could without thrusting her head through it.

"See anything?" he asked.

"Nothing noteworthy. I am trying to see if I remember any of the... right there, I remember visiting that baker on our left."

"Is it worth the visit?"

"It's bread. It's what you expect," she said.

"I'll take anything at this point. How long has it been since we last ate?"

Semi continued to look out the window, not paying heed to his complaints.

Distant shouts pierced their carriage, growing in intensity. "Do you hear that? It sounds like a mob."

She nodded. "It's coming from the center."

He shifted his glance to the cityscape outside of his window. More people stood at the edges of the street, but the small window blocked any clear view ahead.

"Where is the coachman leaving us?" inquired Yetrik. "Safely away from this crowd, I hope?"

"East of the square, though we will pass through the area," responded Semi with no sign of concern.

She must be used to mobs and controversy, he thought. She was an Endowed. After all, they are the fulcrum of society's divisiveness.

"We should find a safe, preferably quiet place for the night. Do you know where we should go?"

She shook her head. "I doubt the coachman does either. He is just here to transport."

"Anyone we could ask for directions?"

"I think you overestimate my experiences here."

"You know, Semi, I could use some bread from your *friend* right about now." He tried to suppress a grin.

She laughed. It felt like the first genuine laugh he had heard from her.

"I don't know if a *friend* is the proper word, but it is worth a try to see if he knows anything. I'll tell the coachman to stop."

"How? He's outside of the cabin!"

"You'll like this one," she opened the door enough to provide space for her to lean out. With the voice of Thane Gett, she called out of the cabin door. "Coachman! Take us back to that bakery."

"Yessir," the coachman replied, pulling on the left bindings of the ghete to change their direction.

"Well done," Yetrik said as she returned to her seat. "Wait a moment, doesn't he know that the Thane never came with us?"

She shrugged. "It worked. I just needed a voice of authority to get his attention and Thane Gett ordered the carriage for us."

"Are you sure you want to divulge that you're an Endowed?"

"If Thane Gett wanted to keep it hidden, why would he have sent me?"

"I cannot argue with you there."

As the coachmen left and would meet them later in the evening, Yetrik peered through the bakery window, which was partially obscured with clouds of flour, and found the inside to be dark and barren.

"What do you propose?" asked Yetrik.

"At this point, I am willing to accept any option. Let's ask someone if they know anything about the protests. If we are lucky, maybe things have swayed back in favor of harvesting and we do not have to be so worried about staying away from them."

Yetrik followed her down the south side of the street.

"Excuse me, Sleffman," she said to catch a man's attention, "could you explain what is happening here?" She gestured toward the city center.

"Here?" he said, turning toward her. He was shaved bald and wore a vest without an undershirt. Holes and patches of mud covered his tattered pants.

"Where've you been all this time?" His eyes inspected Semi and Yetrik's clothing, eyes like a snake tracing their bodies. "You look like you're not from here".

"No, we are not. That's why we need some guidance," Yetrik said.

"Couple of high-borns. Here to punish us?"

Semi didn't move. "We are just here to check out the riots."

"I'm sure you do," he said. "Then you can run off and tell your Thanes about what bad people we are. I see what you're wearing. Quite the difference when compared to our rags. You're the real beasts here, making us live as you wish, killing children and all."

Semi wore anxious confusion on her face. Yetrik bit his trembling lip and was ready to flee on her signal.

"Yeah, I could tell you were a Gruthwoman from the moment you stepped out of that carriage. You know what? I don't recall having a full week's wage! I think you can help me with that one, miss. You look like you have some coins to spare."

How odd, Yetrik thought. *They are not willing to transgress their law to have money, but this man is willing to steal.*

Semi shook Yetrik's shoulder, pulling him from his reverie. The man was three arm-lengths ahead of them, but his pace was quickening.

"Um, Semi, I think we will need more reliable informants than these, um... friendly gentlemen." He and Semi paced backward with arms raised in surrender.

"Please, leave us be."

"What are you willing to offer?" he asked, sticking his hand in his pocket.

"We have coins."

"I'll be wanting a little more than that, Gruthwoman. You nobles are worth much more that petty coins."

A couple of other Sleffmen rose and started to gather around them.

"I command you to stop!" Semi shouted in a deep voice. It reminded Yetrik of thunder. Her Shiftling voice mimicked godly possession.

His sense of shock was evident as he nearly fell down. His sense of awe changed to malice as he angled his brows and stood with a smile that voiced vile intent.

"Hey, Sleffmen! Look over here. I think we got ourselves a child eater. Let's show her what we think about that." Some of the approaching Sleffmen pulled stained daggers and knives from their sides.

Are these the rioters? What else have they been doing with those weapons? Yetrik seized Semi and led her into an alleyway. *Where is a Gorger to protect you with their godlike strength when you need one?*

They continued taking quick turns to lose their pursuers. They heard the mob close behind with the sounds of battered shoes on cobblestones.

"Where should we go?" he said, low on breath.

"You're the one that ran. Don't you have a destination in mind?" She replied with no sign of exhaustion.

"I figured I would start and you would finish."

"Well then. Let's find somewhere!"

After a few more turns, the distance between them and their pursuers grew. Semi pointed to the right, toward an open tavern door. Many Sleffmen would see them there, but not their pursuers.

Semi ran ahead of him and slowed before she reached the door. Yetrik followed like a child running after his parent.

Pipe smoke filled the tavern. Stained windows cast a variety of yellows across the tavern. Five Sleffmen sat in the dining area, three of them at a table, and the other two on their own. A man with long, greased brown hair filled large mugs of mead for the lonesome drinkers. Six wooden tables stood throughout the room.

Semi directed them to a table on the left side of the room.

The man with greased hair walked toward them, wiping his hands on the stained white apron around his waist.

"If he asks, we're here to join the protests," Semi whispered to Yetrik.

"Heloath! What can I get you?" he said as he reached the table.

"Heloath, Sleffman. Do you have any woodland mead?" Semi asked.

"We have Priess Delight, Inland Heat, Seafarer Soother, Middleman's Bane, but I do not believe we have any woodland brews in stock... would any of those suffice?"

"Middleman's Bane is fine," she replied with a smile.

"And you, sir? Any of the meads? We have a fair selection of wine, if you prefer."

"Do you, perchance, have any teas?" Yetrik replied.

The man chuckled. "Feltleaf, tearfruit, possibly some jentail."

"Feltleaf would be delightful," Yetrik replied.

"I'll bring them right out," the barkeep said, returning to the counter.

"Middleman's Bane?" Yetrik said with a quiet accusation. "Are you trying to spend your time here intoxicated?"

"I want to appear comfortable. Maybe they will mistake us for immigrants. Any *true* Sleffman delights in Middleman's Bane, and I want to pry some information from this barkeep. As a Shiftling, I can manipulate how my body processes food and drinks. I can eat an entire swine and be hungry within minutes. Likewise, I can drink every drop of fermented fluid in here and walk out like I drank your feeble Feltleaf tea. At least try to seem competent, if you can."

"I abstain from heavy drinks. I want nothing to distract me from reality. Tragic or joyful, I will face life as it is."

She rolled her eyes.

The barkeep delivered their drinks and left them to themselves. The earthy aftertaste of the hot beverage reminded him of cold Thaust mornings with his parents. He was fond of his current life, but he often reflected on the past with longing. Nostalgia can be a positive sensation, yet it can become destructive if one obsesses over the past without progression.

Leaving his tea to cool, he saw that Semi had finished half of her drink. If anyone else were to drink that much, their body would have rejected the substance and forced it out violently within moments.

"You know, Yetrik, if we are ever in need of coin, I am sure to win any drinking bet."

"Great idea. What is more altruistic than stealing from the poor?"

Semi laughed and drank more ale. "Once you finish, I'll beckon him over. I can pay for the drinks, though I doubt the prices in this sector are low. Taverns nearest to the center are the most expensive."

"Call him over now," Yetrik said with another sip. "I'll need more time to finish."

She nodded, then hit her glass on the table with force, though not enough to shatter it. She caught the barkeep's attention and raised her hand to invite the man over.

"Sleffman, my friend and I are ready to pay for our beverages. How much will it be?" Semi asked.

"Two petiir for the Middleman's Bane, three for the tea."

Yetrik was surprised that the tea was more than alcohol. Nevertheless, he fished for the coins and set them, piece by piece, in the barkeep's grime-stained hand.

"Excuse me for asking, sir. I do not want to assume any political opinions, but we are here to *learn more* about the riots in the center. Can you tell us anything about them?" Semi asked.

"You are pursuing dangerous work." The barkeep's face grew serious. "If you were to enlist, now would be the time to do it. It isn't a quiet city anymore. How can I be of service?"

'Enlist?' Did these rebels see themselves as a military force? How deep did their ties run?

"Could you explain what is happening? Pardon our ignorance, but we have been traveling."

The barkeep pulled a chair from a nearby table and sat with the back against his chest. "Well then, prepare yourself for a revolution.

CHAPTER SEVEN

THE HARMONY ALLEGIANT

The man in yellow approached the edge of the balcony. Bronze-capped edge of the railing still dripped with the Krall's blood. The central square was a sea of hysteria. Screams and attempts to flee through bottlenecked alleys only invigorated their panic. He removed his gold-lined hood to reveal his face to the audience. They were close enough to see his nationality, if the Sleff-yellow cloak was already not enough.

"We are The Harmony Allegiant!" A woman at his side shouted. It was clear that she was a Shiftling, an Endowed who manipulated her voice to be heard over the roar of the Chussmen. Though many had fled the square, the voice would have been heard by the entire city. "Here to rise against the tyrants who slay our children."

An Endowed speaking against harvesting? What is happening to Facet? Phenmir stared at the balcony as Meira and Hir tried to push him away from the square. The speaker called for peace, but panic continued. What else would one expect with the death of their leader, regardless of the fallen monarch's conviction? Though Phenmir did not wish for the rule of a man who overturned morals, he did not wish for war. War was a feral activity between beasts and prey. War was not for an established people, but in eccentric actions of opposition, emotional irrationalities caused humankind to lose all stems of logic and bid them return to a primitive state.

The orator continued to address the multitude. "We are not here to disgrace your people, but to save you from the ideology of the wicked. We are here to make Facet a land in which parents no longer fear losing a child in the grasp of the nobility's greed.

"Our footmen will contact your Thanes and captains of office. With them, we will find ground upon which peace will be established. Sleff stands with Court Chuss!" The assassin then raised his hand in the Chuss salute to win the favor of the people.

Meira turned to her husband and grasped his hand as they shared a look of consternation. He noticed the fear in her eyes, not fear from their current circumstance, but a fear of how *he* would react to this escalation. He despised harvesting, and his last assignment had pushed him beyond hatred. His grip tightened on her hand, but he knew that only made her fear more.

❧ ❧

Colrig Fesst felt a rush of energy accompanied by triumphant relief. He had dethroned the Krall of Court Chuss, beheading the traitor.

He had organized the forthcoming events of the day. Before all else, he would need to finalize his proposal for the Chuss Thanes. The footmen had left a few minutes before concluding his speech and would arrive at their designated recipients' Forthold within the hour. He made sure that they spent the previous days studying the map of the city so they didn't get lost.

A troop of armed Sleffmen surrounded him with short spears, providing protection from any remaining loyalists to the Krall, though he doubted many existed.

"Well performed, Sir Fesst," said the councilman to his right.

"Thank you Teethir. I could not have executed it so well without you," he said. "I'll meet you and the others in the late Krall's council room. Please excuse me. I need to visit the washroom." Teethir nodded, corralling the councilmen to leave Colrig.

Colrig was relieved to enter the vacant washroom. The water developed a pink tone as blood washed off of his hands.

He faced himself, free of the need for justification. He shed the blood of a man for *the hope of the people*. Naked of shame, he faced the reality of what he'd done. *I am no Zealot*. He tried to convince himself that he was only a peacemaker, but knew that he was just as bad as any crazed activist. He had taken justice into his own hands. Killing to prevent more killing. He did something terrible so that terrible things might cease. He was the worst kind of zealot, one that believed that he was more just than any other person.

With a small linen cloth on the basin's right edge, he wiped away a tear and the few remaining spots of blood that specked his clothing.

For Facet. I live for Facet. He reminded himself, adopting the composure of a commander as he left the washroom, banishing any feeling of regret. Only the coming days would reveal the Chussmen's reception of his unorthodox gift.

His councilmen and the associated party members stood at attention in the Krall's council chamber as they awaited his presence.

Upon entering, Colrig waved for them to sit. The room impressed him, as it seemed to be more of a library than a council room. Large cases and shelves of assorted books lined the walls, reaching up three levels.

He assumed most of the literature was decorative, based on the books located high above them out of practical reach. Colrig sat upon a chair, a conglomerate of wood, fur, and decorative stones, making it the closest thing to a throne that he could find.

The councilmen fixed their attention upon him on the throne, though he had no intention of becoming a Krall.

"Hail New Sleff!" Shouted a man in the back of the room. Following his call, many joined in the chorus to produce any army's chant. "Glory to The Harmony Allegiant!"

Colrig gave them the Sleff salute, placing the heels of his palms on his temples and extending the fingers upward, invigorating the cheering.

"Sleffmen!" he called. "Sleffmen!" he exclaimed, catching the group's attention. "Put aside your celebrations. I want you to flood the streets with our message. Tell all who will listen that we are here to liberate them from the treachery of their fallen Krall. Invite any willing to stand against harvesting to join us! Remember Sleffmen, this is no mere revolution, but a turn for greater peace and justice for the young!"

<hr />

Phenmir stepped through the front door of his house and fell onto the nearest chair, still shaking after their frantic return. Hir joined him at the table. They shared a solemn glance, connecting as father and son.

Phenmir's laugh interrupted the silence. Meira entered from another room. Her face revealed her bewilderment, prompting her to question their behavior. Hir seemed to struggle to decide between smiling or cowering.

"What did I miss? What is so humorous that you two would laugh after a public assassination?"

Phenmir stood and greeted his wife with a pleasant smile, resting his hands on her shoulders.

"Meira, look at what has been done. We have hope! That tyrant will no longer change our way of life. I do not want to celebrate death, but I cannot contain my sense of relief. I expected to return home today, fearing to learn who would be the first Chussman to lose a child to the harvest."

"You support these radicals?" Meira was aghast at his irreverence. "These actions breed war! What do these Sleffman think they are going to achieve by assassinating the nobles of another Court? How will the other Kralls view this act of murder? The Gruthmen and Priessmen? Cheric forbid, the Zhaesmen?"

"Do you know who supported the Krall accepting a Graft?"

Meira responded with silence.

"In the worst case, these Sleffmen breed a war of their own. Our fate as a Court is yet to be determined. The time for action will come."

"I'm worried about the future. Phenmir, I cannot fathom Facet at war. What of our Court? What of Court Tchoyas? Will we all be forced to join their cause?"

"We will learn more about their intentions once they meet with the nobility. I am interested in learning what the so-called '*Harmony Allegiant*' hopes to accomplish. Meira, I will do all in my might to ensure safety for you and our family. Cheric is with us. If the man who addressed us in the city square will advocate our conviction, we have gained a new ally."

Do I feel the need to advocate this murder because I have been desensitized by the harvests performed by my hands?

"Leave me to talk to Hir." he said. "Enjoy your evening. Read, sleep, and do what pleases you. We will face the state of the Court once the Sleffmen clarify their motives, alright?"

Meira held her husband longer than usual, then smiled at Hir in passing and left for her room.

Phenmir returned to the table. "Your mother worries sometimes more than she can handle. I remember the first time I informed her of an assignment outside of the Court. You could not pay me enough to repeat that experience."

Hir smiled, easing the tensity in his shoulders.

"Be faithful that the events of today were for the best."

Hir nodded. "You are not considering joining in foreign protests, are you?"

Phenmir shook his head. "No, I will leave the rioting to the mob."

"Then what will you do?"

"I am not declaring my loyalty to these Sleffmen. I only recognize the demands of war if it comes. I just want your mother to be prepared for anything that might arise."

"Do you think the Zhaesmen forced the Krall to accept the graft?"

"Not exactly 'forced,' but I believe they influenced his choice. I doubt any man would overturn his morals without incentive." *Who is responsible for the actions of the Krall?*

❧❧❧❧ ❦❦❦❦

Silence swept the council room as Colrig returned to his seat. The eight Thanes of Court Chuss had joined him, heeding his invitation. The sun had fallen below the horizon line and the time for the council was due.

"Where is your Caser?" He exclaimed. Out of the corner of his eye, he saw a young man with a crimson overcoat and brown pants rise from a wooden chair. He wondered how well the boy was treated among the Thanes, who all sat in leather chairs that were designed for comfort.

"Here, sir Sleffman," he said with the Chuss salute, which Colrig accepted with the Sleff salute.

"What is your name, Chussman?"

"Jeith... sir."

"Thank you, Jeith. You may return to your seat." Colrig turned his attention to his audience, who quieted their arguments, but maintained occasional grumbling. "I recognize you would like an explanation for the *occurrence* this morning. All these matters will be addressed, but I would like to get to know you, as I like you to get to know me. We are not diplomats here to persuade you to live by our law, but are people of a righteous cause in search of allies. Seeds have been scattered throughout Facet and especially throughout your Court. A countermovement to Harvesting has been growing ever since the Pact of Province. Now it is time for the reaping. Today we expose our efforts."

"We have heard of harvesting rebellions," one of the Thanes shouted. "But you beheaded our *perding* Krall!"

"You Chussmen are pacifists, am I mistaken? More has been building up to this moment than you can see. The Zhaesmen, among others, had hoped that his graft would be a great triumph for harvesting, but we came to prove them otherwise in a demonstration most bold." Silence. "I did not want to act until it was necessary. A Krall attempting to join the harvesting cult warranted intervention." He paused. "I am Colrig Fesst, a mere Sleffman. Now, Jeith, please introduce the stalwart Thanes who sit before me."

Jeith stood once again, following Colrig's request without a sign of hesitancy. "Yes, sir! Each Thane, please arise upon your introduction...

"Thane Ream Tolst of the Forthold of Progress

"Thane Lann Prence of the Forthold of Scholarship and brother of the Patriarchy

"Thane Greth Hult of the Forthold of Diplomacy

"Thane Kevim Fren of the Forthold of Utilities

"Thane Aernim Reizh of the Forthold of Agriculture

"Thane Steef Mortriff of the Forthold of Endowment

"Thane Garen Renss of the Forthold of Haleness

"And Thane Phentov Belm of the Forthold of Veneration."

Colrig captured the eye of each Thane before dismissing them. He had already forgotten their names, but held confidence to act like he already knew them.

"I thank *each* of you for attending this council. Without a Krall, you govern the Chussmen and represent the Court's voice until a new Krall takes the throne. You are the Court that lives after the Ideal of endearment and charity to each man and woman. Most obvious in your refusal to condone harvesting. Respected Thanes, all I ask is that you extend your care beyond your Court. Aid us in removing future harvesting in *all* Courts."

"This is no new battle, as you said, Sir Fesst," said one of the Thanes. "Your efforts, while noble, will be fruitless. We do not wish to resurrect the conflicts created during the forging of the Pact of Province."

"Who are you to make such a decree?" asked a short, burly Thane. "You are no Krall or Thane of Court Sleff. No matter how sincere your pursuit, war cannot be led by protesting radicals, regardless of their roots."

Colrig remained unshaken. "I seek not to defend my title, or lack thereof. I am only here to extend a hand from a revolution that has *already* caught momentum. You must understand that I am not the only man responsible for the rising rebellion. Since the harvesting began, I have worked beneath the public eye to forge alliances with the Sleffmen who opposed harvesting. I have some connections with your Court and some with the Tchoyasmen, but now is the time for an official pact. We, *The Harmony Allegiant*, are no longer *a group of Sleff rioters* but a force. Chuss Thanes of the Allegiant, I believe that I have exposed too much to return. Might I reveal you?"

Four of the Thanes nodded and stood. The other Thanes turned to them with wide eyes.

Colrig spoke with hands spread. "Thank you Thanes Tolst, Reizh, Hult, and Renss. These four have been members of the Harmony Allegiant since its early days. I would not have come so far if I did not already have the allegiance of at least half of your Thanes." He waved for the Thanes to return to their seats. "We still need to strengthen our alliance with the rebels in the other harvesting Courts."

"So it was you who inspired riots in your Court?" asked Thane Prence. Prence was hard to forget, seeing that he was a Scholar of the Patriarchy. All Patriarchal Scholars dressed in the same white robes, regardless of their Court.

"You must recognize that this extends beyond harvesting. We will save the lives of the Endowers, but it does not end there. The Zhaesmen are responsible for this forced ideology. Our Court is too reliant upon the Zhaesmen for financial aid. The Priessmen do that which pleases them, regardless of our divine laws. The Gruthmen just echo chamber Zhaes preachings. The Chussmen and the Tchoyasmen are the only ones who escaped the grasp of the Pact of Province, but the Zhaes influence only grows further. This is about freedom of belief. This is about maintaining our agency beneath a greater tyrant. Do not let them attempt to control your next Krall."

The Thanes who had not yet joined the Allegiant became silent. Colrig waited as sweat streamed down the side of his face. He had poured out his emotions out to the men before him. He had slain their Krall as a bold call to action.

"The path of history is paved by the choices of the bold," said Colrig. "This is no childish rebellion to be taken as a thing of naught. We have collected momentum. We only require fortitude."

"Might you dismiss us to discuss this in private, Sleffman?" The Thane with the braid said.

"By all means." Colrig began to stand, but the Thanes escorted themselves out of the room instead. He should have been beyond confidence, already having half of the nobility as allies, yet he still spun the ring on his finger.

They returned after what seemed like an hour. "We have discussed your proposal," began Thane Prence. "It was determined that we shall join your cause, though we would have never been convinced you had not already recruited some of our Thanes. They offered sound advice to calm our concerns now, but we will have to speak later about other risks. We would like reassured incorporation of our opinions in the progress of your 'Allegiant,' especially in the case that war becomes necessary to eliminate harvesting."

"Yes! By my god and yours, I thank you, Chussmen! I will remain here with some of my men over the next few days to establish a base of operations in your Court. You mention war. Do you have a head of military? What about you Chussmen who were already members of the Harmony Allegiant? You have not reported anything of the sort to me."

The bald Thane spoke up from among the bewildered nobility. "Excuse me, Sleffman, but there has been no need for military command or resources for as long as I can recall. Perhaps other Courts have a structured militia, but try to remain passive pacifists when possible, though I suppose our passive era is being forces to close."

Colrig rested his chin on his fist. "Perhaps one of you would like to take up the role?"

Mumbles arose among the Thanes. The bald Thane once again spoke. "In war, both sides fall into defeat if death arises on either side. We have no man that who delights in the desire of bloodshed among us, nor any tactician."

"No true commander *desires* loss on either side," replied Colrig, "but they must understand when it is necessary. The worst individual for this calling would be one who seeks bloodshed. We need a Chussman or Chusswoman who lives the core faith of Chuss while having the deepest abhorrence for harvesting, one of precise skill that would not let the thrill of victory overcome them."

The bald Thane pressed on. "I fear that we have no one of such stature." Shouts echoed in the chamber. The Chuss Thanes argued, to no avail. None among them wished to take up such a mantle, nor did they suggest anyone that they all agreed upon.

What are politics without disputes? Colrig began to stand and call for silence, but remained seated as he spotted a silent Thane with a raised hand.

"Might I offer a proposal?" Thane Renss said.

Colrig waved his hand to prompt Thane Renss to continue.

"This individual is one of the finest Chussmen that I know. He lives by his faith. I know of no other man who detests harvests more than he. I believe he would be capable of military organization and would not be held back by pride or anger. He works as a medic to preserve life. His attitude would be similar towards warfare. This man knows scientifically how the harvest works more than anyone in Sliin."

"What do we have to gain from a medic?"

"Who better than a man who knows the heart of this conflict better than any other? Our Court is filled with self-proclaimed pacifists, yet I feel that he will be willing to give himself for the unspoken voice of the young. I received word from him stating just before our gathering that he recently deflected a position in Court Zhaes near those who direct harvesting."

"Who is this Chussman?" asked Colrig.

"I propose this position be delegated to my commanding advisor, Phenmir Stolk."

A few Thanes nodded.

"Well then," said Colrig, "we shall see that he is extended the offer following this council, though he does not sound fit for a general. He shall be appointed as my high advisor. A Chuss voice at my side who will command as a general when I see fit."

"Besides appointing a general, who will pay for the troops and their sustenance?" asked the Thane with the braid. Colrig was glad that some of them had such defining features as most of their names were well beyond his memory.

Thane Prence turned to him in an audible whisper. "They likely hope we might fund their militia. They are Sleffmen. How else could they pay for a new government?"

"Only the bigots who despise our Court see us as greedy. I assure you, good Thane, we do not seek to gain anything but justice and preservation of our individual faiths. You are not mistaken that we ask for financial assistance, but we can provide aid tenfold. Tell me, Thane, what do you know about Sleff Endowed?" asked Colrig.

"They are not my concern," he replied.

"Thane of Endowment? As the leader of the Chuss Endowers, you must know about the Endowed in the harvesting Courts, even though you do not have any of your own."

"Endowed are placed throughout the Sleff bureaucracy, as it is with each harvesting Court," replied the braided Thane.

"As would they have you believe." Colrig smirked. "And our Thane of Endowment, who works with these people, tell me what you know of him."

"We have never met, but I hear he is a fine man."

"And from whom did you hear this praise?"

"I confess, I have heard very little of him. I only hoped not to offend."

Colrig straightened. "As I assumed. The Endowed of my Court are as reclusive as the men who oversee them. The Thane is of no further concern, though the Endowed require an explanation. As you have suggested, Thane. Most Endowed are dispersed within the nobility. The people believe as they are told, trusting in blindness. You will find an occasional Endowed among the foremost authorities, which makes it easy to assume that Sleff simply has fewer Endowed. This, of course, is another falsehood." The room was silent. "Have any of you heard of *the Northern Colony*?"

✻✽✾ ✾✽✻

Phenmir turned toward his wife as she slept. Peace molded her features. The rising sun followed the Krall's demise with gold, a sign for a new era. He yawned and stretched like a cat, the fatigue of travel still laying heavy on him. The movement woke Meira.

Motionless and silent, they stared into each other's eyes and shared a smile. She blinked slowly.

Thoughts of the Court circulated in his mind. *Who will take up the title of Krall? Will he take the graft that was offered to their previous Krall? What is the public's reaction? Is anyone angered by the assassination? What of his widowed wife?*

The bed dipped lower in the center as he reached to kiss her on the cheek before rising. Yesterday's clothes sat in the corner, providing an easy target for the day's attire. He exited the room and dressed in the hall to keep his bedchamber silent enough for Meira to continue sleeping if she so desired.

He sat in a chair in the front room and noticed a book on a short wooden stool. He grabbed it, bringing *The Tome of Charity* into his lap. As he opened the dust-covered volume, a light knock on his front door interrupted him.

He felt uneasy as multiple voices spoke beyond his door. After checking to ensure that he had shut his bedchamber, he opened the latch and to the front door.

"Thane Renss?" Phenmir said in a voice only a notch higher than a whisper. With squinted eyes, he viewed the ornately dressed men outside his door. "Is this about my letter?"

"I have not received any letter yet, but some of my associates saw you return from Kzhek," replied Thane Renss. "May we enter?"

"I would invite you in, but I fear you would wake Hir and Meira. They had a long evening and could use the rest."

"Understood. I will keep this brief. We desperately need your expertise."

"Sir, I cannot return to Zhaes. I will only work for Chuss from now on."

"No, no, no, Phen, that is not what I was implying. We need your precision, your knowledge of grafts, and even your hatred for harvesting. We need a man dedicated to the well-being of Chuss. We need you, Phenmir Stolk. I would not have any other man."

"Sir?"

"Phenmir Stolk, my commanding advisor and trusted friend, will you serve your Court by taking the mantle to lead and protect? Will you stand with your brethren in the face of war?"

"If circumstances would arise, I would do anything for my people. You know that."

"Then, Phenmir, serve us in recompense for aiding the enemy in harvesting."

"Thane Renss," he addressed the man with squinted eyes, "what do you mean?"

"Help us lead Court Chuss to eradicate harvesting. Aid us to overturn the Pact of Province. Become the high military advisor for the battle ahead. Become our Thane of Harmony."

INTERLUDE 1

Clouds filled Bashin's vision. He sat at a table near the door and clenched his head. The room was a library made into a slaughterhouse. Entrails were dragged across the floor, twisted as if to spell some message, though they were not long enough. The victim's mouth was cut from cheek to cheek, making his mouth that of a screaming demon. Coins scattered the floor covered in crimson.

"Everything alright, Feelman?" asked one of the two Zhaes deputies accompanying him on the investigation.

"Yes, suppose I just forgot to break my fast this morning."

He read the deputy.

"Weak lie. I thought these Endowed were supposed to be worth something."

He was something! He was Inquisitor Feelman Bashin! A title that received no applause, only sleepless nights of work.

At least the deputy said nothing, merely thought about it. Was he too dull to remember that Bashin was an Endowed who could read his thoughts? *Forgive my weakness, you kulf. You may be a servant of the law, but it's not every day that you happen upon the corpse of the Krall's treasurer smeared across the floor.*

Bashin had accepted the organ, and it had its costs. He was loved by some and hated by what seemed like many more. Thank Laeih the walls were thick enough to block out the mob's shouts in the city center.

"Feel... read... learn anything? What does it say?" The second lawman asked. The more sensible one. Maybe his large head was worth something.

"What does it say? You expect the perding corpse to speak? *Who killed your master treasurer?*" He spoke as if reprimanding a disobedient pupil. "Enough of this. I've seen the body. Where are the palace guards? I want to speak to the witnesses." He turned to his deputies, pulling himself up with the back of his chair. "You two look around for any promising leads."

His vision cleared as the scent of blood and crushed organs left his nose. *Having accepted the organ of a child, one would have thought that I could handle the macabre.*

He passed by a pair of Zhaeswomen by a window. Each sat behind a cup of tea, though one remained untouched and near the middle of the table. He read the owner.

"*Doesn't she know that I disdain feltleaf? Perhaps she–*" Her thoughts were cut as Bashin drank the entirety of her cup.

"Excuse me?" she said in disbelief.

"I'm a Feelman," he said. He returned the cup to the table and turned to the other Zhaeswoman. "She prefers jentail tea."

Ignoring their astonishment, he wiped his mouth.

Revered by some, hated by others. Life of an Endowed was not as easy as those without abilities might believe. Some were seen as gods among men, but Bashin was not one of them. *Perding idol worshipers.* Too often, Endowed were no greater than the likes of him. Feelmen used to solve petty crimes, though this was an exception. Gorgers forced to construct buildings on their own. Shiftlings forced to use their bodies to entertain a nobleman's guests. Perhaps the deputy lackeys had it better than him, never expected to dedicate their life to a single skill.

He slapped the sides of his face and shook his head. *Enough self-pity, go find the treasurer's murderer.*

CHAPTER EIGHT

PURSUIT OF DOMESTIC BLISS

26 YEARS AGO, COURT PRIESS, YEAR 306 IN THE CLERICAL ERA (CL. ER. 306)

F aeth saw her ten-year-old daughter hiding behind the wall. She focused on her husband, hoping to shield the girl from the worry of being spotted.

She took a deep breath, trying to quiet her own anxieties. "Why *this* week? I had hoped for another week's wage!"

"If we were to remain any longer, we could lose our chance. I acted, hoping that we had already saved enough." Derlik, her husband, pulled her into a tight embrace and stroked her dark hair with careful fingers.

Her daughter stepped closer, causing the floor to creak. She only hoped that Aerhee did not think they were fighting. It was merely a *tense* discussion.

"I have a way for us to escape." Derlik spoke softly. "You remember Ferth, right?"

"Of course, I know Ferth! It's not like you have him over every week for late-night mead!" *Stay calm. Stay still, for her.*

"He has a ghete carriage, said it was a goodbye gift, but we have to use it immediately or he would 'lose a proper bargain.' I *trust* him, Faeth. Can you trust me?"

"I do Derlik, you know I do. I just worry about the border and finding a place to settle. And... the faith... You know how particular they are with 'sinners'. Do you think they will accept us?"

"They are not as welcoming as Court Chuss, that's for sure," Derlik said. "But these people believe in a good god, one that embraces change, right?"

"They do," she said, nodding against his chest.

"And you believe the Zhaes faith to be the one for you?"

"Yes."

"Then so do I," he whispered as he pulled her close. "If there is a god, then I trust him to allow us to leave our faithless Priess culture to join those who worship him."

She smiled, tasting salt as a tear streamed into the right corner of her lips.

"Aerhee," Faeth called, turning toward her daughter with red eyes. She extended her arm toward her.

"What's going on?"

Faeth tightened the grip on Aerhee's hand. "We are going to have to leave home for some time.

"Your father and I have been looking into the other cultures of Facet. They are all beautiful in their own way. Each land has its own belief, as you know."

Derlik looked at his wife as if to say, *"Just tell her."*

"We have been in Priess our whole lives. This is ... not the best place for us. We want you to live somewhere you can grow up to be a proper woman, one of honor."

Derlik reached in for Aerhee's hand. "We are going to Court Zhaes. You can learn so much there and will have a better life than if we remain here."

Faeth looked at the floor. "Aerhee, do you know what a 'god' is?"

She furrowed her brow in thought as Faeth rubbed her back. "The scholars say that gods are statues that the other Courts love because they give them rules. Some kind of Krall, right?"

"That is what they tell you, but can I tell you a secret?" This was the best way to entice her daughter.

Aerhee nodded and turned her ear towards her mother's mouth.

"There is a god–"

"Faeth, maybe that can wait."

She turned back to Aerhee. "Court Zhaes has beautiful mountains, new creatures and animals to see. I know you will make plenty of new friends there." *Ones who will not hurt you.*

"When are we leaving? How long will we be there?"

"Your father said that we need to leave soon. Do you think you can pack your belongings by tonight?"

"But how long will we be gone?"

"A while." She tried. "Take all that you can fit into this." She walked over to the closest to remove a large brown sack crafted from darkly stained leather. "Take only what you need, Aerhee."

Aerhee's sniffles rose like an emerging storm. Her lower lip quivered. Derlik called her name, getting her attention.

"We have to leave tomorrow. You remember Ferth, right? With the short beard and hair that looks like it grows from his ears? He has prepared a farewell gift for the road to Zhaes."

"New boots?" Aerhee asked.

"Not quite, but good guess," he replied.

Another thing to add to the list, Faeth thought, hoping they would have enough reserved coinage to purchase a new pair in Zhaes. At least for Aerhee. Faeth could go a long while with the holey shoes that she wore. She would do anything for her daughter, and so would Derlik. *Aerhee will have a good life. One free of pride and with enough funds to sustain herself.*

"He has a ghete-drawn carriage for us. The trip will be a lot shorter now, won't it?"

Aerhee's demeanor lifted to joy. They had never given Aerhee the opportunity to ride in a carriage or mount a ghete, even though most did not learn how to ride them before their fifteenth year.

"Really?" she said, turning to her parents.

"Really," he confirmed. "Now go pack your things, then get some sleep. We will have to wake before sunrise."

She nodded, taking the large bag, and dragging it towards her room.

The old hinges of Aerhee's bedroom door woke her as Faeth entered. "Little one, it's time to leave."

"Mmhm," she moaned as she adjusted her head on her pillow. Faeth lit the candle at her bedside, hoping to keep her awake.

Derlik snuck in, retrieving Aerhee's bag. Faeth left her daughter, knowing that she would wake with the sound of their guests.

Deep, cat-like growls sounded beyond their walls. Aerhee nearly tripped as she ran outside. Faeth followed with a hopeful grin. Two large beasts, each taller than Aerhee, were roped to the carriage with leather attachments around their head and shoulders. Their fishlike scent reminded her of the Gruth dishes that Derlik had attempted to cook from a borrowed recipe, ending each time with apologies for his "inauthenticity."

Derlik continued to load their belongings into the carriage as she rested an arm around Aerhee's shoulders.

"That's it. Anything we might have forgotten, Faeth?" said Derlik after loading their last bag.

"Did you grab Aerhee's bag?"

"First one in there."

"That must be it. Ready to leave?" Faeth said, looking for Aerhee's response.

Aerhee nodded and tightened her grip on her mother. Faeth attempted to move, but Aerhee slowed to turn back and look at the house. Aerhee was only ten years old. She had only ever known this home. Nostalgia would one day hit her with a strike delayed by childhood immigration. Her life would not be a calm pond, but a rough sea. Perhaps that was not a tragedy, if she could remain above the water.

Derlik lifted Aerhee by the waist into the carriage and she migrated to the far end of the bench on the cabin's right side. Faeth followed in and sat by Aerhee. Derlik joined and closed the door to sit on the opposite side of them.

Their coachman fed the ghete some unknown meat—at least Faeth assumed it was meat—then took his seat to start their journey. Their carriage shook as it accelerated down the road, away from their home.

Only Faeth had ever been to Zhaes. Despite her experience, she could not recall how long the journey would last. She prepared some small meals to stave off hunger; food options in roadside villages would be too expensive for their limited currency.

She felt Aerhee's head on her right arm. With their daughter slumbering, they could discuss the sensitive financial matters of their immigration without worrying Aerhee any further. Derlik watched the passing scenery through the window as she turned to look at him.

"Explain now, while you can," she said, maintaining a quiet yet commanding voice.

"What?"

"Your work."

"I have a job in fine materials."

"You know how vague that statement is, Derlik. I need to know the details."

"Well, I will work long days, late nights, and early mornings."

"And that would mean…"

"I will work a lot. Nights without seeing you or Aerhee."

Her frustration showed in her increasing volume. "Get to the point. Derlik. 'Working in fine materials' doesn't tell me anything. Are you working with fashion for the wealthy? Constructing fineries, or…" he cringed as her heart dropped. "No Derlik! You cannot do that!" she whisper-shouted.

"Whoa, whoa, be quiet. Aerhee doesn't need to worry about money. I haven't told you what I am doing. Why are you so anxious?"

"Long days? Fine materials? Pay to sustain us with no prior training? You are going to the mine bronze at the Cloven Gleff, aren't you? "

"Faeth…"

"You are!"

"We have no other choice!"

"What a wonderful way to feed into our identity as the 'poor immigrants'! You know the Zhaesmen see mining as labor for the poor! They practically use it as a secondary prison. I know we need the income, but mining is no job for the father of a ten-year-old girl! She needs you to be present in her life! *Laeih forbid* you to die there!" She felt empowered to swear using the name of her new god.

Derlik grasped her hands, her arguments drifting off as he met her eyes. "They take us for a thing of naught, regardless. We are Priessmen! Their equivalent to anarchists. Don't you think I've already fought these questions myself? I understand the danger of working in the mines. I won't have as much time with Aerhee, but at least she will be in a safe home, away from the Priessmen who prosecuted us for our faith. We will have a home, food on the table, and that is enough for me. Without a proper income, we will be deported back to Priess. Trust me. *Please*, Faeth. I will give my time and effort, my whole self, so that Aerhee might have a good life in our new home. I want her to have all that I never did."

Faeth covered her face, tears seeping through the cracks of her fingers. Derlik gestured to the space next to him. He removed his jacket and placed it in a personal bag for Aerhee to rest her head. She continued to sleep as though she had never moved. Faeth rested her head on Derlik's shoulder as they embraced.

"This is not the end," he whispered into her ear, "just the beginning, a stable foundation. Maybe this will only last a few years, then I can find another position."

Faeth muffled her sobbing with her hands. Whether it be the revelation of his labor or thoughts of raising Aerhee on her own, she could not tell.

Fears of immigration costs and legal entrance into Zhaes added to her anxiety. It was as if a land could proclaim freedom, but people still bow to the elite.

Their carriage calmed its motion as it slowed to the end of the rocky pass to the Eastern Zhaes border. Derlik returned The Tome of Measure to his worn leather satchel.

※※※※ ※※※※

"Are we there yet?" Aerhee asked.

"Not quite," Derlik replied as he watched the passing scenery. "We have to pass through the Zhaes border regulation."

"Border? We never had to pass through a border to Sleff."

"I know, little one, but the people of Zhaes are precise."

Faeth caressed Aerhee's cheek, still red from leaning against Derlik's bag. The night had passed, but Faeth had slept no more than a couple of minutes. A ten-year-old could not comprehend immigration regulations. Faeth herself could not understand why people would restrict anyone from living wherever they pleased.

Faeth feigned confidence with a smile at her husband as they exited their carriage with documents in hands.

Aerhee accompanied her parents to the immigration office. Inescapable for any who wished to immigrate to Zhaes, the chancery stood a minute's walk beyond the border. Aerhee clenched her mother's palm as they took their first steps into Court Zhaes, approaching the building that guarded the path to their future.

CHAPTER NINE

DIMINISHING SECURITY

Yetrik and Semi adjusted their seats, anticipating the barkeep's explanation as would a peasant reaching for a royal cuisine.

"The riots have been going on for a while, but it has taken a... less than civil turn. Too many rumors circulating to guess how it started. The revolt began with a group that calls itself 'the Harmony Allegiant.' They kept their meetings small, then invited the attendees to 'indoctrinate' the others. I was invited to one of their gatherings, but I am not the political type. Harvest or not, it's not my problem. I've got no wife, no younglings. I keep to myself."

"So they staged the riots?" asked Yetrik.

"That's my theory, it is too much of a coincidence. Sects host their secret meetings and then rioting begins?" he nodded. "I believe their leaders had something more sophisticated than riots in mind. People say they have been gathering in the shadows since harvesting began. With five years to plan, they must have more in mind than petty riots. Time will tell. Are you certain you want to join them?"

Semi took the lead. "We were sent here for business, but by happenstance, we found some people who shared our beliefs."

The barkeep seemed skeptical.

He swept his hand out to gesture at the room. "As I said, I keep to myself and just observe. No need to fret about crafting a story."

His nerves relaxed. The barkeep repeated his supposed "disinterest" in politics, yet continued to preach personal philosophies. Semi turned toward Yetrik. She made a motion towards the door while the barkeep was looking at his hands, rambling on about his past mistakes.

As the barkeep took a breath to fuel his discourse, Yetrik interjected his words. "Thank you, Sleffman, for the fine company, but we should leave."

"Yes, yes, yes." He waved them away. "I am sure you have many things to accomplish. Riots to feed, kingdoms to crush, and so forth."

They bid the man farewell. Yetrik followed Semi out the door.

Distant shouts still echoed, but fewer people filled the streets. "I think the inn that Thane Gett reserved for us is not far from here." Semi said. "Shall we head for the night?"

"I wouldn't mind some candlelight reading," Yetrik replied, taking quicker steps.

"Sounds good. I think I have seen enough of the city for the day."

"I couldn't agree more. We are only here to spend the day. I am sure Thane Gett would have us focus only on our work in Zhaes."

"Yes." He thought she sounded uncertain. "We must keep our minds on matters at hand." Was she frightened by the attempt on their lives?

"Semi?"

"Yes?"

"I am a Gruthman by blood, and I stand behind our Court's Ideal. You know that, right?"

"Yes, why?"

"I live as our Court teaches. I condone harvesting. I recognize the necessity of it, but ... does all of this protesting bother you? You know, being an Endowed yourself? How do you feel about Courts rejecting the gift given to them?"

Semi stopped and looked into his eyes, as if this were the first genuine conversation they had shared. "There are two sides to every coin. I hate to see people reject a divine gift. I know the woman who gave me her child's organ saw it as part of the will of the divine. Part of me still worries that she hates me for accepting the gift. I am sure that each Endowed occasionally doubts themselves, but people who protest the process fail to see how the abilities help us. Even Chuss and Tchoyas would fail without our Endowed. Our sacrifice compensates for their ignorance. We have become dependent on them. I fear how we would survive if we were stripped of our power."

Yetrik nodded as he watched the stones pass beneath his feet. He was comfortable being held a captive listener by her soft, melodic voice. The rhythm of her speech suggested a slight eastern Gruth accent, though he was not willing to bet a coin on it just yet.

"Gorgers have revolutionized labor forces. Feelmen have prevented deception by reading the minds of the guilty in courts of law. Eurythrins have allowed unprecedented medical advancements, and those are only the most common types! They say we have only seen the smallest fraction of what is possible. I've heard that some can control people's actions and others who never tire. We can now solve medical problems that would have meant death only ten years ago. Now, it seems the Courts are on the brink of war.

"They say that most Endowers die before their first year. Thank Deilf that only some children are born as Endowers. We know that very few children are born as Endowers, but every time one dies before they can grow, we waste an Endowed. Each premature death of an Endower is an

Endowed that we will never have. People may call us 'power-hungry child eaters' as they please, but a proper analysis of what the Endowed have done for Facet would silence the cynics. I am grateful for my identity and those of my kind, but we must not forget that we are all human."

He knew today was far from the only time she'd been ridiculed for what she was. He had always worried that many Endowed saw themselves as gods among men. Power can corrupt the humble, making one deem oneself superior to the one who created them. Such as it was with the heretics of Court Priess, though they would argue otherwise.

With a greater distance from the commotion, Sleff seemed to be a respectful and peaceful Court. Poverty was apparent, but money was not life, but rather a commodity that was used to survive.

"How well do you know Thane Gett?" Yetrik asked. Though the Thane recruited Semi, her timidity during their first meeting led him to wonder how deep their relationship ran.

"We've worked together, though I have kept our relationship strictly bureaucratic. I have no desire to know the man beyond business."

Yetrik nodded.

"Do you disagree?" she asked. "I do not loathe him. I simply prefer to work with more personable individuals."

"Perhaps you never knew him well. True, he is dogmatic in his views, but does not wish to offend others."

She nodded with pursed lips. "Perhaps you're right." He doubted her sincerity.

Their inn was decorated with torchlights along the outer gates, providing stark visibility for a safe return as the night struck. Every seat in the inn's tavern was occupied. It seemed to be a purely Sleff crowd, but Yetrik noticed a few individuals with a sickly pallor. *Why would Zhaesmen be congregating with Sleffmen so joyously, let alone in this political climate?*

Strong cheeses and fatty sausages filled the air. The party of Zhaesmen drank strong, aged meads from murky bottles with small, tarnished labels. They seemed to be in mourning or celebrating some victory, intoxicated under either circumstance. Semi ascended the stairs, and he felt it better to consult with her before pursuing contact with any civilians.

They shared a room with two beds and a single candelabra between them on a small nightstand with two drawers. The bottom drawer was lacquered shut, but Yetrik was able to force the top one open. Inside, he found the Sleff scripture, *The Tome of the Meek*. He had heard a few verses from the script quoted but had never taken the time to read it himself.

Returning the tome to its place, he glanced at Semi, who was looking at herself in the mirror in the washroom. She pulled her hair back, straightening it from the small braid which she had worn for the day. Sienna curls were left in her clean locks, complimenting her beauty that was not hindered by the sweat of traveling.

He admired how she cared for her appearance but was not governed by beauty. He could see her gray irises in her reflection. She left her lips their natural color, but a slight shade on her eyelids gave depth to her eyes. Embarrassed at being caught staring, Yetrik shifted to face the wall. As she returned to sit on her bed, Yetrik noticed a blush dissipate from her cheeks.

"Was there anything else you wanted to do today?" Yetrik asked to draw attention elsewhere.

Semi rubbed the bed coverings between her fingers. "Nothing comes to mind. I could use the rest."

"Did you notice the crowd in the tavern?" He hoped that intrigue would overcome her fatigue.

"The drunken louts who will probably continue to shout until morning. I chose to ignore them after I heard one call the other a derogatory term for an Endowed. I prefer not to associate myself with those who will not enjoy my presence."

"Well, true, but did you notice the Zhaesmen among them?"

She scowled at him. "Zhaesmen? Here? Most Zhaesmen would rather drink alone in the mountains than in Sleff, especially with all the riots."

He shrugged.

"Do you think people have come from Zhaes to join the protest?"

"It's plausible, but why wouldn't they protest in their home Court? Why travel so far to join the public unrest?"

"Are you proposing we ask them why they are here?"

"I see no reason not to."

Semi had already removed her boots but put them back on. With the energy that was thrashing through the Courts, perhaps a blade would not be a poor investment, but he had nothing more dangerous than a quill.

"Ready?" she asked with a motion of her head. He nodded, and they pulled the door open with enough force to generate a small gust.

Most of the candlelight in the hallway had been extinguished, but the wood panels were still visible by the light of a single candle at the end of the corridor. They heard voices below, but not the shouts from before.

To his disappointment, he found only the innkeeper speaking to the barkeep, who was drying the used glass steins from the evening's customers. The Zhaesmen had left, but they had been present. Of that, he was sure. Some form of Zhaes business was being conducted in Court Sleff.

Yetrik woke before Semi the next day, anxious to leave Sleff and continue their journey. While Semi remained motionless in bed, he took *The Tome of the Meek* to awaken his mind for the day. He had read *The Tome of Measure* twice, *The Tome of Stability* countless times in his youth, among a few other Court scriptures, but he had never felt compelled to read "the book of the poor" as some had called it. Despite their dysfunctional economy, he believed that he could find something of worth within their scripture.

The edition from the drawer seemed to be abridged for simplistic travelers who lived their beliefs in a manner of tradition rather than devotion. The tome was worn with yellow-shaded pages to testify to their years of usage.

He opened three-fourths into the book and read from a chapter heading.

Seek thine fellow Sleffman's pleasure over the bounties of nobility

Yetrik admired their dedication to humility, but it led too often to self-degradation for the benefit of others. *To endure in righteousness, one must ensure their own state, then seek to strengthen those around him.*

Semi's covers rustled. He could not tell if she was just shifting or preparing to rise for the day. His bed creaked louder as he placed feet on the floor and walked to the washroom. He stared at the washbasin, recognizing his thirst. He left the room quietly to fetch a drink.

No one was in the tavern except for the barkeep, who leaned against the wall and smoked from a pipe as long as his tattooed forearm.

The barkeep was burly and balding. Serving as a Krall's guard would have fit him better than running a tavern. Bushy eyebrows of the same yellow as his beard covered his eyelids in his scowl towards Yetrik.

"Heloath, Sleffman." Yetrik raised his canteen. "Excuse me for bothering, but might I have some water?"

He squinted at Yetrik and took his canteen.

"A Gruthman, eh?" he asked with his back to Yetrik as water filled the jug.

"In the blood." Blood had nothing to do with it. His Gruth skin was a fair mediator between the Zhaes pallor and the dark tone of a Chussman.

After capping the canteen, the Sleffman reached his hand into the left pocket of his apron. "I assume you are Yetrik?"

"Yes?"

"This arrived from your Court no more than an hour ago, and I do not recall seeing another Gruthman spending the night." He removed his hand from his apron's pocket to reveal a small envelope made from a green-dyed parchment.

Snatching it, Yetrik read his name on the front fold above the stamped seal of the Canton of Utilities. *Only a Feelman could time his message so precisely.* It seemed that Thane Gett knew exactly when they would arrive.

"Must be an urgent matter if it is from a Canton." He reached into the apron's other pocket to remove an oil-stained rag as he returned to the bar counter.

Yetrik tore the envelope's seal but tamed his excitement to share it with Semi.

He gave the door a tap to warn Semi of his entrance. "Semi?" He cracked it open, waiting for her response before peering inside and entering.

He heard a light groan and a raspy "Huh?" from her side of the room.

"Semi, we received a message from the Canton of Utilities."

"What? What happened?" She sat up. The covers fell from her chest, but Yetrik was relieved to see that she was modest enough to sleep clothed. He had heard rumors of how loose the eastern Gruthmen were with nudity, especially during times of leisure on the seaside.

"The barkeep handed me a letter when I went down to the tavern room to fill my canteen. He said that it arrived via raven in the early hours of the morning."

She beckoned him forward with a finger motioning towards herself. Rather than handing it to her, he walked over and knelt beside her at the bedside and read from the bold ink.

Semi and Yetrik,

Due to political contention throughout the Courts, I request you make for Zhaes directly, avoiding Court Priess. My abilities as a Feelman warn of danger. I have seen horrific visions of the coming days. Do not delay, the Zhaes nobility will help you prepare. I wish I could say more,

May Deilf endure with you.
Firm is the foundation,
Thane Fortik Gett of the Canton of Utilities

CHAPTER TEN

CALLED TO SERVE

S weat beaded on his sideburns, though he could not determine if it was from the heat or the imposing figures seated before him. Phenmir sat among the eight Thanes of Court Chuss and a man who claimed to be leading a force against the "harvesting despots." The eyes of the nobility held him like archers aiming loaded bows.

"Our gratitude for the hospitality, Chussman," said the self-proclaimed leader in Sleff-yellow robes. If he was not mistaken, this was no innocent man. He had seen the Sleffman on the Krall's balcony before the city fell into disorder. Now he could clearly see the curls in his dirty blonde hair and an unshaven stubble.

"I would like–" began the Sleffman.

"Stop right there," said Phenmir, as his memory clarified his suspicion. "Were you not the man who was on the balcony today? You were the assassin."

"Allow me to introduce —" began Thane Renss.

"Thank you." Phenmir stood. "Thank you for doing what no Chussman would do." The words felt odd, yet not wrong. He should have opposed violence as a Chussman. Did he still? Years of injustice caused him to praise any promise of change. Harvesting required a permanent end, not a temporary cessation. Murder did not seem the best option, but it cleared an obstacle. He did not condone the Sleffman's decision, but it was a step towards justice. He extended his arm to shake the man's hand. "I may disagree with your methods, but I know when proper measures must be enacted to ensure the state of a population and their beliefs."

The Sleffman extended his arm to shake Phenmir's hand. "Colrig Fesst of Court Sleff, leader of the Harmony Allegiant. It is a pleasure to make your acquaintance."

Colrig turned to the Thane on his left. "Thane Renss, would you care to explain our proposal to Phenmir?"

"Phen," began Thane Renss, "Colrig leads a group that fights to remove harvesting and push back the Zhaes hand from the politics of Facet."

Hearing that one wished to overthrow the system of harvesting would sound preposterous from any other man outside the nobility. Their titles held credibility, strengthening his meager hope for change. "Respected Thanes, with no offense toward your capabilities, how do you propose such an insurrection?"

Colrig told an abridged version of the story he previously shared with the Thanes.

After speaking, he offered Phenmir a pause to take in the river of information. "My good Chussman," Colrig said, "I fear to admit that war will break out before we achieve our goal, but such a price is required for the crowning payoff."

Their unexpectant call to action coincided eerily well with his departure from harvesting in Zhaes. If Cheric desired to make his hand visible, now was the time.

"Would you have me advise the militias? Organize the structure of an army? You know that we Chussmen avoid conflict. I am no man of war."

"Very few are, but one can always learn. You would be my high advisor until you are prepared to lead as a proper general. I have spent years building up to this, secretly growing the Harmony Allegiant's forces. The Sleff troops are ready once I call them to march. Some of your Thanes have been at my side since the beginning and have troops willing to fight if necessary."

If he were to accept, what would Meira and Hir think of it? Would his people see him as a heretic and traitor for participating in a war? A true Chussman would sacrifice himself for the lives of others. He would be willing to be seen as human filth if it meant a safer state for Endowers and his Court alike.

"Chussmen, Colrig." He looked at each of them. "I should be reluctant to take upon myself such a responsibility, but the will of Cheric compels me to accept. That or my impatience with the Zhaesmen. I am honored by your call and wish to accept it with each part of my soul."

The men clapped and cheered until Phenmir called for their attention.

"However, I must speak with my family. May we meet again tomorrow?"

"Of course! Attend to your family. The family is the reason that we fight for the lives of the young, is it not? I look forward to tomorrow, Phenmir."

⚜⚜⚜⚜ ⚜⚜⚜⚜

As the final Thane exited the cottage, their small troop of guards followed the party closely.

Colrig approached Thane Renss, who avoided glaring at the surrounding unrest.

Colrig was not bound by such hesitancy. He looked up with complete sobriety, facing what he had done. He chose to slay the Chuss traitor, recognizing that not all would support him. One must be willing to accept the consequences for any violence they instigate.

Ravenous moles hounds dug through looted markets. Spinerats scattered from overturned barrels and devoured fallen produce. Dilapidation tarnished the Chuss capital with shredded tents and pillars on the edge of collapse. Fires burned in the distance as smoke billowed to taint the white clouds. Rogue gangs shouted for justice for their fallen leader. Others stirred up orange dust as they threw red rocks at any who stood with the Krall. While many denounced the Chuss pacifism in favor of an uprising, most hid in their homes and shops. Fearful eyes gazed through cracked curtains for any hope of peace.

"Is all well, Thane?" asked Colrig with a hand on the Chussman's shoulder. "Besides the state of the Court."

Thane Renss rushed them forward, guiding them through empty alleyways. Though conflict filled the city, contention was concentrated on the central streets. "I worry about Phenmir."

"Why?" He faced Thane Renss. "Have you recommended a criminal to join us?"

"It's not that." Thane Renss looked up and directed the group leftward. "Phenmir is back in Sliin because he has forsaken his career for his beliefs. I knew it was inevitable, but it frightens me that we have reached his tipping point. No matter how well you understand the atrocities of harvesting, your knowledge does not compare to Phenmir's experience."

Colrig looked at him in confusion.

"Phenmir is a surgeon. He has traveled throughout the Courts as a renowned practitioner. The nobility pays a fine price for his services, especially outside of Chuss. Phenmir has been a... harvester on occasion."

Colrig studied him.

"I pray Cheric forgives me for encouraging him to proceed with such work. If there is any guilty party, it should be me for providing him with the opportunity. Thane Hult, of our Canton of Diplomacy, and I were trying to mend old wounds with other Courts, but it seems to have cost us in the end."

❧❧❧❧❧ ❧❧❧❧❧

Meira sat on her bed with the covers over her legs as Phemir entered their bedchamber. She was reading from *The Tome of Charity*. *She was always the saint among us*, Phemir thought as he sat at his wife's side on their bed.

"Meira, I—"

"I heard. Our walls are not as impenetrable as you would hope."

He traced his fingers along her thigh. He looked up at her face with the eyes of a regretful hound. Her skin was like polished stone, smooth and buffed through years of living amidst the Chuss sands.

"What would it mean for you?" she asked. "For Hir and me? I am a spouse loyal enough to not criticize the heart of my lover, but I need to know how deep your conviction is."

"I do not worry about what I should do, but more so about the state of Facet. War, Meira. They mentioned war. Have we returned to such barbaric practices?"

"You know as well as I do." Her hand covered his. "A saint shall not quell offense amidst dominant hatred." She always stilled his soul with the holy words. "*The Tome of Charity* does not tell a saint to yield in the face of the enemy's avarice of hatred. We are to do as we feel proper to ensure the fair treatment of humankind."

He turned his hand to clasp hers, tightening his grip. "You're not opposed? Would you support my enlistment? Becoming their 'Thane of Harmony'?"

"My husband, a nobleman? Am I enough of an honorable woman for such a valiant knight?" They shared a laugh, but he could read the anxiety hidden behind her sarcasm. "I will stand by you no matter what. But that does not mean that I am giving you to be their object. They will not mistreat you. Go where you must, but I want to attend tomorrow's meeting by your side."

Her care had always made her the perfect mother. He jested that Hir's successes were her victory, but he meant it.

"And Hir?" she asked, without moving from his arms.

"Hir is a year shy of manhood. Soon enough, he will be a Scholar and therefore above us. I trust he will understand."

She rubbed her head on his chest; he took it for a nod. His work had already stretched their family. He feared it would only become more difficult in the coming months.

"Meira, you will never understand how much I appreciate you. Let's spend the day as a family." He sat up. "Though I trust Hir's maturity, I worry that recent events have shaken him. Not every child gets to live through the most eventful period in a historical text."

"And what do you propose we do?"

He captured her gaze. "Have you ever ridden ghete over open planes?"

<hr />

Colrig shaded his eyes from the midday sun. He walked up the steps to knock on the door to Phenmir's home, hoping not to alert anyone besides Phenmir. Colrig had a wife of his own back in Sleff, but he could not deny the beauty of the woman who opened the door. She stood tall and slender, with piercing eyes and shoulders held high to demand obedience.

"Heloath, Sleffman!" She waved them in, giving a slight bow to each Thane who accompanied him. Incense burned from a small pedestal near the door. The musk of sage and lavender reminded him of the chapels in his home Court.

"To you as well, Chusswoman." Colrig searched for Phenmir, to no avail.

The woman who had let them in sat on an orange wooden chair, gesturing to an assortment of objects in a semicircle. "I hope these stools, boxes, and chests will suffice for seats. Excuse us, but we are not used to such a large company. My husband will join us soon."

"Join us?" She acted as though they were her school pupils and she was the educator with a stern voice. Colrig sat on a stepstool and nodded for the others to follow.

The door on the left side of the hallway opened as Phenmir approached the party in the white garb of a medic.

"Pardon my delay, Chussmen, Colrig, I have a matter to attend to following this meeting in Western Sliin. Less work abroad, more at home." He sat beside his wife, who then placed her arm on his thigh and glared at Colrig.

"I assume you have some questions, Phenmir," Colrig said.

"I stand with you, Thanes of the Court, in service to our people." He turned to his wife, who nodded. "What will you have me do?"

Colrig blinked. "You accept?" His surprise was obvious.

"Indeed, Sir Colrig." Phenmir laughed. "I will do all within me to preserve our freedom and the freedom of the young who perish for the Endowed. If such a calling permits my loyalty to Chuss and my Lord Cheric, I will be at your command."

Colrig bit his lip, eyes squinted in valiant determination. "Well then, Thane Phenmir...."

"Stolk," whispered Thane Renss, earning a smirk from Phenmir.

"Thane Phenmir Stolk, welcome to the force of change. Welcome to the Harmony Allegiant. We have chosen you as the Chuss Thane of Harmony. You will be the commanding officer of the Chuss members Harmony Allegiant. You will help lead the military of the Chussmen under me as my high advisor. While I remain in command of the Allegiant, I will delegate certain responsibilities to you. We understand the lack of clarity surrounding your calling, but it will develop in form as we proceed forward. The Allegiant has formed over years, but this is the first time that we face public conflicts, including war."

"When is he leaving and for how long?" asked Meira. The only reply she received was a grimace from Colrig.

"Are we to sit in counsel within the coming days?" Phenmir asked.

"To a degree," he glanced at Meira. "Noble sacrifice comes with substantial change, Chussman. To see the end of harvesting, we must labor beyond the boundaries of Court Chuss. I request that your wife and son remain here, safe at home, in the meantime."

Phenmir locked eyes with Colrig as he bit his inner lip. "You will ensure the safety of my family?"

"I will assign my footmen as their personal guards during your absence."

"Are all the Thanes leaving the Court?" Meira stared at Colrig. "Surely you are not so ignorant of our Court's unrest to leave us without leaders."

"You can rest assured that only a few of your Thanes will journey with us," Colrig replied.

Zeira stared at her husband, then turned back to Colrig. "While my husband serves abroad, I will lend my efforts to the remaining Thanes to restore order to the Court. I am no woman of insignificant political influence."

Phenmir gave her a reassuring nod. "See that she is given the opportunity to serve as she wishes and I will join you, Sleffman."

"See to it, Thanes, and make sure their son is given ample protection." Colrig commanded. "Thane Stolk, tomorrow we journey to Court Tchoyas."

CHAPTER ELEVEN

DIGNIFIED ASSOCIATIONS

Aerhee had left her home to study the Sleff history books she had taken from the Athenaeum. She made her way toward Kzhek's center, unsettled by the less than amiable atmosphere for study. An army of torches arose from the crowd before Aerhee, appearing like a bonfire above the crowd. She had never experienced civil unrest. Zhaes was the Court of order. The riots in Sleff initiated the unrest, spreading to plague her city. Was it too late to study Sleff's history to find an origin to their unrest? Had they lost their opportunity to stop the growing rebellions?

She had faced many trials in her life. Loss, poverty, rejection, persecution, but never had she feared war or terrorism. They were unlikely possibilities that existed only in a bard's tale. That belief held no longer. War was the demon one never hoped to meet, but feared that they might.

She had forgotten how fear felt. As the crowd raged ahead of her, mutilating the Canton of Endowment, she stood in somber silence. As the rioters targeted the Canton of Endowment, the very building that led Endowed research, their objective was clear. The anti-harvesting riot was already attacking the core of Court Zhaes.

The largest members of the mob struck the building with large hammers. All other rioters used what they could to deface the Canton. Even some children joined in to throw stones through its windows. Sweat-stained merchants joined high collared aristocrats, all screaming defamations against harvesting.

Not only were the pillars of the Canton losing stability, she thought she had seen bodies amidst the stomping feet. How primitive had these people become to allow a difference in opinion to turn them into savages?

The city center had been home to inspiration and Zhaes piety. A Cathedral stood tall next to a shrine of Laeih. Across the square, she saw a chapterhouse of the Patriarchy of Scholars. Decadent stone benches with bronze edges were now tarnished and broken. Zhaesmen tended to frequent the city center for studying and worship. She had come for a sanctuary and received the antithesis.

She stepped back to flee, but found herself stopped once again by a dreadful sight. A Zhaesman hung above the crowd from the Canton's balcony. Rioters below threw stones and rubble, causing the body to swing and bleed.

The corpse was gaunt and wore bronze, signifying a higher rank. She recognized him instantly by the thick silver streak down his dark hair making him look like a skunk. Fheen Euress, the Proctor of Harvesting in Zhaes and the understudy to the Thane of Endowment, swung as a trophy to the revolting audience. Aerhee did not particularly enjoy the man's company, but she respected his accomplishments. She tried to numb herself against death. Those deaths closest to her had broken her for too many years. She tried to hold firm, but felt her heart give way. No one deserved to die like that. Aerhee prayed for him and his family, and turned before she was forced to ponder his death even more.

Aerhee needed to find shelter in another Canton. Part of her feared it would become another target, like the Canton of Endowment, but they had no reason to attack a building that was not associated with harvesting. *Or would they?* She needed to make it to the peacemaker. The Canton that bound differences between Courts. She could reach the Canton of Diplomacy within a few minutes if she walked quickly enough. Sheath Leisa, the Zhaes Thane of Diplomacy, would be sure to offer her some help.

The Zhaes image of perfection was growing worse with each act of vandalism and terrorism against the Court. The dissenters would likely be apprehended, their actions condemned by the high Krall, but when would the city see the light of justice?

She heard footsteps behind her, picking up pace.

She ran. She struggled to breathe, but pressed on with what little bravery she held.

The shouts seemed closer than ever, but it was all a mess of sounds to her.

This was not the Aerhee seen by the public, but the Aerhee that she had hoped to have tucked away in her adolescence. Caser Aerhee Kleeh was a confident woman, stern and exact in her actions, instilling fear in subordinates.

Now, her anxiety showed. She bit on her lip to muffle a scream that tried to creep its way up her throat.

The Canton of Diplomacy stood high before her, like a parent to save their child from the dark.

Her shaking hand found the handle, and she entered with feigned confidence.

26 years ago, the eastern border between Court Zhaes and Priess
Year 306 in the Clerical Era (Cl. er. 306)

The immigration office was uncomfortably cold. The stern administrator and the stone building intimidated Derlik like a ghete eyeing him as prey. He strengthened his grip on Faeth's hand, knowing she must feel likewise. After the man before them left through the front doors, Derlik and his family stepped forward to meet the Zhaesman who stood behind an ornate wooden desk.

The Zhaes immigration officer had a receding hairline with flat brows and lips as flat as the horizon.

He extended a hand. "Documentation, *Priessman*."

Derlik pulled out his leather satchel and removed three sheets of parchment and handed them to the Zhaesman.

"*There are three creatures in this world without emotion. The ravenous beasts of the field, the stones of the mountain, and bureaucrats,*" he recalled telling Aerhee once after visiting the Priess Thane of Diplomacy.

"Where is the official seal?" He pushed the papers across the desk, back to Derlik.

Derlik's blood drained from his face.

"From your Canton of Diplomacy," the man pressed.

Derlik steadied himself. "We left in haste. Departing from Priess is not as simple as you would presume. Please, sir." He moved to the left, making Aerhee more visible. "I'm sure a pious Zhaesman like you would understand our predicament."

The Zhaesman's eyes never turned to Aerhee. "Without Canton authorization, you must pay the immigration fees. One hundred and seventy jame is the charge." His face did not even hint at empathy.

"Sir, we cannot afford that. I am already consigned to spend most of my daughter's life laboring in the Gleff. Is there another way?"

"You may pass without charge, but that would be trespassing, a matter of illegal immigration. I would then be obligated to call for the authorities to seize you three and your belongings."

Derlik looked at his wife.

"We're already here," she whispered.

Derlik carried his family's savings in his satchel. He removed sufficient coinage, leaving only thirty jame, enough to sustain them for a few weeks, for their resettlement.

The bureaucrat took the money and the documents, signing the bottom of each page.

He returned the documents, dismissing them with a wave. Faeth held Aerhee's as they returned to the carriage. Derlik did not want to look at Faeth, scared that she would see him as a failure.

They boarded the carriage, closing the door once they had all taken their seats. Faeth sought Derlik's hand and twined their fingers together. They shared a glance, eyes in contact to pass a wordless conversation.

The carriage rode onto a finer-paved street and continued to the center of Court Zhaes.

Derlik held his Faeth's hand with a sweaty palm, the same one that had provided the Zhaesman with One hundred and seventy counterfeit Jame. The plans for leaving Priess were well executed. The Priessmen who had given him the fake coins were unable to forge or provide official documents to ensure immigration, but they had helped where they could. He owed his life to the Priessmen who were willing to aid in his family's escape. He had paid with counterfeit currency and left unpunished.

❦❦❦❦❦ ❦❦❦❦❦

The Present
Cl. er. 332

❦❦❦❦❦ ❦❦❦❦❦

Aerhee approached a group of Zhaes diplomats behind one of the four large pillars within the front chamber of the Canton of Diplomacy.

"Greetings, Zhaeswoman." A Zhaesman turned to greet her. "How may we be of assistance?"

"Where is Thane Leisa?" Aerhee asked.

"Might I ask why you are here? The Thane is quite occupied at this hour."

"Please inform her that Caser Kleeh needs to meet with her."

The Zhaesman straightened his shoulders and adjusted the collar of his deep blue overcoat. "Caser, I did not recognize you! Please forgive me, I—"

"Do not burden yourself with formalities, Zhaesman. Now, the Thane? "

A tall, thin woman descended the spiral staircase at the back of the room. Midnight hair fell to her right breast in a braid streaked with silver. She wore a gown of gray silk similar to Aerhee's, but her bronze hem extended to drape across the floor. *Impractical wear outside of one's home.*

Aerhee waved for the diplomats to resume their conversation as she left towards the staircase.

"Aerhee, it is good to see you. It has been weeks. I must have you and Zeir over soon to dine with us!"

"It is good to see you, Sheath." Aerhee tried to hide her concern, but knew it was useless in the presence of a Feelman.

She grasped Aerhee's hand. Sheath's smile dropped to concern. Aerhee could tell that Sheath was using her abilities as an Endowed to read her thoughts. It was not quite a physical chill, but as if something touched her soul.

"Come to my study." She grabbed and pulled Aerhee's hand.

Sheath led her down the hallway of the second floor and invited her to sit at her desk. The room was decorated with a new flower each time Aerhee visited. This time, two vases of pale blue roses stood on pedestals on each side of the room. Aerhee tucked her feet in under the chair, worried that she might track mud on the white pelt that spanned half of the room. The room was just as cold as any other canton office, but Sheath tried her best to make it seem otherwise.

Sheath sat down across from her. With steepled fingers, Sheath brushed her own chin with manicured fingernails, pondering in silence with the stare of a concerned parent.

Aerhee looked away from her, but knew that eye contact had nothing to do with Sheath's abilities as an Endowed Feelman.

"Will you tell me what bothers you?" Sheath asked.

"You already know." Aerhee scowled.

"Even if I can read your thoughts, it is not the same as a conversation."

Aerhee shook her head. "Sleff riots gain in numbers, *our* Court has joined their rebel movement, and the Chuss Krall has been assassinated? What are we to do, Sheath? Are we facing war?"

"The Thanes have been talking about this." She paused to read Aerhee, squinting her eyes. "So you have been working with Thane Lettre on his Sleff investigation? There is a lot to discover there. Zhaes and Sleff are closer than many would believe, like siblings."

"How so?"

"We have harbored Court Sleff like a parent to a lost child. Their economy is reliant upon our Court. I've spoken with Thane Lettre about this. As a Feelman, he thought I could be useful." She smiled. "I found it interesting that when the rioting began, it was in the Court least equipped to lead a rebellion. I *see* that you spent time researching their history in the athenaeum, but to little avail."

Aerhee nodded.

"I, too, have been working with Thane Lettre, discovering some anomalies regarding the missing Sleff Endowed. I have learned that our Zhaes Thane of Endowment opted for control of the Sleff distribution of Endowed, in trade for 'revolutionizing' their society through Endower usage. The Sleffmen allow our Canton of Endowment to manage their Endower, we fund their organ research, and seal a promise of more grafts for their Court. Our Canton of Endowment had Control and the Sleffmen would benefit by having more Endowers. In theory, it sounds quite attractive on their side

"In Court Sleff, you are likely to meet Eurythrins, Feelmen, Shiftlings, among other, if you are in nobility. As it is with every Court, one can expect some of their Court's Thanes to be Endowed. Most of the others Endowed are assigned to labor throughout the Court. The general Sleff population goes on trusting that the Endowers are just beyond their typical social circles. After some time, few suspect anything odd and just live without worrying about the Endowed in their Court.

"Then where are the promised grafts from the Thane of Endowment?"

Sheath shrugged. "Your findings regarding your predecessor, Caser Zhil, align with my discoveries. She worked with the Sleff Thane of Endowment as well as with ours, Tyrith Sorn. You read this on paper, but I learned that there was *more* to their relationship than what was shown on the surface. From what I remember of her, she had a severe distaste for the idea of harvesting before it was put into the Zhaes law."

"Then why did she work with the Thanes of Endowment, who *leads* harvesting in their Courts?"

Sheath smirked. "Why not ask her ourselves?"

"Do you know where she is?"

"No, but Thane Gromm will. As a member of the Patriarchy of Scholars, we can rest assured that a brother of the Patriarchy has access to the whereabouts of former nobles."

The Patriarchy. Aerhee's displeasure shone through her eyes.

"I haven't had the best interactions with them," Aerhee said.

Sheath sat in silence.

Hiding her past trauma was futile. She knew that Sheath was reading her, digging deeper into her derision of the Patriarchy of Scholars.

A joyous grin from Sheath's jest swiftly dropped like a falling stone to a frown of sorrowed concern. "Aerhee…"

Aerhee sighed. "Enough, Sheath. I try to avoid *those* memories and you should, too. We will meet with Thane Gromm as you suggested."

Sheath nodded, forcing a polite grin. Aerhee saw right through it.

"Thank you, Aerhee. We will see him in the morning. It's too late to travel through the city safely. I don't want to send you home this late. The tavern crawlers have likely joined the riots in a drunken rage, regardless of their opinions on the matter. I will have a room prepared for you to sleep here tonight."

"Thank you, Sheath."

"I'll meet you downstairs at the entrance at dawn."

Aerhee nodded and stood.

"Sleep well, Aerhee. Try not to worry."

If anyone was able to maintain professional composure as still as a statue amidst a storm, it was Aerhee. A woman who had fortified herself to become the ideal Zhaeswoman, living by the law in every way and not letting emotion misdirect her journey.

She offered Sheath a nod as she departed, knowing that her memories of the Patriarchy would haunt Sheath worse than any phantom ever could.

CHAPTER TWELVE

THE THANE OF AGRICULTURE

Yetrik was relieved to see the bronze-lined structures of Kzhek. Soon enough, they would meet with the Zhaes Thanes to settle matters they had traveled for–Bronze procurement for Thane Gett.

The closer they rode to the center, the more Yetrik's sense of awe dwindled. Merchants' stands and shops were abandoned. Debris from broken walls and windows littered the street sides. Disheveled and dirty Zhaesmen marched down alleys that lead to the highest building in the city. Their appearance suggested days, even weeks without bathing. The rioters were congregating in the center of Kzhek.

As the carriage veered away from the center,

Yetrik removed the roll of parchment with Thane Gett's directions. *Royss Belik - Thane of Agriculture. Canton - Northwest Kzhek, Alloy district.*

Few people filled the streets and light rain fell. Most of them wore long sleeves and high collars with no sign of dishevelment. They held their chins high and walked with elegance, seemingly ignorant of the damaged streets not too distant. Bronze statues, small and large, stood atop what he took to be churches. Zhaesmen rushed into their doors like water through the cracked hull of a boat. Yetrik wondered how long it would take for the street to fall victim to the rioters. He counted himself an optimist, but knew the dangers of a plague that is permitted to grow.

Semi's face was hard as she stared out the window with her chin resting on her palm.

The carriage slowed, and Yetrik was the first to open his door. He looked up to see that they had arrived mid-day, as the sky was covered by rotund storm clouds that blocked direct sunbeams, casting the tranquility of a Gruth twilight.

He turned back and offered a hand to assist Semi from the carriage, but she swatted him away.

"If anyone needs help, that would be you, Yetrik." She smiled to take the sting from the words.

In place of the cobbled stairway they'd find in Gruth, they found marble polished to reflect the ever-constant storm clouds. Spherical lanterns held onto the walls, providing light amidst the gloom. He held love for the buildings in his home Court, but could not help feeling as if the Zhaes architecture was years, or decades, ahead of the other Courts.

They entered the Canton to find twenty or so Zhaesmen, speaking in reverent tones, the opposite of a Gruth tavern on a feast night. Large portraits of a godlike being took up the right and left walls, likely depictions of their god, Laeih, in a metallic lacquer.

Yetrik noticed Semi ahead of him and made haste to reach her, cringing as each step echoed across the hall.

"Where are you running?" he asked.

Semi waved for him to follow, keeping her attention forward. "To find someone who can lead us to the Thane of Agriculture."

He felt tension in her voice, but felt it better to comply than to complain.

Semi veered to a man reading in a large black seat, spectacles resting on the bridge of his nose.

"Heloath, Zhaesman," Semi said. "Where might we find Thane Belik?."

He looked up, disappointed by the sight before him, and returned his focus to his reading.

"Hey, Zhaesman!" Semi commanded, changing her skin tone to match the blue leather that bound his book.

"Mistress, allow me to be your guide," the studying Zhaesman stood and motioned them down a corridor.

"Some Zhaesmen should be taken for blasphemers for their idolization of Endowed," she whispered to Yetrik as they walked a few steps behind the scholarly man. "Show them your power and you are as proper as any native in their eyes."

"Are you sure we should reveal your gift here?" Yetrik asked.

"We are in a Canton, not in the city center. I don't worry about any persecution here. Showing that I am Endowed will only earn respect."

The Zhaesman left them at the Thane's door, bidding farewell with a bow.

The murmur of voices was audible from behind the arched wooden door. Semi reached to grasp the door's bronze circlet and knocked.

Warm candlelight bled through the crack as the door opened to present a Zhaesman in lengthy gray robes with golden hemming. Damp black hair was slicked back to touch the base of his neck, matching a meticulously groomed beard.

"Thane Belik?" asked Yetrik.

The man at the door turned his head toward the two Zhaesmen further into the room. "Thane Belik, your presence has been requested."

A different Zhaesman approached the door, his demeanor a pleasant contrast to their greeter. He had the countenance of a miner that had bathed himself an hour ago; contrasting themes, but it fit him well. His facial hair was unkempt and much thicker than the other man's. If his skin were a bit darker, Yetrik would have mistaken him for a Gruthman.

"Heloath, Gruthmen! Excuse Thane Gromm. He treats each situation with excessive solemnity. Thane Gett speaks highly of you two. Come in. Lettre and I won't bother you." The Zhaesman reminded Yetrik of his favorite uncle. Genial, yet with a countenance that seemed to demand respect.

Thane Gromm seemed hesitant to allow their entry, scowling as they passed to sit on a gray cushioned bench. "Thane Belik, might we speak privately?"

"No need," replied Thane Belik. "Gett trusts them. Yetrik and Semi are your names, unless I am mistaken."

"Correct, sir," Semi answered.

"Well then, Yetrik and Semi, you have already had the *grace* and *pleasure* of meeting our Scholarly brother at the door, Thane Gromm, who presides over the Canton of Scholarship." He turned to the other man in the room. "This is Thane Lettre from the Canton of Veneration, head of Court worship and law. And as you might have concluded, I am Royss Belik, *the* Zhaes Thane of Agriculture. "

"The pleasure is mine, Gruthmen," said Thane Lettre. He was a typical Zhaesman. Tall, thin, with dark hair trimmed short.

Yetrik had never been in the presence of so many foreign dignities, let alone a non-Gruth brother of the Patriarchy. Thane Gromm's intimidating demeanor lived up to the Patriarchy's reputation.

"Thane Belik–" began Yetrik

The Thane interjected. "Titles are for peasants. Just call me Royss."

"Yes, Royss." The words felt uncomfortable in his mouth, like partaking in a five-course meal at the table of a poverty-ridden family. "As you know, Thane Gett has sent us to discuss his need for your mined products–"

"Yes, yes, the equipment is already..." Royss glanced at Yetrik. "You know what he is pursuing within the Canton, correct?"

Yetrik shook his head. "He informed me that he needed imported bronze, but that's all I know."

"What a tease. Send a boy on a quest to pursue an unknown prize. Maybe he sent you here for you to prove yourself before giving you his complete trust." Royss said, prompting an awkward laugh from Yetrik. "With the riots, we have more urgent matters facing us. I am sorry, but his requests will have to wait. But why not utilize your presence while we have you here? You Gruthmen are masters of the sea. Why not help us tame these waves of rebellion?"

"Thane Belik," interjected Thane Gromm, "such matters are not to be discussed with civilians."

"On the contrary," said Royss, "the state of one harvesting Court affects the state of another. Harvesting is a mere tenant of our problem. If the insurrection continues here, it will reach Court Gruth soon enough. Thane Gromm, I appreciate your sense of security and will keep this counsel within their jurisdiction."

"What are you talking about?" Semi asked. The situation had become no clearer.

"Gruthmen," began the Thane Lettre, "welcome to our council. We have been discussing how to best approach the riots that are tearing our city apart."

"We need a way to maintain order before we lose the city," said Royss

"And why do you think we can help?" asked Semi.

Royss grinned. "Thane Gett is a Foreteller. I've heard about his visions enough to know that he has sent you for a reason."

"Enough to bring them into *this* discussion?" challenged Thane Gromm.

"Have a little faith, Zhaesman." Royss replied. "What would you have of the public unrest?"

"It is a danger to unity in Facet," said Yetrik, "and a threat to all Endowed." He smiled at Semi.

"Ah, you're a Shiftling, right?" asked Royss.

Semi nodded.

"Then you are even more crucial." Royss slapped Thane Gromm on the back. "Come on, Gromm, these two are a gift from the Lord Laeih himself! We may be a part of the nobility, but we too are concerned citizens. Though you two have no authority within our Court, perhaps you may have some influence in your Court. Civilians today, Thanes tomorrow." He winked.

"How widespread are the riots?" asked Yetrik. "When we left, Sleff was the only Court in protest."

"You heard about the Chuss Krall, right?" asked Royss.

"In passing. So it really is true?"

Royss nodded. "The current state of Facet is subject to change from one hour to the next. As of today, the only anti-harvesting riots in harvesting Courts are here and in Sleff."

"So is Sleff completely overtaken by the rebels?"

Gromm cleared his throat and spoke. "Not entirely. Sleff is in a delicate balance, now leaning towards refusing harvesting with their population revolting against the choices of their 'oppressors.' Reports claim that some of their Thanes, though I have heard nothing of their Krall, are in favor of outlawing harvesting. Priess, Gruth, and Southern Zhaes are all in favor of the harvest, remaining loyal to the Pact of Province. Northern Zhaes is currently in a less formidable state. All reported Thanes remain loyal, as well as the Krall. Our Thane of Endowment has not yet reported his persuasion, though we can safely assume that he is in favor of the power that his very Canton controls. Tchoyas is in opposition as they have been since the pact. Chuss remains in opposition, though the consequences of their Krall's assassination are yet to be seen. Our informants wait patiently within their Court boundaries."

Thane Lettre lifted his hand. "It seems more likely every day that Sleff will fall into the hands of the rebels. They have grown too large, but we still have time to prevent the worst happening to our Court."

Royss turned to face Semi and Yetrik. "But don't worry, we have not entirely given up on the Sleffmen. Lettre has been working with our Caser to identify the origin of Sleff rebellions. There is a lot to uncover there, but if we can find that origin, we can find the heart of the rebellion and crush them at the center. If we leave the head of their rebellion alone, we will never be able to put a permanent end to this all."

"What solutions have you already discussed?" Semi asked.

Royss dismissed her comment with a smile. "We have some *early* ideas, but perhaps your perspective could help. Once we have a probable solution, we can approach the Krall to implement it."

"What have you discussed so far?" asked Yetrik.

"As Thane of Veneration," said Thane Lettre, "I could use the influence of the church to influence the rioters."

"But we do not want to militarize the church," challenged Thane Gromm. "It must always remain a beacon of hope, not of fear."

"What about the Patriarchy of Scholars?" Yetrik asked? "Their influence is greater than any single ruler."

"*Our* influence is attacking the problems of Facet from a different angle," said Thane Gromm.

Yetrik wondered what he meant by that. He tried to brush it off, knowing that the only people who understood the Patriarchy were the members themselves.

"And now you see why we are yet to find an answer," chuckled Royss.

"Why not sell the opportunity to become an Endowed to the community?" asked Yetrik? "I am sure you would secure the loyalty of the most affluent protesters. You could even–"

Thane Gromm raised his hand to stop Yetrik. "In an ideal world of perfect morality, that would be possible. Do not forget that the affluent are rarely the most ethical. If we were to permit the purchase of God-given abilities, it would be taken and monopolized by the corrupt. The empowered would become more empowered, eliminating the voice of the lower classes. As my fellow Thanes have said, this is a matter greater than harvesting itself. It is a matter of social order that is being challenged by deranged zealots."

Yetrik nodded.

"What if the Sleff Endowed join the rebels? Maybe they feel remorse for the child's life that was taken for their abilities." Everyone directed their focus to Semi in as if she had just prosecuted herself. "That would only make the riots even more dangerous. Unless I am an exception, every Endowed has wondered what would become of the children who gave up their organs."

Royss nodded. "I agree, though I am interested in another point that you raised. If the Sleff Endowed rebel, which they may already have, what will happen to our Zhaes Endowed? It is reasonable to suggest that the conflict which we are now facing will not close within the coming weeks, possibly months, or even years. The more time we give the anti-harvesting Courts, the more time their young Endowers have to grow into adults, therefore becoming greater threats."

"If we wish to persuade people to remain committed under the fright of opposition, we must hold their attention by drastic means," uttered Gromm. "The protesters have attacked our infrastructure and a price must be paid. Fear-mongering, though the tactic of a lowly man, is effective for obtaining obedience. If we were to execute half of the central mob, the remaining half would be forced to comply with our offer of peace. If our Endowed, perhaps Gorgers, serve as the executioners, they will recognize that harvesting is no force to oppose."

Royss nodded. "I must agree, Gromm. We must punish them before they can infect the rest of the Court."

Yetrik felt a cold bolt of energy fly through his spine. He had begun his quest and now was no time to withdraw. *Killing people because they fought for what they believed in? Where was the line between righteous justice and brutal punishment?* Semi appeared to be as unsettled as he was, though he wondered if she was thinking the same four words.

Firm is the foundation.

CHAPTER THIRTEEN

MASKED LOYALTY

P henmir stretched his legs as he exited the carriage. Days had passed since their departure from Sliin. Due to their party's size and need for discretion, they avoided inns and well-traveled roads, making camp each night on the barren roadsides. The Chuss desert gradually shifted from yellow sunbaked sand to the moist swamps of Tchoyas. Roadside desert rodents were replaced by amphibious putle, the large blue frogs with giant nostrils and an even larger rib cage.

He could not tell they had arrived in Fayis–the Tchoyas capital–or another village.

"Is this Fayis?" asked Phenmir. "Just ahead," Colrig pointed to the structures ahead, beyond mossy walls. "Too many suspension bridges in the city for ghete, so the carriages will leave us with some distance to walk. Have you been here before?"

"Yes, but it has been years."

He accompanied Colrig as the company marched toward the city. They had left the ghete carriages on the eastern border, giving the beasts a much needed rest.

"How many of the Chuss Thanes did you invite?" Phenmir was only able to see three, and the company was too large enough that he had missed the chance to count.

"Three came with us. Although your Thane of Diplomacy left with one of my chief officers for a journey to Sleff for more recruits."

Phenmir nodded.

Fireflies the size of gulls swarmed through the dense air and a variety of reptilian animals crawled over moss-covered rocks that stuck out of the deep blue water, an odd hue for a water so polluted by the grime of the marsh.

"Tell me, Chussman," Colrig pointed at a Tchoyasman with the mask of an ox. "You're a medic. How can their faces be bound to wood? Or is that just some rumor?"

"Oh, it's true." Phenmir looked at the other Tchoyasmen he passed, noting their masks but trying not to stare too long. A young girl with the mask of a squid held her mother's hand. On the mother's face he saw the mask of a human face, but one that held an expression of worry with arched eyebrows. "What do you already know about them?"

"If it's true, when they outgrow their mask, there is some changing ritual, and that their masks cannot be removed under any other circumstance."

Tchoyasmen were an uncommon sight in Sliin. Colrig's reaction suggested that they were an even rarer sight in Sleff. "Do you know why?"

Colrig shook his head.

"Although I specialize in digestion, I have worked with skin conditions. Working with skin entails training with mask exchanges." Colrig's attention was captured like a fly in a spider's web. "They are born without the outer layer of their skin on their face, requiring immediate coverage postpartum to prevent infiltration of disease or damage from the harsh environment. When they outgrow their mask, a private meeting is scheduled with a medic for a changing of masks. The procedure is a quick change, preventing prolonged exposure to the open tissue. The inner lining of each mask, though wooden, is crafted with a putle-derived substance that allows mucosal binding. Straps hold the mask on for a period but are later removed once the mask is fully attached."

Colrig stared at the muddy ground with squinted eyes, nodding slowly to take in the information. "Why are they so private?"

"Privacy is not a mere aspect of health, but a tenant of their beliefs." Phenmir lifted his right arm as if to make a proclamation. "'One of loyalty has no need to question the true face of another.' I recall hearing something like that when I asked a similar question. Nudity is not a concept among them. Sexual organs are no private matter in comparison with the sacred nature of their face. Regarding their tendencies, be aware of their 'open' nature if such a thing offends you."

Colrig nodded.

They entered the larger walkways and Phenmir spotted a wooden sign hanging from an arch. *Fayis - Steadfast is the Honor*, it read to proclaim the Tchoyas Ideal. Along the neighboring buildings hung two vast banners the size of a small sailing ship, bearing the Tchoyas sigil of a blue head putle on light gray. Large vine-covered willows decorated the riversides and ponds. Night had not yet fallen, but thick clouds warned of rain. The foul stench that stained the land outside the city had been replaced by a mineral musk of petrichor and herbal aromas from nearby plants.

"Will we be staying at an inn?" Phenmir asked.

"In due order, Thane Stolk, after we speak with the Krall. Have you met him before?"

"I haven't had the opportunity, but I've been looking forward to it ever since you mentioned the chance. When did he commit to the Harmony Allegiant?"

Colrig chuckled. "The Sleff Thane of Diplomacy was one of the first noblemen to join our cause. I led the group to ensure that we had an alliance with your Court, and he came to do the same here. Luckily, the Tchoyas Krall still held true to his anti-harvesting beliefs."

Phenmir shuddered as he thought about his Krall's death. He had to ignore it. If he thought about it too much, it would only cause him to question Colrig's methods.

Phenmir thought of his son and wished he could see this. He had tried to be involved in Hir's life, but had done far too little in showing his son the world outside of Court Chuss. Hir was soon to be an adult, but that did not end his calling as a father.

The pathway atop the quagmire continued into the inner city, though stone began to replace the wooden walkways. The center of Fayis was compact and busy. Children chased fireflies, a band of four played tubular instruments with a deep harmony, and older Tchoyasmen conversed outside of a tavern.

A monumental structure of gray polished stone stood before them, taller than any building in the area. The Krall's palace. Blowing in the light breeze, a Tchoyas banner confirmed its identity as the Krall's palace. Guards stood at each side of the entrance, each one clasping a spear. Their hoods hid any hair, obscuring their identity to only reveal their masks. One displayed a look of pain, as if the face was just informed of the loss of a close friend. The second bore a hopeful gaze, a pleasant contrast to the first.

Colrig stepped before the company to lead them into the entrance chamber of the Tchoyas Krall's palace. Five paces behind the dark wooden doors stood a stone podium. A Tchoyasman stood still behind it with the mask of a boar.

"Greetings, Tchoyasman," said Colrig. "I am Colrig Fesst of the Harmony Allegiant."

The figure remained still.

"Krall Trhet has requested our presence. Might we see him?"

Stepping down from the podium, the masked figure invited them forward with two fingers. Other Tchoyasmen were scattered throughout the corridor, ten by Phenmir's count. Only a careful listener could hear whispered conversations, as if they passed through holy sanctuary.

A Tchoyas guard pulled open one of two large doors, each one had a silver rim with the Tchoyas sigil in its center. Dim sunlight leaked through the stained blue glass, casting a misty glare across the chamber's occupants. A cacophony of voices fell to a sea of whispers as they entered.

The Krall's throne room was decorated with the finest adornments. Sapphire chandeliers hung from the high ceiling and silver seemed to be as abundant as wood. Phenmir admired how the beauty of the people contrasted with the begrimed quagmire. Juxtaposition highlighted the finest of the world's hidden beauties.

"Colrig of Court Sleff, come forth." Old age resonated from a voice ahead of them. The Krall spoke with the sound of a powerful whisper, each *s* ended with a whistle. He wore an owl mask with an extensively protruding silver beak with golden circles around the eyeholes.

As Colrig approached, the Krall arose from his throne that sat at the top of a staircase.

"It is a pleasure to make your acquaintance, Krall Trhet."

Phenmir stepped forward to see the source of whispers that had remained since they entered the room. He stepped through the company to see a large group of Tchoyas children, each one with a unique mask. He was perplexed as to why so many children were present at a diplomatic meeting related to an impending war. By his count, he estimated thirty of them. Phenmir studied their small, masked faces. Some seemed comforting with cat-like faces and pleasant smiles, while others were more unsettling, namely one with a deer skull and another with the mask of a fanged imp. He turned away from them, focusing on the diplomatic exchange before him.

"... departed for Court Sleff not long before our trail reached your city," concluded Colrig.

"We have likewise been establishing a military. Your Gorgers will be tenfold our worth if you have as many as you claim." The Krall walked towards the congregation of children, meeting one in a wolf mask as he stepped forward from the younglings.

"Though young, this is one of the finest men in Tchoyas." With a boney pointer finger, the Krall motioned to the wolf-masked boy. "Voln Zertef, *captain* of our Endowers." he announced as the boy made the Tchoyas salute, placing interwoven fingers over his mouth "At ten years of age, he was one of the firstborn Endowers in our Courts. It was his idea to assemble them into such an organization, recognizing that Tchoyas would be strengthened with all Endowers allied as they came of age."

"Sir Voln, I look forward to working together," said Colrig. Phenmir could feel the unease in Colrig's tone. How was one expected to treat a mere child with a political role?

"*Sleffman,*" said Voln as he shook Colrig's hand. Colrig stumbled backward, ripping his hand from the boy's grip with fright as the boy's hand transformed into a wolf's paw.

"As made manifest before you," said Krall Trhet. "Voln is one of our most talented Endowers. As a Shiftling, he has perfected his craft."

Colrig turned to the Krall. "As far as I was aware, Shiftlings are limited to voice manipulation and changing skin tone. I saw hair grow from the back of his hands and claws grasped my palm. How is that so? Have you been able to modify their capabilities?"

"Ask him yourself. He deserves as much respect as any Thane of the Court, if not more."

"Forgive me Voln," Colrig replied as he looked at the boy.

"'Sir Voln' sounded better."

"Yes, 'Sir Voln,' Enlighten me. How are your skills so refined to match folktales and fantasies?"

Voln looked at the Krall, who nodded. "We Endowers can learn to have greater abilities than those who steal our organs. You are wrong to believe that power comes only from our intestines. Endowers, if they are taught to, can use more power than an Endowed. As a *true* Shiftling, I have learned to change more than my voice and skin. Wolfmen are nothing more than a bard's story, like you said, but I can change my hair, bones, and more. Because I was given a wolf mask, I chose to study their bodies so that I can look like one."

"Remarkable! If I even need a carrier raven, I know where to turn," Colrig jested, though he was surprised by the wisdom of a boy of only ten.

"Can't do that," said Voln, without a hint of laughter. "My body size has to stay roughly the same. You can't create a castle from a single brick or a lake from a chalice of water."

"Right," Colrig responded, reverting his attention to the Krall.

"There is a lot ahead of us, Colrig. At dawn, one of my men will guide you to my high council," the Krall said and flicked his fingers, dismissing them. "It was a pleasure to make your acquaintance. Let me be the first to welcome you to Court Tchoyas." His ghastly tone now seemed more inviting.

᠉᠉᠉ ᠍᠍᠍

Night had fallen and illuminated lamps hung from large posts through-out the city. Moths and other insects swarmed around each light and the fireflies glowed even brighter. Spices filled the air to accompany the aroma of freshly baked bread. The Tchoyas people thrived at night, leaving their festivities until the workday had ended and family and friends were about.

Phenmir walked alongside a Sleff footman wearing company garb.

"Tell me, Sleffman." Phenmir said, "why did *you* personally turn away from the harvesting policies of your Court to join Colrig?"

"Perhaps you would not understand my Sleff view as a Chussman, sir."

"Try me. Our beliefs may not be as different as we are led to believe."

"My belief guides my way of living. My life is lived to glorify Heitt, my god. Am I a man of priestly composure? No. I try to improve, try to achieve something larger than myself to show my dedication to my god. True, our people show their devotion by giving their income, but can I honestly say I follow that decree? No, but I still give some to show that I have not become a heathen.

"As I walk here, away from all that I value in my home Court, I hope Heitt will recognize the sacrifice of my *life* as one much greater than any payment. I believe that Heitt has chosen Colrig to lead us out of this dark era."

Phenmir gave a satisfied, yet surprised nod, as if he had just found a coin in an old jacket. "Sleffman, what is your name?"

"Tarrn, sir."

"Sir Tarrn, that is the most justified claim for a fight that I have heard in all my years. I respect a man who lives his beliefs for a higher purpose. Whether he serves my god or his, we are brethren in spirit. Giving your soul is the noblest of sacrifices you can offer."

"*Payest thou me in spirit. Thou are the refined coin of mine eye's desire.*" quoted Tarrn with conviction.

"*The Tome of the Meek*?"

Tarrn nodded. "Have you read it?"

"I cannot say that I have, but we have a similar passage in *The Tome of Charity*. '*Sellest thy soul unto me, for thou art priceless as thy fellow man.*' I suppose you could call my decision to join the Allegiant a *spiritual quest* similar to yours."

Tarrn watched the road with a smile. "Many see the beliefs of other Courts as rivals, opposites in the colosseums of eternity. I find the similarities a spectacle. I like to envision that our individual gods, Charic for Chuss and Heitt for Sleff, are the finest of allies."

❦

They spent the night in shared rooms throughout several inns. Phenmir shared his room with nineteen others.

In the morning, Phenmir sat at a table, reading. His eyes turned from the page to see Colrig standing and stretching.

Other people had arisen, their whispers woke the remaining few who still tried to sleep. Tunics were buttoned and belts were fastened as they prepared for the morning meeting with the Tchoyas Krall's council.

Colrig approached Phenmir, kneeling at his table to speak.

"Phenmir," said Colrig.

"Yes..." Phenmir closed his page as he finished reading the final paragraph. "Yes, sir?"

"You have had time to see how the company functions. Remember that I want you to lead when the time comes. Now is a great time to assert your role as my high advisor and practice leading. Take your office as Thane of Harmony. You were not left in Chuss to attend to matters of bureaucracy."

"What do you want me to do?"

"Gather and direct them through the day's duties. We have the council to attend and they have trainings."

"What trainings?"

"You've seen them practice and drill. Choose something for them to do. That is not as important as the connection I want you to foster with them. Show some authority. They know who you are, now earn that respect." Phenmir glanced back at his tome on the table's edge. *The Strategist's Dilemma*. He had enjoyed the writings of Lord Noh Detti, the battle captain who led the northern colonies in the last recorded war, many years in the past. Phenmir was not a comparable replicant to Lord Detti, but he was willing to risk his very being to become what the people of his land required.

Phenmir stood without another word. *Engender a spirit of unity among your men. A captain is no greater a being than the frontman,* he recalled in his reading.

"Chussmen! Sleffmen! All who join us! Lend me your ears!" He shouted with the spirit of a mighty bear, capturing everyone's attention.

"On this day, we bind a treaty with Court Tchoyas. Soon we shall depart to write a new history for the Endowers of Facet." He felt a bead of sweat trickle down his ribcage from his armpits as he forced composure. He recalled seeing them work on their endurance and sparring during stops along the road to Fayis. "I want you sparring with one another until we finish our meeting with the Krall." He pointed to a Sleffman who still sat on the floor. "Lead the drills as usual and inform the others of what you are to do?"

"On with it!" shouted Colrig. He gave Phenmir a nod. All arose, finished donning their gear, and ran through the door.

***

The palace appeared more lustrous as the clouds cleared enough for a sunbeam to fill the chamber with a rainbow of lights through the stained glass windows. Two men stepped ahead of Colrig, opening the doors for them.

They were once again met with the silent chamberlain with the mask of a boar. Without a word, he stepped down to meet Colrig and lead the company up a wide stairway to the Krall's council chamber on the second floor.

The room seemed to span half of the palace's length. Walls of polish gray stone carried sound well. Arches decorated the walls near the ceiling three immense Tchoyas banners stretched over them. A dark wooden table spanned the floor. An astounding amount of chairs lined each side and end. Though it was deemed a council room, it seemed to be designed for large feasts.

Krall Trhet sat at the head of the table with Voln to his right with the other Endowers nearby. Some Tchoyas Thanes had joined them, identifiable by their silver and blue robes. Phenmir and Colrig sat down and were brought tall chalices of copper containing the finest of Tchoyas wines available to the region.

"Thank you for joining us, Sleffmen and Chussmen." said Voln.

Phenmir wondered if a boy of yet ten years would head the session.

The Krall began to speak. "I look forward to having your intentions clarified. I was surprised to hear that some of my Thanes had joined this creed of yours years ago, but I must admit that I am somewhat apprehensive."

Phenmir was not surprised to hear that Colrig already had members among the Tchoyas nobility, just as he had with the Chuss Thanes. He wondered how prepared Colrig was to execute his plans, but each day made Phenmir more confident in the Sleffman.

All the eyes on the table turned to Colrig.

"That is why we have come to this council, Your Grace. Brethren and sisters, we express our gratitude for your aid and will. As you all have probably heard, riots are now causing a tumult to rise in Court Zhaes. Their Court is facing an unprecedented unrest, and it is too early for their nobility to form a proper defense. There is no better time than now to go forward into the Court who powers harvesting more than any other. 'How do we win them over?' you may ask, but more is afoot than acts of diplomatic persuasion. No individual can convince an entire Court to swear off their source of power. Zhaes is being pulled by warring parties. More of Sleffmen are with us than Zhaesmen, but this is just the beginning. Seeds of revolution have been planted ever since harvesting began. Now we must reap. I understand the risks we take, but we must march our troops into Court Zhaes to turn the tides of this conflict in *our* favor."

One of the Tchoyas Thanes, a woman with the mask of a lizard with silver horns raised her hand. "I don't understand. What is there to gain by joining a bunch of rebels in Court Zhaes?"

"Thane Holmn?" Colrig gestured to another Thane near her. This one had the mask of a bestial face with silver fangs. "You were one of the first to join the Allegiant before we made ourselves known. Will you help clarify?"

Thane Holmn cleared her throat. "You know as well as any of us, Your Grace, that Court Zhaes was the most influential in initiating harvesting. Likewise, they have remained the most powerful Court through their abundance of Endowed. If we can gain control of Kzhek, we will have a promising chance at abolishing harvesting."

"And you think you have enough power to overthrow the capital of Court Zhaes?" asked the Thane with the lizard mask.

"We have been building an army among the supporters in our Court during these past years," said Thane Holmn. "Now that Colrig has come to bring the Harmony Allegiant to light, we can bring them out of the dark."

Colrig nodded. "Alongside your troops, we have the Chussmen and my Sleffmen, more of which are coming to join us for this stand in Kzhek. We have the plans set to succeed, Krall Trhet. All we require is your support."

The Krall nodded, taking a moment to breathe. "After the Arrival of your Sleff emissaries, Thane Holmn told me about your plans to end harvesting, I just never envisioned it would be so *bold*. Nevertheless, you have thought this through. What might the cost be for such an operation?"

"We need some of your Thanes to join us on the campaign. Thane Holmn is expected, but I would like at least two more. Aside from the troops, we need food, resources, and complete support from you and your Court. A few Tchoyas Thanes on our side will no longer be enough."

"You really believe you can do this, Sleffman?" asked the Krall.

"I swear by my god and your god."

Krall Trhet paused again, but was interrupted as he started to speak.

"What about us?" Voln shouted, sitting taller.

"What might you propose, Sir Voln?" asked Colrig, a smile easing back onto his face.

"How do your scouts plan on obtaining information? Zhaesmen are not the type to share."

"I have people who are trained in espionage."

"Might I suggest Endowers? Shiftlings are worth twenty professional scouts. Diplomatic matters are less of a threat when you have deception on your side," Voln said.

"War is controlled by the deceiver and lost by the blind," Phenmir quoted from *The Strategist's Dilemma*. His morning reading had indeed been worth the time. "The historic Lord Noh Detti said such is one key to a strategist's victory. Endower Shiftlings would be an invaluable resource."

Colrig turned to Phenmir. "You agree with him?"

"If he is offering Endower aid. We would be fools to disregard such an advantage."

"Would you lead them to search for allies in Kzhek, Phenmir? Perhaps I have not thought of everything, but paving the way for us to enter their Court would be worthwhile. If the heads of the Zhaes rebellion knew we were coming to join them, we could be even more sure of our victory." Colrig turned to the Krall. "Phenmir shall depart with my scouting party this evening. Voln will choose some or one of his Shiftlings to accompany them. Two would suffice. While we await their return, we shall prepare to march forward with our collected party and the late arrivals from Chuss and Sleff. Once Phenmir, Thane Stolk, returns, we can march into Kzhek with even more confidence."

"You will have the best of us, Sir Colrig," Voln said. "Kaela is the second best Shiftling that we have. She and I will accompany Thane Phenmir."

The Krall stared at Voln to ensure that he received an opportunity to speak, free from another interruption by the cocksure Shiftling. Averting his gaze back to Colrig, he inhaled deeply. "You propose we send two of our Endower Shiftlings alongside your Thane and scouts. My chosen militia will then join yours in preparation to march into Kzhek. What are we to do after that?"

"This is by no means an assault on the city. I do not want lives lost to senseless acts of violence. Enemy or ally, it does not matter, but that does not discount the inevitable casualties who violently oppose us. This may seem to contradict the Chuss Krall's assassination, but that was a necessary spark to start our fire. Further killings, should they be necessary, will only come on the battlefield. Ideally, we gain the attention of those who organized riots and join their forces. With their help, we will capture control of the Cantons and the Thanes within. From there, we move to the Palace and capture the Krall. I expect surrender more than a violent defense from them. Little has been done to quell the riots within their city. We shall go forth armed to intimidate but prepared to control."

"And how do you plan to stave off complete chaos in all of the Courts?" asked the Krall.

"Chaos already reigns. It will continue to grow until we are able to stop it. With Zhaes in our grasp, we will be on the way to have four of the six Courts standing with the Harmony Allegiant. After Khzek we move to Gruth, then Priess. This is not the beginning, Krall Trhet. This began years ago, as I have said, but now is the time for our efforts to pay off."

Banter resonated throughout the room as the attendees discussed Colrig's proclamations. Colrig glanced around, judging the excitement among the people, whether it be inspired by fear or determination. His eyes grazed past the Krall but reverted to glancing at his masked eyes. Krall Trhet remained silent, focusing on Colrig as he expected an owl would.

The Krall raised his hands to beckon attention.

"Silence, you perding kulfs!" Voln shouted.

"Thane Holm," said the Krall, "You believe that this will work."

She nodded. "It may seem abrupt, but there is no better time. If we delay, the harvesting Courts will only be more prepared to destroy the riots and rebels. The time is now."

"Colrig," said the Krall, "let us go forth."

CHAPTER FOURTEEN

HIDDEN ROOTS

S heath and Aerhee approached Thane Gromm who was just leaving his study on the first floor of the Zhaes Canton of Scholarship.

"Thane Leisa, Caser Kleeh, what has brought you here?" asked Thane Gromm, his hand still on the handle

"Caser Kleeh and I would like to ask you some questions."

"And what might those questions be?"

"We are working with Thane Lettre to investigate the Sleff riots," said Sheath.

"Very well, proceed." He sighed and pulled the door open, stepping back to let them into his study. The room was uncomfortably barren and lifeless, like a corpse left to dry in a spacious mausoleum, with the cold to match the chill of the dead. He likely spent his time elsewhere; all that was in the room was a large desk, three chairs of minimal comfort, and a shelf with four large tomes bound in white leather and lacking inscriptions on their bindings.

Sheath sat to her right as Aerhee adjusted her dress as she sat down in her seat. Gromm stacked some parchment on his desk and moved his quill and inkwell to the right side of his desk before giving his guests his attention.

"How might I be of assistance?" he said.

"We need information related to former Caser Felta Zhil. As the Thane of Scholarship, we thought you might have the means of locating her."

Thane Gromm raised his eyebrow. "As *your* predecessor, I would assume you would be aware of her current location, no? Well then, let us have a look." He arose from his chair and walked toward the door. "It seems you are quite adamant about making me move as much as possible today."

They followed him out of the room. Gromm paced ahead of each of them, giving no notice to their delay. Aerhee and Sheath quickened their steps and approached him like snow rabbits in a quiet flee. Large tomes sat atop pedestals along the hallway, though no one stopped to read. Even when it might seem impractical, those in the Canton of Scholarship were sure to show off their wisdom even in the decor.

"Though most of the records are well maintained within the Athenaeum of Kzhek, we keep a personal library of the records of the Zhaes nobility in our Canton in more *secure* hands."

Away from prying hands like mine or the hands of other Thanes? Is your loyalty pledged to your Court or your society? It was hard for Aerhee to assume the best from a man like Thane Gromm, despite his loyal history.

The trio passed a flight of stairs and then down a long hallway before reaching their destination. Gromm removed a set of keys and chose the eldest on the ring, and unlocked a large wooden door.

The Canton's library seemed to be more of an undercroft and outmatched the coldness of Thane Gromm's personal chamber. Bronze shelves stretched forward, covered in a veil of dust. Gromm took a small lamp off a shelf to his right, lighting it to continue onward in his search.

"Mind the darkness," Gromm warned. "Unlike many of the refined athenaeums of Facet, this one wasn't built with windows."

"Did you know Caser Zhil well?" Aerhee inquired.

"Not as well as Thane Sorn. With as much time as they spent together, one would assume her to be a part of the Canton of Endowment."

Gromm slowed, whispering to himself as he pointed down the shelf. "*Casers of Court Zhae*s," he read aloud, grasping a container. "Take this, will you?" he told Aerhee as he handed her the lantern.

He combed through layers of parchment before removing a sheet that appeared to be in much better condition than those beneath it with worn edges and a yellow stain.

"Not far beneath your records, Caser Kleeh, we have those for Caser Zhil." He traded the sheet for the lantern.

Aerhee gave Gromm a polite bow.

"Return her record within a week, if not before."

"Our gratitude, Thane Gromm," said Sheath.

They shared the Zhaes salute and parted ways.

Little time remained for the day's pursuits, and the Canton of Diplomacy was closer than her home. Aerhee was sure that Zeir would not mind if she stayed another night away from home, especially with the rampant riots. Knowing it would be most productive to leave for the previous Caser at dawn, Aerhee agreed to spend yet another night at the Canton of Diplomacy.

"Where can we find her?" asked Sheath as she watched Aerhee read from the document. "Is she still in Kzhek?"

"She lives in Traedus," replied Aerhee. "Why would she leave to southern Zhaes and not stay in Kzhek?"

❧❧❧❧❧ ❦❦❦❦❦

26 years ago, Court Zhaes, Kzhek
Year 306 in the Clerical Era (Cl. er. 306)

❧❧❧❧❧ ❦❦❦❦❦

Zhaes had grown since Faeth's last visit. The cityscape seemed more affluent than any town in Priess and she could not imagine what a Sleff-man would think of the architectural wonders. It was the first pleasant surprise in their journey.

Aerhee walked between her and Derlik as they neared the center of Kzhek for the first time. They had been in the city for two days but had spent their time in the city's outskirts.

Townsfolk were accepting enough out there, but their neighbors tended to keep to themselves. Faeth tried to assume the best of them. Faeth, Derlik, and Aerhee were not as pale as the Zhaesmen. With dark hair and pale skin, anyone outside of Zhaes would not think twice if they claimed that heritage, but the Zhaesmen knew otherwise.

Derlik was scheduled to work in the Cloven Gleff the following morning. Faeth was relieved to have one more day together before he left.

"Mother," Aerhee tugged on Faeth's arm. "I'm hungry. When can we eat?"

"Soon." She kept her reply brief as her eyes shot through each passing alleyway.

"Why? There are a lot of places *right here*! Just look, that Gruthwoman is waving for us to come to her booth!"

"We will get something soon. Wait a little longer," pleaded Derlik, though he too walked uneasily, glancing from side to side. Faeth gave him a nod, trying to hide her own fear of persecution. They had heard the worst of rumors regarding the treatment of Priessmen in Zhaes. Their time had been peaceful so far, but Faeth remained cautious.

They approached a large building in the center of the city, made of white-gray with bronze rims to outline the structure. Zhaesmen in refined clothing entered and exited with unfriendly glares.

They walked up the staircase, but Aerhee ran to the top and waited for her parents.

"Why did you run here?" Aerhee asked, standing in their way.

"Let's go in, Aerhee," Derlik pushed her toward the doors of the clothing shop.

The inside was more captivating than the cityscape. Marble statues wore clothing that looked as expensive as their home. Intricately woven dresses with beautifully embroidered patterns hung from the right wall, with men's clothing on the left. Despite their glamor, the style seemed restrictive. Faeth's dress was open to nearly exposing her breast, whereas the Zhaes makings left little of the neck to be revealed.

Faeth grabbed Aerhee's hand and led her to a quiet area near the back of the shop, while Derlik left towards the men's clothes.

She knelt beside Aerhee. "As you may have noticed, the Zhaes style is quite *different* compared to our clothing from home."

Aerhee nodded.

"Our hair and skin already set us apart," Faeth told her.

"What is wrong with that?"

"People don't always accept those from other lands, especially here in Zhaes."

"But why? Can't they see us walk and talk just like they do?"

She smiled at her daughter's innocence, brushing the side of her cheek. "Aerhee, the people here might not want us living in their Court. If the city guards see us walking about, they ask how we got here. Despite our documents, they might require payments, especially because we were

Priessmen. We need to dress like they do. We are now Zhaesmen and are going to live like it."

"If it is so dangerous here, then why did we even come?"

For our faith that would never be allowed in Priess, but you cannot yet understand that, Aerhee. "Life will be much better here. You just have to trust me. It may be hard now, but things will be better soon."

Aerhee nodded.

"Aerhee."

She looked up with the eyes of a beaten hound.

"Let's buy a new dress that would make all of your old friends in Priess jealous."

Aehree smiled as Faeth led her through the shop.

Soon after they found Derlik, they purchased clothes with the little money they had remaining. After changing into their new outfits, they stuffed their old outfits in a travel bag and left.

Derlik glanced around the city square.

"Mother?"

Faeth remained focused on her husband, waiting for his direction.

"Mother?" she repeated.

"Yes?" She tightened her grip on Aerhee's hand.

"What if I want to wear my clothes from back home?"

"You are a Zhaeswoman now, Aerhee. If anyone asks you where you are from, you are to say Kzhek. If anyone asks why you have a different shade of hair or skin, you say that your parents were born in Eastern Zhaes. You must leave Priess behind. Do you understand?"

Aerhee nodded.

"Where are you from?"

"Kzhek," she replied.

"Why do you look different?"

"My mother and father are from eastern Zhaes, near Court Priess."

"Why do you walk with imperfect posture?"

"I read too much." Aerhee hunched over as if she was reading at a desk.

Her mother smiled. "You are as quick as a thunderous bolt, Aerhee Kleeh." She hugged her and approached her husband. "Is there something wrong, Derlik?"

He turned to his wife. "No... it's fine. Is Aerhee still hungry?"

"Probably."

"Aerhee," he said, turning to his daughter, sneering at her with a pompous demeanor, "let us savor Zhaes delicacies. Will you join me for fine cuisine?"

Faeth rolled her eyes, but she was thankful for her husband's playful personality. He brightened even the most somber days.

"I could not ask for a more proper evening," Aerhee replied with feigned refinement, as if she was a Thane.

Derlik smiled and took her hand. "Lead the way, Zhaeswoman."

* * *

The Present
Cl. er. 332

* * *

Aerhee watched the passing roadway through the small carriage windows. They were nearing their journey's end on the way to Traedus to meet the former Caser Zhil, having left early in the morning from their last inn.

Aerhee felt she was persuasive enough to get information from the former Caser, but was relieved to have an Endowed at her side, especially a Feelman. Sheath would be better than any hired interrogator. *Interrogation* did not feel like the proper word, perhaps an *informative discussion*. She only hoped and prayed for Sheath's ability to read Zhil.

Was the previous Caser an Endowed? She cursed herself for not knowing enough about her predecessor.

"Aerhee."

"Yes?" She pulled herself from her reverie and smiled at Sheath.

"How are you? I don't want empty words. I want a real conversation. You avoid them too much. How is this all *truly* affecting you? The riots? The chaos in our Court?"

Why was she asking how she felt? She was a Feelman and she could read a person better than they knew themselves. Aerhee disliked it when Sheath read her. It took away from the relationship. At her plea, Sheath tried to avoid the readings during her interactions with Aerhee, though she was not always perfect at keeping that request.

"I am well."

"And what of the Patriarchy? You kept your composure while meeting with Thane Gromm."

"Can we talk about something else?"

Sheath frowned and sighed. "Did you find anything of note in Zhil's documents?"

"I think so. Let me take another look." She scanned the document. "All the information they have recorded makes me wonder what they have collected about me. She has no family listed or close associates. You mentioned her infatuation with the Canton of Endowment, but it seems she stopped working with them before I took office."

"Perhaps she was preparing for a life away from the city?" said Sheath. "I know many people in high offices look forward to a reclusive retirement."

"It's possible, but I would have assumed she'd stay in Kzhek to continue working in the Canton of Endowment based on her previous interests. You knew her, Sheath. What did you think of her?"

"She was quite reclusive and kept matters to strict bureaucratic standards."

"After serving as Caser, I can understand why she would keep to herself. People become exhausting. I've learned to appreciate my time at home."

Unease emanated from Aerhee, like rays of the sun in the Chuss desert. She felt Sheath reading her deeper.

"Aerhee, how are things at home? How is Zeir?"

Aerhee scowled. "Sheath, *please*, leave me to my thoughts."

"I'll read more if you don't want to talk."

Aerhee groaned. "You are quite the *kulf* when you are not given what you want. Zeir and I are doing well, as fine as ever." She forced a frustrated smile.

"Calling *me* a kulf? Since when have you used such coarse language? As fine as ever? That is a lie. When are you going to draw close to him?"

"We don't argue. We never have."

"You need to *embrace* your differences. While you care about aiding the Court as a whole, he wishes to aid those within his circle. For people like him, it is hard to see the impact of a single coin on the scales of justice. You, however, see that each person will benefit from that coin as they learn to give theirs. You may see him as your opposite, but you complement each other well. Marriages accomplish the most when each spouse strives for a separate good rather than the same goal, unifying their pursuits to create an amalgamation for their mutual benefit. A farmer reaps a larger harvest by planting many seed varieties rather than planting a single crop. Branch your gaps. He is offering his side, but cannot complete the connection without you. Does he still believe your parents are from eastern Zhaes?"

Aerhee bit her lip.

Sheath shook her head. "Do you think... could you ever think it possible to bond with your spouse when you lie to him about your past? How does he not know you were born in Court Priess. Or has he finally figured it out?"

"No," refuted Aerhee, "and why would he? I am more Zhaes than the Krall himself. Sure, I looked more like a Priessgirl when I was younger, but you could never tell now. I live each day as if my residence were a gift, never forsaking my parents' sacrifice for my life here."

"Then why refrain from telling him if you are so bound to Zhaes? He will only appreciate your honesty. Zeir would never think less of you."

"He would think me a heathen! Priessman are as valuable as street vermin in Zhaes!"

"Times have changed, Aerhee."

"Sure, but that does not change the opinions of people, especially the elders."

"Aerhee." Sheath waited for Aerhee to compose herself. "My husband and I were not aligned by the stars. We had to labor for our relationship. Many people in Zhaes will have you see marriage as a convenience or a mere political ordeal, but that is their flaw. You can trust me. Expressing some degree of love does not make you any less a Zhaeswoman."

Sheath had always seen things in a more radical, controversial way than most Zhaesmen. Perhaps her popularity among the nobility was derived from her unique perspective. Aerhee knew that her marriage was not unlike most of the stern Zhaes population, but Sheath would not allow that to continue. If one were to speak with Aerhee and Sheath for the first time, they would likely assume Sheath was the Priessborn among them.

"Your wellbeing matters," said Sheath. "By reading you, I can tell that your marital distance is causing you distress. If you keep obsessing over Zhaes law and perfection, you will soon enough become a lifeless statue."

Aerhee sighed.

Their carriage halted before a small cottage, with a flat roof and red walls. Evening was approaching as the orange-tinted sky matched the shade of the warm candle within the cottage's window.

With force enough to wake a beast from its slumber, Sheath knocked on the door.

Footsteps approached the door from inside. The lock clanked as metal slid across metal. The door pulled back to reveal a woman not much older than Aerhee. Though her hair had gone gray, she bore few wrinkles. She wore an evening gown of a pale red, nothing to impress, but a step above casual homewear.

"Caser Kleeh?" The former Caser Zhil said. "Thane Leisa? What in Laeih's name brought you here?"

"We came to speak with you."

"I live away from Kzhek for a reason, you know." Her scowl lifted with a wave. "Come in, I'll make tea. Wipe your feet. The dirt clings."

"Thank you, Caser Zhil," Aerhee led the way into the former Caser's abode. The cottage smelt of old wood and dust. The decorations were older, the wood on the chairs and tables were well worn. A tapestry of the Zhaes sigil hung on the wall above a desk with scattered parchment and a quill out of its inkwell.

"Felta is fine. I appreciate the formality, but you are the only Zhaes Caser now." She entered her modest kitchen and hung a pot of water over dancing flames, tossing in a handful of orange flowers and herbs.

Leaving the pot to warm, she returned to the company and took the seat across from her guests. "How is my old office?"

"Fine, thank you."

"And you, Sheath?"

"As well as you might expect," said Sheath.

Felta nodded and stirred the tea.

"Mistress Felta," said Aerhee, "tell me about your work with the Canton of Endowment. I heard that you worked alongside Thane Sorn." She did not have to be a Feelman to notice Felta growing tense.

"Thane Sorn…" Felta paused. "Yes, we made many remarkable accomplishments for the Court, most in relation to Endowed placement. We utilized the strength of Gorgers to help build up the smaller villages, Feelmen judges in judiciary systems throughout the Court's villages rather than only in the large cities, and so forth. I enjoyed our time together, but I am happy now." She grabbed three glasses. "The tea is ready."

They would not need her to speak about her connection to the missing Sleff Endowed, only to direct her thoughts to matters of Sleff and Zhaes in order to make her thoughts clear to Sheath's skill. If the desired information was on Felta's mind, Sheath would read her thoughts and reveal all that they needed.

"Perhaps you saw my garden. I grew this tea myself." Felta offered each woman a cup, placing a small cloth around it to prevent a burn. "Fool's Wisp and Harvest sage. It is said to be good for mental clarity, though who knows if that is true? Ever since Eurythrins came into this world, all health-based studies are based on testing them and the other Endowed. I enjoy the spice of it though and hope it will entreat you."

Sheath and Aerhee nodded, each taking a sip of tea. It tasted bitter, yet with a spice similar to cinnamon or camel's clove.

"While we appreciate the hospitality, we have come here for a more serious matter," said Aerhee. "As you likely have heard, many riots have arisen throughout Facet, including in Sleff and Zhaes."

"Perhaps I had heard it mentioned in passing," replied Felta. "I dismissed it as a rumor. Little happens here in Traedus. The community is always in search of some story to tell."

"I regret to inform you that they are more than rumors. We have been investigating the origins of these uprisings. While searching for a lead, we came across your name, Felta. Hearing about your work with the Canton of Endowment, we thought you might be able to help us answer some questions"

"I have little more to provide than what I told you. I simply enjoyed observing the work of the Canton of Endowment. Ever since the Endowers were discovered, the supernatural abilities of these beings have fascinated me."

"She's lying, trying to hide information," said Sheath, her face as sober as a Zhaes priestess. Aerhee recognized the distinct focus in Shealth's glare. She was reading Felta's mind.

"Ex... excuse me, Sheath?"

"You have more to tell, Felta. I know you were more involved with Thane Sorn."

"What are you *suggesting*? I worked with each Thane the same as Caser Kleeh does!"

Sheath turned to Aerhee. "She was sleeping with Sorn."

"You prying *kulf*, I..." Sheath raised a hand to silence Felta.

"I am sorry, Felta. I truly am, but I must continue." Sheath leaned closer.

Felta grew anxious and looked as if she would jump from her seat. Aerhee wondered if she should reach over to keep her still while Sheath continued to dig into Felta's thoughts.

As the reading progressed, Sheath's face grew tense. The previously sorrowful gaze cringed into a grimace of accusation. "You traitor! How dare you!" shouted Sheath.

Aerhee stared at Sheath in confusion.

"It is wrong, Sheath!" Felta shouted. "Their practices are a crime to humanity, a crime to Laeih!"

"Do not take our divinity's name in vain!" said Sheath. "Laeih would be ashamed of your ungrateful spirit! You might as well be a Chusswoman, you *perding* turncoat!"

Aerhee was shocked equally by the vague revelation as much as she was by Sheath's vulgarity. The situation must have escalated further than they presumed if it invited tainted words to escape Sheath's righteous lips.

"And Thane Sorn? What of him?"

"I have not seen him in months. I swear by all that is divine," Felta cried.

"Sheath!" Aerhee called.

Sheath turned to face her.

"Please elaborate! In case you have forgotten, I'm no Feelman. I can't see what you are reading."

"Felta bedded the Thane but did not leave it there."

"They were wed?"

"No, such relations might spark rumors of nepotism. Felta bore a child two years after the binding of the Pact of Province."

The year before I took her position. Aerhee was stunned.

"And what of the child?"

"It was born with two umbilical cords."

"And?" Aerhee said.

"The child of a Caser and Thane was killed. They were both struck with the loss of their child."

"Those murderers gave me no choice but to rebel!" Felta stood. "You would understand if you were the mother of an Endower."

"What did you do?" asked Aerhee.

Felta shook her head. Resistance was futile.

"The Thane of Endowment should have understood the need for harvesting better than any other Zhaesman." Sheath said. She turned to Aerhee. "If she won't admit it, I'll tell you what she is hiding. She worked with Thane Sorn to overturn the Pact of Province to allow Endower children to be born free of harvest."

Aerhee was aghast at the revelation but dared not interrupt Sheath.

"Though Thane Sorn did not reveal all of his works to her, hoping to keep her safe in ignorance, they were responsible for numerous dissenters. Thane Sorn needs to be held accountable for the impact he had on his people. He might be responsible for turning the whole Canton of Endowment against its own Court."

"But what did *she* do?" Aerhee pointed at Felta.

"As a Caser, she had influence throughout the Court and *those under its power*."

"The Sleffmen!" Aerhee hissed.

"Stop!" Felta shouted. Tears fell from her eyes. There was nothing left for her to do as her secrets fell from Sheath's lips.

Sheath nodded. "She worked with Sleff rebels to establish small villages for Endowed in Sleff. They built up something that they called '*the Northern Colony.*' A village of Endowed."

"But why? Were they building an army?"

"They were preparing an army to combat the very source that gave them strength." Sheath shook her head. "It was a perfect crime. The only ones who would notice the Endowed number discrepancies would be those within the Canton. Perhaps they even worked with the Chuss and Tchoyas Canton of Endowment, though I read nothing of the sort in her. I fear we are on the very cusp of their plotting that has been under construction for years. If we do not stop this movement soon, this Northern Colony will be detrimental. They have an army of Gorgers in this Sleff village. Nearly every graft that was sent to Sleff was redirected by Thane Sorn to build up this village for the rebels to use against us."

"You planned on overthrowing harvesting with Endowed, the very things you were fighting against?" Aerhee almost laughed at Felta.

"The harvests happened regardless of our actions," said Felta. "We took what you harvesters were making and were preparing to use it against you."

"The basis of her augment does not matter now," said Sheath. "They have a Gorger army. If her knowledge is not mistaken, the Sleff Gorgers *far* outnumber our Gorgers. War would be detrimental with so many behemoths on their side. "

Aerhee approached Felta, though stood back from a safe distance. "What about Sorn? Where is he now?"

"I don't know!" Felta shouted. She started to breathe faster and clenched her fists.

"Did you see the Canton of Endowment before we left?" asked Sheath?

"I saw it on my way to your Canton. The riots were attacking it, but it still stood."

"Right before we left, one of my informants told me that it collapsed. The rioters reduced it to rubble. We will not find Thane Sorn there anymore. It was undoubtedly a part of their plotting."

"How did you even start the riots in the harvesting capital of Facet?" asked Aerhee.

"We are not alone in this," said Felta. "This rebellion has been growing for years. We even had some of the members of the Canton of Endowment on our side."

"What else is she hiding?"

Sheath focused on Felta and took a sudden step back. "*By Laeih's law!*"

"What is it, Sheath?"

"The Krall of Chuss, that opted for a graft?"

"Yes?" Aerhee nodded

"These rebels worked with local Sleff revolutionaries to plot the assassination of the Krall, hoping that it would politically charge the Chuss population and invite them to their cause. Due to their absolute abhorrence of harvesting, they knew the Chussmen would join their cause."

"So what do we do with her now?" asked Aerhee. "You've outed her as a traitor."

"What about her?" exclaimed Aerhee as she gestured to Felta.

"She must face the law, as does any who transgress it."

"No," said Felta.

They turned to her. "As followers of Laeih," stated Aerhee, "we do not tolerate transgression of Court law. Your crime is too destructive to be dismissed by a mere prison sentence." She turned to Sheath with a concerned glare, receiving a nod in return.

Sheath stood. "We will escort you to the Patriarchy."

Felta ran to the corner and grabbed a broom, holding it like a sword. "Please, Sheath! You do not grasp the entirety of this. You are as blind as any of them!"

Seize her? Aerhee thought while looking at Sheath.

Sheath nodded to show that she had read her mind and grabbed a long shawl from a wooden chest in the corner. She returned to Aerhee, both an equal distance from Felta.

Three, two, one she thought to Sheath. They ran at Felta to corner her, but the former Caser vaulted over a short armchair. Her dexterity was surprising for her age. Felta ran to the dining area and removed a worn cleaver from a drawer.

"Sheath," Aerhee said. She cast her thoughts, knowing Sheath would read them. *Watch and follow.* She took a vase from a nearby table and hurled it at Felta, who braced . While Aerhee distracted Felta, Sheath ducked to seize her around the waist.

"Heartless wenches! Ignorant kulfs!" Felta grunted. She forced the cleaver upward and it down across Sheath's face, slicing from her forehead to the corner of her lips.

Aerhee ran in amidst the chaos and pummeled her fist into Felta's stomach, causing her to seize over. Aerhee retrieved the cleaver with startled hands and pressed her weight on the woman to tie her up with the shawl from Sheath's hands.

She gave up the fight and cried with arms pressed to the floor.

Sheath clenched her face as blood dripped like hot wax through the cracks of her fingers.

Frightened that Felta would escape, Aerhee remained sitting but reached toward her companion. "Sheath! By Laeih's glory! Can—"

"It's fine, Aerhee. Take Felta to the carriage while I find a rag to stop the bleed."

"Is the cut deep?"

"I don't think so. We can find a medic before leaving the village."

Sheath closed her eyes and felt around the dining area for a cloth. She dabbed at the wound with a crumpled rag and hissed with pain. She pulled the rag back and turned to Aerhee. Her right eye looked like a ripe grape cut open by a kitchen knife.

CHAPTER FIFTEEN

DIRE OFFERINGS OF RIGHTEOUS SINNERS

"Trust me Yetrik. I am a Gruthwoman and I'm not opposed to harvesting. I only question the means by which the Thanes plan to stop the rebellions," said Semi.

"Do you think that I do not have my own doubts? Of course I do, but I trust their authority," Yetrik replied. He was called to Zhaes to perform a single task, speak with the Zhaes Thane of Agriculture about bronze procurement for Thane Gett. Royss, the Thane of Agriculture, had other preoccupations, but he would serve as he was told. Without cooperation and allegiance, unity is as achievable as counting the sand grains of the Chuss dunes.

"This *'experience'* of theirs... How experienced are they with preventing a revolution? Has that occurred in their lifetimes?"

Yetrik shook his head. "No, but they are the Thanes and we are but messengers."

"Yetrik," she said, placing her hand on his shoulder. "When you work with the nobility as much as I have, you learn that the only true authority in this world is given by Deilf. People are flawed."

"Then what do you think we should do? Stand atop a crate before the rioters and kindly ask them to stop? 'Return home. Change your ways, you vile heathens!'" He shook his head. "That won't work. I value your opinion, Semi, but let's just see where their plans lead. Who knows if they will even go through with this?"

"So you think they are a little extreme, too?"

He shrugged. "I have too many questions in life to expect them all to be answered at this moment. Trust and patience are what we need."

She nodded. "I guess you're right. I only wish that there was an option without civilian massacres to 'teach the people properly.' These Thanes act in questionably."

"Then tell them you're concerned!" replied Yetrik. "You will accomplish little by rejecting them, but perhaps you can help them modify their strategy in favor of peace."

She pondered for a moment. "Broken buildings are made stronger by destruction and rebuilding. Sometimes a forest needs to burn to make way for new growth."

"Yes! Yes! Firm is the foundation, Gruthwoman!"

She laughed. "Firm is the foundation."

❧ ☙

A large map of Kzhek lay across the grand table. Thane of Court Zhaes, except for the Thanes of Diplomacy and Endowment, stood around the illustrated land.

Royss stood at the head of the table to address the company. "Excuse Thane Leisa, she is attending to *delicate* courtly manners with Caser Kleeh. Both are expected arrive to soon."

"And Thane Sorn?" asked one of the Thanes.

"As many of you know, the Canton of Endowment has fallen victim to the mobs. We expect an excavation of the ruins when it's safe to do so, but his whereabouts are currently unknown." Many bore shocked expressions.

"Laeih bless him and his kin," said Lettre.

"Many of you have noticed our guests," said Royss. "The Gruth Thane of Utilities sent Yetrik and Semi to offer their insights." Royss gave them a wink and a nod, maintaining a smile in the gloom of the room.

"One of our Cantons has fallen. If we do not put an end to these rebellions soon, more will fall, destroying the only order in our land. Do not let their plight cause you to doubt. Harvesting is as divine as Laeih himself, for he gifted it unto us for the sake of humankind's progression.

"It is our responsibility as the head of Facet's harvesting to prevent its downfall. These rebels are no more than attention seeking children. Riots have done little more than disrupt the lives of all Zhaesmen. Do you think the bakers are pleased when their markets are closed by their undignified neighbors? What of the spirits of our Endowed? Many are among us this evening, who are told they are monsters and devourers of children. What of the city guards that leave their spouses each night not knowing if they will return to bed that evening? Their opinions are loud, but few. If we can stop them here, I am sure that order will return. Royss sat down and gestured to Thane Gromm.

Gromm nodded and stood to study the map. From a side table, he took a handful of small wooden figures and a thin pole with a curved end. He placed half of the figures in the center of the city and the rest in a circular formation in surrounding streets, lacquered red and gray, respectively.

"I see who you think the perpetrators are," said Royss as he pointed to the four Chuss-red pieces in the city center. He earned a few light laughs, though sounded anxious and forced.

"Noble, Zhaesmen," Gromm began. "Having met with Thanes Lettre and Belik, we seek your counsel. If those rebelling act like children, then they will be treated as such. We will execute half of these disasters and force the others into compliance, lest they too will face execution."

"If we tolerate *their* terrorism," Royss said, "our Court will fall to anarchy. If anyone desires to propose an alternative solution, please let it be known."

Yetrik was astounded by the unanimity. They all seemed to agree with the plan without any arguments. He would have expected more questions or doubts from the other Zhaes Thanes, but it was as if Royss had spoken with a voice so hypnotic that he'd convinced everyone that this was the only solution. Certainly, there had to be another way to stop the mobs that did not involve so many deaths. Fear of the Thane's unspoken power began to contest Yetrik's adoration of him. *How deep does his influence reach?*

"I appreciate your trust. We would never wish to be in the current circumstance, but Laeih himself has appointed us to stop the infection before it tears at our infrastructure." He took another moment to look into the eyes of the other Thanes. "Thane Lettre, the floor is yours."

Thane Lettre arose with tended eyebrows, spinning the rings on his middle fingers. "Ideally, only a few victims will be sufficient to make the rebels surrender. I emphasize a *few*. We do not need a massacre, but to put out some of the largest flames of the bonfire. We will surround the central square with city guards and a force of Gorgers. They will serve as a blockade to capture and arrest those who try to escape. In the end, we will remove some rioters and hold them in our city jails. We will free those remaining to warn their fellow Zhaesmen from pursuing the same path to civil unrest."

"By what means do you wish to see this through?" One of the other Zhaes Thanes asked. Royss had introduced them, but Yetrik had already forgotten most of their names.

Royss opened his mouth but was interrupted by one of the Thanes. "I cannot condone this. Murder transgresses the divine law." With the face of a disappointed mentor, he glared at each Thane. "Have we forgotten who we are?"

Gromm lifted his chin, tightening his jawline. "Have you forgotten about the slaying of Fensil by the hand of Rein in *The Tome of Measure*?"

Yetrik nodded alongside the other Zhaes Thanes, but was unfamiliar with the story. Yetrik had glanced over a few passages in the Zhaes scripture, but did not know it well enough to know the story.

Gromm continued talking about the scriptural tale. "Do you not recall the revelation that commanded the hand of Rein to behead the tyrant Fensil for the prosperity of his people? Holy events repeat themselves."

Whatever it was, Gromm's story seemed to be some reason to justify killing when necessary. There were similar stories in the Gruth scriptures, but Yetrik remained hesitant about trusting Thane Gromm's reasoning. Even if their god had commanded a beheading in such a story, times had changed.

"Sometimes our god requires such a punishment," said Gromm. "Thanes Belik, Lettre, and I feel that this punishment is the will of Laeih. Do I believe that he delights in the slaying of his people? No, but I know this is what he wills. War is never ideal, but the righteous must prevail when threatened."

Royss nodded to Gromm. "Do any of you believe us to be at fault?" No one spoke. "Let us return to a concern that was raised. How are we going to do this? How will we terminate a portion of the central mob?"

"A combustible, capable of producing a fatal detonation within the central square," responded Thane Lettre. "Thane Sentree, do you have anything of the sort?"

Yetrik remembered Thane Sentree now that she was pointed out. Like Thane Gett who had sent them from Gruth, Sentree was the Thane of Utilities, the Court's head of innovation and engineering. She was a hard sculpted woman, who had seemed to have pushed through years of physical labor before settling among the nobility.

"We've used combustibles in the tunnels of the Cloven Gleff." Her voice reminded him of his aunt, deeper than most women's voices and somewhat rough. "I presume we could have a reasonable amount sent to us from the mine's Proctor."

"How soon could we expect to have them?" asked Royss. "The sooner we act, the more likely we are to succeed."

"I will sign a decree following this session. We should have them in a few days."

"What of the Gorgers?" asked another Thane with a half-raised hand. "How will we secure their cooperation in the absence of Thane Sorn?"

"Thane Sorn's departure was unexpected, but not insurmountable. Although he led the Canton that oversees the Endowed, his absence does not mean that the Gorgers are out of reach." He turned his attention to the table. "Do any of you have a suggestion?"

Aren't some of you Endowed? Yetrik wondered.

Semi raised a reluctant hand. "Are any of you Shiftlings?"

"Unfortunately not," said Royss. "Why so, Gruthwoman?"

"You asked for our help, and I might have a suggestion." She replied in Royss' exact voice while shifting her skin tone to match his. "If you need to convince someone to *lend* you a force of Gorgers, I might be able to coerce them."

Royss smiled, baring his teeth. "Are you trained in deception and espionage?"

"As all proper Shiftlings should be," she replied.

"Well, then, perhaps you can join me. You can pose as a member of our Canton of Endowment to speak with the Krall. He trusts us well, but is quite *firm* on the boundaries and jurisdictions between each Canton. He's almost as bad as Caser Kleeh." His comment earned a few laughs from the council. "Though you are not Thane Sorn, we should be able to convince the Krall to cooperate."

Semi smiled. Yetrik was relieved to see her happy after a previous spurt of reluctance.

"Well then, Zhaesmen, Gruthmen, we have a place to start." Royss leaned forward. "Let us reconvene here in two days to discuss our progress. Are there any further questions?"

With the Zhaes salute, Royss closed the meeting. The other Thanes left while Royss remained.

"Did we impress you well enough, lad?" Royss asked Yetrik.

"I am impressed with how serious you were. It was like seeing a ghete serving tea in fine dress," said Yetrik. "I do have a question for you, though."

"Yes?"

"I know you have all of this to focus on, but can you tell us why Thane Gett *really* sent us?"

"That coincides with what we were discussing today."

Royss took the nearest chair and sat.

"You may have believed that Fortik, or Thane Gett, if you insist on using his title, sent you on a diplomatic mission, but it is more than that. He likes to keep the more intimate visions private. Perhaps he sent you here to assist as diplomats without even knowing it, that crafty Foreteller."

"What do you mean?" Yetrik leaned in with his elbows on his knees.

"Fortik is one of the most skilled Foretellers in all the land, if not the best at his craft, as I am sure you are already aware."

"Of course, but what do you mean by private visions?"

"He's a showman, but his graft is sacred. Some of us could learn reverence from him. He shares certain visions with others, but those are more foresights rather than *visions*. His visions are kept sacred and private unless he feels the need to share them. There is a spiritual side to the organ, allowing its host to tap into a divine source of power. Not all Endowed can access this depth of their power, but Gett is one of the few who can. Foretellers on their own may predict events, but if they can gain power from the divine aspect of their body, they can see visions of the future. *Actual visions* with unfailing accuracy. Such are never received by choice but granted as a gift from the gods. And so it was with Gett. His god allows him to see a shadow of what is yet to come."

Yetrik's mind raced. *Can other Endowed tap into this higher degree of power* "What did he see?"

"Like the events in our holy times, it was vague, but symbolic. He saw a field of grain, some rows of wheat, some amaranth. One half of the field was continually harvested and used for food, the other was left to grow. In time, the half that grew, grew so high that its crops swayed among the clouds. The stalks grew higher, yet never grew in thickness. Their length was too great to hold the structure of each reed and the unharvested field fell on the other crops, killing them all. As the large stalks lay broken atop the shaded dead ones, the harvester saw his field left to waste. To begin anew, he cleansed it with a flame, even taking the lives of those that remained, leaving only black soil under a sheet of ashes.

"Though it may sound cryptic, Gett was struck by it as if he had seen the spirit of his late mother. He recounted this during my last visit to Gruth."

"What did it mean? Destruction of people? A condemnation of those who reject harvesting?"

"He knew these riots would come. He knew that war was imminent. That is why he sent you. He sought bronze to forge an army's worth of armor. I feel we may have acted too late."

Yetrik nodded. He was never sent as a diplomat, but as a Gruthman to help his people brace for a conflict. "What can I do while you and Semi see the Krall?"

Royss smiled. "Have you ever worked alongside a Beastling?"

Beastlings, the Endowed capable of reading and mimicking animal reactions. Yetrik was interested. "I know of some who are skilled shepherds and farmers. They say that they can direct the animals how they wish. Why do you ask? Do you want to send me to a farm?" He understood that if a war were to arise, the armies would need sufficient food, though he would not want to go down in history as *the one who fed the warriors*."

"Beastlings are very skilled and valuable. If war were to escalate, as predicted by Thane Gett, we would need more than just footmen. How would you like to accompany our Beastling companies to recruit some soldiers from the forest?"

"Are you suggesting that we recruit bears and eldeer?"

"Not quite, but that could be of use. With the best of the Beastlings, we could entice *kaesan* to join our cause."

Kaesan, the bipedal nightmare that was embroidered onto the Zhaes banner. A creature said to feast upon the sinners who disgraced divine law. He thought them a thing of myth, straight from the under realms. They bore thorny antlers, large teeth, and the face that was a cross between a ghete and a vile mare. If anything would intimidate men enough to flee, it would be kaesan.

INTERLUDE 11

"Inquisitor Bashin!" shouted the deputy with the large head. *The bright one. Please have something of worth.* The other followed close behind. *By Laeih, even that one's nose annoys me.*

Less than an hour had passed since they stared at the massacred corpse of the late treasurer. Was that enough time for these two to accomplish anything? Had *he* accomplished anything? Sure, this was an important case, but he was tired of servitude, especially as the city dwindled further into unrest. He would rather be lost in a book, letting his mind be entertained by history rather than living it.

Bashin attempted a glare, but surrendered to courtesy and feigned a grin.

"What have you found?" Bashin could have read the deputy without speaking, but that removed humanity from the exchange. *Hold on to the normalcy that you have.*

"One of the Krall's advisers recommended a Proctor from the Canton of Endowment. This Proctor met with the treasurer nearly every day last week. The adviser told me where we can find him."

Bashin seized the note from his hand. "Our first suspect. I suppose this is a start." *What good is a man who visits the treasurer?* He read the conversation from his associate's mind. *Vehement conversations before the reported murder? That is much more than frequent visits, you kulf. Speak clearly next time.* "Thank you, Zhaesman. Send for a carriage."

During the carriage ride to the edge of the city, Bashin grew bored enough to remind himself of his deputies' names by reading them. He was not so bored that he wanted to ask them. The dull one, Yellin, was the kind who acted interested in small talk. Bashin was not going to talk about the unchanging weather, nor would he discuss irritation with the ever-present inflation. Deim, the large headed one, would have agreed with Bashin. He read Deim enough to learn about his personality.

The ride was short, ending in less than ten minutes. Grey light shone from the doors as Bashin followed his two deputies out of the carriage. It was well past dusk, but Bashin did not expect the Proctor from the Canton of Endowment to be asleep. If he was already in bed, Bashin did not care. He came to read the Proctor's mind to see if he had any connection to the murder of the treasurer, not to have a pleasant visit. This was a matter of Zhaes law. It would not be interrupted by courtesy.

The Proctor lived in a standard, wealthy Zhaes house. Bashin's house would serve as a nice shed for this bronze lined feat of architecture. Their homes were both in Kzhek, only a small walk away from each other, yet the Proctor had two floors, stained glass windows, and bronze sculptures in his yard. Bashin was an Endowed. The Proctor *worked* for people like him. Equality was a figment of the aristocracy's imagination that they told each other to make them feel better about themselves.

Deim and Yellin gazed up at the house as Bashin walked between them and entered without an invitation. The deputies' heavy footsteps followed him into the house.

"Who goes there?" A spectacled man glared up from *The Tome of Measure*. Tented eyebrows suggested more fear than anger.

"We are here to—"

Yellin's explanation fell away from Bashin's ears as he began reading the Proctor. Yellin and Deim were competent deputies, but were often more of an obstacle for Bashin's interrogations. The deputies would mention the murder, causing thoughts of the event to fill the Proctor's mind. He could not read everything about the Proctor's past, merely what was on his mind.

What business did you have with the treasurer, Proctor?

It felt like focusing on whispers. Bashin took a deep breath, exhaling slowly to center himself. Regardless of his experience, his Endowed ability would be rendered useless without concentration. Whispers gained clarity, like a rippling pond reaching complete stillness.

"Seize him," Bashin waved Yellin and Deim forward. "You kulfs are better investigators than I thought. He is our guilty party. Our first suspect, how convenient." *Maybe I will sleep tonight after all.*

"What? You must be mistaken! I–" The Proctor grunted as Yellin held him from behind in a bear hug. Deim held his hands in front.

"I'm a Feelman," Bashin shrugged. "Struggle if you wish, but your conscience incriminates you." *The poor fool wanted to aid those radicals. He wanted to prove that harvesting was not necessary in our society, yet he was caught by an Endowed. A poor irony to prove the necessity of harvesting through your own actions. Perhaps I am worth something more than a convenience to the nobility myself.*

"You sure, Inquisitor?" Yellin said through clenched teeth and he squeezed the struggling Proctor tighter. Deim removed the pair of manacles from his side bag, pulling the Proctor's hands behind his back.

"No."

Yellin scowled. "Then why–"

"Of course I am sure, you perding kulf!" Bashin's shout fell to a hiss. *Who would have thought my deputy would enrage me more than our captive?* "Take him to the carriage."

"What did he do?" asked Yellin.

"Why don't you tell them yourself, Proctor?" said Bashin. "You can't hide anything else from me."

"I only did what I needed to set our Court on the right path!" shouted the Proctor.

"Can you be a little more direct?" asked Bashin.

"Perd you! Maybe I should have killed someone like you, you kulf!"

"If you haven't guessed by now, he's involved with those anti-harvesting protesters."

"I killed that perding treasurer because he bribed the Chuss Krall to accept that graft! *He* is one of the people responsible for stirring chaos in Facet."

"Says the man who works with rioters," Bashin chuckled. He turned to his deputies. "Much more than money was used to entice the Chuss Krall, but the treasurer was one of the key pieces in winning the Chussman over. The Proctor discovered this, organized meetings with the treasurer to confirm his conclusions, and took his life when the opportunity rose."

Bashin walked closer to Proctor and grabbed his head to stare into his eyes. "I hope you learned that a single murder does little more than make your life worse."

Yellin pulled the Proctor into the carriage. Deim and Bashin followed.

CHAPTER SIXTEEN

YOUNG WOLF OF THE TCHOYASMEN

Phenmir stretched as he walked along the muddy roadway, a few days out from Fayis. He yawned, longing for more than a few hours of sleep, but recognized that this was just a small piece of the fatigue that he would experience on his scouting assignment. They were fortunate to find a small cave, absent of wildlife, to spend the night away from the rain. He was grateful for the shelter, but the stone floor was less than helpful for his aching back.

"Voln," said Phenmir to the boy at his side.

"Sir Voln, if you will," replied the young Tchoyasman.

"Excuse me, Sir Voln."

Phenmir chuckled. "Tell me about the Tchoyas Endowers. Your organization was impressive. In Chuss, we have nothing as refined as your legion."

"It's something new for us as well. Krall Trhet noticed that some of my friends and I were meeting as a small group of Endowers, around two or three years ago"

You have much more ahead of you, boy.

"So the Krall recruited you to be his manservant, did he?" said Phenmir.

"No!" his biting reply startled Phenmir. "Krall Trhet needs us, so does the rest of Tchoyas, but he does not own us. His Thanes are worthless compared to us."

Speaking with Voln reminded Phenmir of morning walks across the Chuss dunes in search of palmfruit pods with Hir when he was younger. The ache of nostalgia stung, but hope for his son's future served as an ample slave.

❧❧❧❧❧ ❧❧❧❧❧

Large needle-tipped cathedrals sprouted from bronze lined buildings. Voln stared up in awe as they entered the Kzhek. Noticeably fewer people walked the streets, their numbers diminishing the closer they drew to the city center.

Evidence of passing rioters decorated the once- pristine city. Shattered glass crumbled into the cracks of the cobblestone street. Chaos among the orderly. Phenmir did not enjoy Kzhek, but it pained him to see the architectural masterpieces made to look like the slums of Sleff.

"We should find an inn soon," said Port, one of Colrig's scouts. He often wore his hood up to cover disheveled brown hair that curled like an artist's depiction of wind. A dagger sat sheathed against his right thigh, hidden beneath a gray coat. Colrig had forced Phenmir to have one as well, despite his protest. He had never held a weapon. It was unlike the medical tools he was accustomed to. Rather than heal, these were designed to destroy. He prayed to Cheric that he would not have to resort to its use.

"Do you know where we can find one worth the price, Chussman?" called Port.

Phenmir shook his head. "We have plenty of options, though I recommend staying in the lower districts to avoid attention. Even prospective allies could pose a threat."

"Lead the way, Captain!"

He was not yet used to his authority. It felt odd to speak of the *military*, *militia*, and *war*.

"Let's first check the commotion in the city center. We need to know what we are working with before we look for a place to start." Voices echoed in the distance from a large crowd. It seemed to be to the north-west. "We will observe from a distance and then return to an inn for the rest of the night."

There were seven men, counting Phenmir. The group included four Sleff scouts and the two Tchoyas Endowers. As they proceeded towards the center, the shouts grew louder. An aura of light shone from above the city square, illuminated by torches and the spirits of rebellion.

"What are you wishing to see there, sir?" asked Port as he approached Phenmir from the left.

"He wants to see the heroes of Zhaes in action, fighting the good fight!" said Voln as he approached Phenmir on the opposite side. "Death to the child-eaters!" he shouted with a deep voice manipulated to sound like a titan.

"Contain your spirit," Phenmir said. "I want to see what these riots actually look like." He turned to the Tchoyas Endower Shiftlings, seeing the wolven face of Voln and Kaela's mask of a serval. "Voln, could you and Kaela shift to look like Zhaesmen? I would prefer to go unnoticed for as long as possible."

Without a word, Kaela and Voln changed their skin to match the pale gray of the sky and adopted black hair. Remarkably, they could even alter their masks to appear as skin. He wondered if he underestimated how close their masks had grown to an actual appendage. Before him stood two young Zhaes children. *Are those their true faces with only a minor color change?*

"Would you like the clothing altered as well?" asked Kaela.

"Is that possible?" said Phenmir.

They lightened their clothes to a Zhaes gray with bronze lining. The style was modified to be more restrictive and to cover the neck and arms. A shimmer reflected off of their shoulders under the lamplight. It appeared as if they had adorned a putle lining to prevent more rain from soaking in. Voln looked up at Phenmir with a self-satisfied grin.

How is it possible? Shiftlings are said to alter the organic materials of their body, reshaping them, but these two can alter anything on them.

"Our Canton of Utilities worked with the Canton of Endowment to make clothing that is embedded in our skin, like our masks. They make it from plant material, allowing its life force to connect to our own and change as we want."

"Fascinating," Phenmir replied.

Phenmir led the way. Beggars glared at them as they passed. Once renowned as the paradise of Facet, one could now mistake the torn capital for an impoverished wasteland.

Stray dogs roamed the streets. Ribs protruded from sickly skin as they snuffled through refuse. Kzhek had become the nightmare of a Zhaes nobleman.

Voln and Kaela walked ahead of their party, but quickly drew back to Phenmir's side. The entrance to an immense building blocked the street. Half was lit by a warm yellow and orange glow, like the sun across a morning lake, enticing them to turn left at the fork.

Shouts grew louder with each step. Smoke from an enormous bonfire bled into the air, staining the sky. The rioting crowd filled the square. The left side of the crowd trampled the ruins of what used to be the Canton of Endowment.

No bodies were seen in the rubble. Phenmir opposed pointless death, but could death ever be justified? Deaths would increase as the tides of war rolled in. He would become numb to it, just as he had to harvesting.

Voln stepped forward, but Phenmir stopped him.

"Now is not the time for investigation," he told the boy. "Even if they are fighting the same fight as we are, they might take the wrong message if we simply walk in. We need to find some allies in the city before we go right to the rioters."

Voln scoffed. The boy could act dignified when he needed to, but childish mannerism still arose in his demeanor.

Port stepped towards Phenmir. "What do you make of the riot?"

The spirit of revolution was inspiring, to a degree. Their disorderly approach made him think otherwise. Hopeful enough to make the lowliest serf believe that change was possible. People went to such extremes in a quest for their desire. Had he not done the same when he fled from Kzhek? "I admire their determination," continued Phenmir, "though their approach is less than civilized."

"Do we not share a goal?" said Port, puzzled by Phenmir's reply.

"Yes, but there is power in order. We have a plan. Their plans seem to be little more than destruction, but I think we can win this city over if we can find a better way to join our people with theirs. A whining child accomplishes nothing. They need direction." He turned to face Port again.

"Like you said, sir," said Port, "we just need to find a way to connect our forces peacefully."

"Let's head in for the evening. We've seen what we need to. Now we can prepare."

As they left, Phenmir noticed Voln focused on the rebellion. An anxious frown showed through his mask's mouth hole.

"Are you well, Voln?" Phenmir asked, noting the boy's demeanor.

He shook his head. "Yes, I'm just..."

"A little frightened?"

"No, I'm no perding kulf of a child who fears a fight. It's just... I didn't think it would be this... I didn't think they would be that angry, that violent. I think I saw blood."

"Don't fret. We all have the right to be frightened. No man in his right mind would ever wish for war." *But am I here as an advocate for what we are calling a righteous war? What kind of Chussman am I, so easily forgetting the pacifism of my people? I claim to be a Chussman that lives by my Court Ideal, but my actions, even my thoughts, speak otherwise. Oh, Cheric, forgive me. I am a hypocrite.*

"Do you think it will come to that? War in Facet?" He turned to look upward at Phenmir. "Killing people for victory? I don't want it to be like that, Phenmir." He sounded as if he longed for a father's reassurance.

Has it not already begun? "Victory does not have to mean killing. Victory means control. Mercy is not always weakness."

He nodded.

"Nevertheless, Voln, do not hesitate to fight if you or an ally are in danger. You are gifted with something from your god himself. Do not let someone take that from you. Fight for what you believe in if you must."

"I will."

He could act as mature as he wished, but he was still a boy being thrown into an adult conflict.

Thunder woke Phenmir with a rumble that pulsated through the inn. The two Shiftlings remained asleep on the only bed.

Ruffling his hair and wiping his face, he stood and stretched his back, aching from sleeping on the floor. He left the chamber and left the children to sleep. The corridor was empty and still. The scouts slept in the next room over, but their room was silent. Was he the only one awoken by the storm? Storms were a rare occurrence for the Chuss desert, but not in Tchoyas.

The lack of sunlight in Zhaes baffled his internal clock. One could rely upon the warmth of the sun to awaken him in Chuss.

Perhaps he could read or have some tea in the inn's tavern. He entered and found a lone barkeep standing at a wooden counter, organizing bottles of alcohol. The inn was not as impressive as those nearest Kzhek's center. The area had only four wooden tables with worn benches and the glasses that hung from the wall were cloudy and stained.

"Excuse me, Zhaesman, but do you know the time?" he asked.

"I'm sorry to say that you just missed the evening crowd."

"The storm woke me. Maybe I'll try to sleep again in a while."

"Zhaes is not fit for all." He turned to face Phenmir. "What brings you here, Chussman?"

"I was sent here on an assignment. I work as a traveling medic." *Hide a lie amidst the truth.*

The man nodded. "Impressive work."

"I suppose so. I enjoy my career, but all of this *political unrest* has made my traveling less than ideal. Can't a man enjoy his neighboring Court in peace?"

"I hear you, Chussman. There is a reason I've settled in the outer city. You can still experience the spirit of Kzhek without binding yourself to politics."

"It amazes me that this undignified disaster began in Kzhek, the *head city* of harvesting. You would expect some gratitude for your Endowed."

He did not feel sick lying, for these statements were far from his true self. The worst lies, those that cause the most destruction, are those close enough to truth to *truly* deceive.

"What a shame for the virtuous Court Zhaes," chuckled the barkeep. "Some say it started with the Thanes, but who knows?"

"Do you know any of them? Do any of them frequent your inn? Those kulfs." Phenmir clenched his fists behind his back and took a breath to still himself.

The barkeep's eyebrows tightened in a squint.

Too many questions.

"No... but their companies pass frequently enough."

"And the guards let them roam?"

The barkeep chuckled. "They've tried to make some arrests, but any guards that try to do so are taken by the mob. Killed, tortured, who knows what they do to them. They still try to apprehend some who wander the city, but I think the nobility has stopped sending in guards while they try to find a better solution to all of this. At least we have some distance between here and the center. Still, the ones that really strike my spine are the troops that march throughout the town in the mid-day hours, spreading their propaganda. There ought to be some leader among them."

Maybe we can find such a leader nearby. Phenmir pressed his face to shade any excitement. "Well, I shall do my best to avoid them."

He earned a smile from the barkeep. "Can I get you a drink, Chuss-man?"

"I'll have to pass on your offer, though I appreciate the gesture."

The barkeep took a pull on his wine and wiped his lips, the blue staining his teeth. "Make yourself at home, don't hesitate to ask for anything. The city structure is a bit odd for an outsider. Even I occasionally get lost on the way to the market."

Phenmir nodded and left to return to his chamber.

Phenmir managed to sleep for a few more hours and was woken up when he heard the whispered voices of the Shiftlings.

"Heloath, you perding kulf!"

"What a dignified way to greet your captain, Voln. It's a pleasure to see you as well. Did you two sleep well?"

"Yes," Kaela said with a quiet morning voice, combing her hair with nimble fingers.

"Yes, and we stayed tucked in as our mothers would wish. I crave her milk already." Voln bit back with his characteristic wit. "We may look young, but you don't need to treat us like children."

Phenmir couldn't resist a smile.

"Before you leave the room, be sure to revert to your Zhaes guises."

They both adjust their clothing and composure, leaving the bed as Zhaes younglings. Port and the other three scouts—it would do him well to learn their names—were likely waking in the neighboring chamber.

"Where's the food?" Voln said. "Shifting is no easy work."

"In our baggage, though I believe"—he reached over to the bedside table and searched through his rucksack—"I have some nuts and dried fruit."

Voln glared at the handful of food.

"Is the little lad scared of proper food?"

"No," Voln said. "I would rather have some meat. I would give my left leg for a camel steak."

"Wouldn't we all?" Phenmir tossed the remaining food into his mouth after Kaela took two dried berries. "We will have something more to your liking. Just hold tight for a little longer."

They heard the sound of approaching footsteps, followed by a light knock.

"Port here."

Phenmir arched his back to stretch. "Come in." He beckoned the four scouts into the room.

"Lead us in today's matters, Thane Stolk," said Port, his voice rough.

"We can discuss investigative tactics after we leave the inn, but I think we know where to start. Some of the anti-harvesting companies march through the city and they sound a lot more approachable. I would like to leave as soon as possible."

Voln groaned.

"Voln?"

"You know what I want, you kulf," he replied

"Our Shiftlings want to eat. Could you see that taken care of, Port?"

"Without question, sir! Though I suggest heading to the market beforehand. It appears some of our perishables have spoiled."

Phenmir nodded for Port to lead the way, passing down the corridor and into the lobby and tavern. Food seemed to last much longer outside of Court Zhaes. Bread never lasted more than a few days, and anything dry-preserved seemed to return to a moistened state after being left out. Kzhek was in the ideal location for humidity, capped by the Great Lake of Zeal and bordered by the Tchoyas Marsh.

The scouts stopped abruptly before Phenmir could see down the corridor. Beyond them, the barkeep stood among a group of four people who appeared to run a blacksmith's shop or an underground contraband ring. The barkeep's companions wore leather straps across their chests and shoulders.

Phenmir's concern deepened when he noticed swords protruding from along their backs.

"Heloath, Zhaesmen," Phenmir said. He stepped forward with his eyes down, only to be halted by the group. Like the cliche conflict of a children's tale, the largest among the party stood to block the doorway. His bald head reflected condescension as he stared down at them.

Phenmir clenched his fists. "Pardon me, Zhaesman. I really need to pass. These two are already late for their morning lectures." He turned to Kaela and Voln, who stood in line with the scouts. *Thank Charic they maintained their Zhaes appearance.*

The barkeep walked before the others. "I really am sorry, Chussman. You can't blame me for questioning why you would be here with some Sleffmen."

"What do you mean?" asked Phenmir. *Please, no. Not here. Not with the Endowers.*

"I am just trying to follow the law. The Canton of Veneration is looking for people who are coming from outside Zhas to fuel the rebel fires here. I just need to have my friend here take a look at you." He gestured to the bald man blocking the door. "He's a Feelman. If you have no connections to the conflict here, you have no reason to worry. If he sees something else in your thoughts, then we might have to take you to see someone in the Canton of Veneration."

"Sir, we mean no trouble."

"Is that true?" The barkeep looked up at the bald Feelman.

He shook his head. "They are trying to find rebels to join. They have troops in Tchoyas and need to make a connection here for their armies to come."

"*Armies?*" said the barkeep. "You must see now, Chussman. We have no choice but to take you in.

The two frontmost men unsheathed their swords. Their blades were of a pristine metal with a luminous shimmer, exposing their virginity to combat.

The barkeep then removed a long knife from a sheath in his belt loop. "Just let us take you in. I hate to make threats, but we need you to follow us."

We can't let them free. They know about Tchoyas. Perd me. "Kaela, Voln, get out of here." *There's an exit in the back. Delay the problem here, let the children escape. At least let them leave uninjured. Alive.*

Kaela stepped back, but Voln remained as sturdy as the palace of Tchoyas during a rainstorm. "No, Kaela," he said, "we stay."

Defense. No shield or sword. He looked around in search of a knife or anything that resembled a blade. *Table? Bar? Supply room? Fire!* He looked at the fireplace on the left. Though he was not a nimble youth, he believed he could reach the fireplace before the others would catch him. They only had five enemies to eliminate, equal to their group without the Shiftlings.

Combat? Violent self-defense? Is this really happening? Cheric, forgive me for what I am about to do.

He dashed to the fireplace. One of the large men pursued him while the other three clashed with the scouts. The weighty fellow was only five steps behind him, enough space for him to receive the fire iron from its sooty metal stand.

Once in his grip, Phenmir swung at the charging figure and met his sword with a loud clang. While the brute stood back to prepare for another strike, Phenmir shook his hands free from the clash's sting.

The scouts attempted to deflect the sword blows with their gauntlets of thick leather. The rightmost scout shot himself like a crossbow bolt at his opponent's legs. He took the man down, to his surprise, but enjoyed a short-lasting victory as the man stabbed him in the chest while they sat on the floor.

Phenmir glanced quickly at Voln, disappointed to see that he remained close. Kaela continued to beckon him away from the battle ahead, but her pleas only hit closed ears.

His opponent knocked him back against a thickly laced rug that adorned the fireplace's mantle. His back ached as if the shaft of a sea voyager had struck it. In desperation, he reached for the fire tongs to his right and removed a lump of red coal. With his remaining force, he tossed the coal into his attacker's face. The hopeful act resulted in only a black dash on the pursuer's cheek and an expletive shout illustrating his now multiplied anger.

In a single quivering breath, the brute was thrown to the left as a shadowy blur hurled him away from Phenmir. Shocked and panting, he stood up and cleared his eyes. A black direwolf had tackled his pursuer, though the animal was slightly smaller than the large Zhaesman and had swiped at his face. Long red lines across his face dripped with the crimson liquid of life.

The other combatants stumbled and turned from their tussles to see what had barged into the room.

Blood pooled from the wolf's victim; the man's throat had been torn out with rough teeth. The wolf turned away from Phenmir, searching for its next target. Chunks of gray Zhaes meat still hung from its bloodied jaw.

The wolf dashed to the barkeep–who was caught defending himself against Port–and repeated the gruesome act on the conflict's instigator. The three remaining men kept their vision split on their opponents and the ravaging beast.

With an adrenaline spike, Phenmir joined Port in combat. He swung the fire pole at his new opponent in unison with his ally. He fought with his remaining strength, but was left weakened by tortuous thoughts. *I did this. I was foolish enough to divulge our pursuit.*

With spring-loaded paws, the wolf ran across the backside of the remaining Zhaes party, clawing at their ankle tendons, not losing momentum. The black bolt met the last Zhaesman and tore at him as if he was nothing more than boiled chicken.

The speed of the beast startled the remaining scouts, but they soon jumped on their fallen opponents to finish the act that the wolf had begun.

Silent, awestruck, fearful. The survivors of the Allegiant stood together as he faced the beast. The furthermost scout held his hand to his chest; a severe break made visible by a disfigured wrist.

The wolf finished digging through the last Zhaesman. Warm breath projected saliva onto the floor. Slashes were now visible on the side of its pelt as it walked with a limp toward Phenmir.

In haste, he searched for the Shiftlings while Kaela hid distraught behind a mead barrel. Her tears had passed, leaving bloodshot eyes and wet cheeks. She ran to meet the direwolf with open arms, like a child running toward her mother's embrace.

"Kaela!" Phenmir shouted with a hand outreached for her. Confusion quelled his fear as she embraced the wolf and knelt at its side.

The wolf retracted its hair as it stood on its hind legs. Skin replaced fur as Voln stood before him, covered with the blood of the wolf's victims.

Phenmir rushed to the boy's side, inspecting the wounds on his arms and across his back. The dripping lacerations cut across his body, yet they were superficial enough that he could stitch them without an extensive recovery. He looked the boy in the face, seeing a red mouth that appeared as though he had just devoured a baked cherry pastry.

"As I promised, Phenmir," said Voln with a shaky voice, "that I will fight for what I believe." He collapsed into Phenmir's embrace, panting and coughing, though still conscious. He embraced Voln–as if he was Hir–like a proud, yet concerned, parent.

"What was his name?" asked Phenmir. Port and the other two scouts turned to the sound of his voice. "Our fallen brother. What was his name?" he repeated.

The female scout pointed at the corpse. "Him?" Phenmir nodded. "Kall." She sniffed as her eyes welled tears. "We grew close during our travels with Colrig."

"Heitt be with him on his journey homeward to the spirits of his ancestors," said Phenmir. "Thank you, Thane Stolk."

"Kaela?" he asked. "Were you harmed?"

She shook her head and wiped a tear from her face and pointed to Voln.

"He'll be fine, but we need to leave now." He looked at the others. "We need shelter and medical attention." "Where shall we go, sir? We cannot travel on the road to Tchoyas in this condition. And what about Kall?" asked Port, his eyes too on the verge of leaking with despair.

The words of Lord Detti came into Phenmir's mind. *A troop's spirit is the captain's countenance.* He banished self doubt. "We will give Kall a journeyman's burial. He's earned it."

"What does a 'journeyman's burial' entail?" Port inquired.

"As recorded in *The Strategist's Dilemma*, a journeyman's burial was a ceremony that would not require the materials and effort of a ground burial or farewell flame. A journeyman was the title given to a traveling soldier and I feel it was appropriate for Kall. As soldiers journey, they have few resources to pay respects to a fallen comrade and their gods. Though it may appear gruesome, they found a proper tribute was to return the soldier's life to the land, giving the body as an offering to the beasts of the field. Their body is not wasted but lives in the realms beyond and within the creatures that roam this plane."

"We can take care of Kall, then attend to our medical needs. Before the assassination of my Krall, I worked in Kzhek for the Canton of Haleness on a labor contract. There, we will have sufficient materials to make sure we can return to Fayis in good health."

"How are we going to enter?" Port worried, his confidence slipping. "Seeing that we are not particularly liked by most of this Court?"

"Fortunately for us, I left my previous assignment in haste, not thinking of returning keys to certain chambers in the Canton." He reached into his rucksack to remove a bronze key. "I was trusted. We will visit the building tonight, when most people should be home. We can bind some wounds here with some rags while we await the night. Though I am not inclined to have you all drink, it can serve to stave off the pain." He pointed to the bar behind him. "I think we have a right to use some of the barkeep's bottles, seeing that he will no longer need them."

The company laughed at the grim humor; fright still slipped through their glares.

Trials bred the finest of people, but they could just as well breed antagonists from those who refuse to adapt and grow from their challenges. *How would they take the loss of an ally? Was this the first, or just one of many in their campaign?*

How will it affect me in the coming days?

CHAPTER SEVENTEEN

MOTIVATION, HEART, AND DUTY

"Caser Zhil?" gasped a Scholar as they entered the Canton of Diplomacy. His hands shook as if in panic, eyes opened as wide as a full moon. "Thane Leisa? Your eye!" Aerhee expected such a reaction. She and Sheath held the former Cased, leading her down the corridors of the Canton of Scholarship.

"Take us to Thane Gromm," Sheath commanded. Red bled through the center of a bandage that wrapped around her head and covered her eye. Redlines ran above and below the cloth to show the full extent of the attack.

"Thane Gromm has been occupied as of late. All the protests and—" Sheath scowled.

"But I will try my best to locate him."

Curious eyes followed the party as they paced through the Canton. Thankfully, Felta was a submissive captive.

The Scholar knocked on the Thane's door upon arrival. The silence behind the door released some tension in Felta's wrists, but Aerhee was not inclined to wait.

"Thane Gromm!" shouted Aerhee, pounding on the door.

"This is urgent!" exhorted Sheath. Blood dripped from her red-soaked cloth bandage after she had agitated the scab.

A chair scraped across the stone floor. Footsteps followed. The door swung open, and Thane Gromm removed his spectacles. "What has called you to disrupt a Scholar's work, my dear Zhaeswomen?"

Sheath and Aerhee dismissed the guard and shoved Felta forward.

Aerhee had never seen panic from a brother of the Patriarchy, but Gromm's mouth fell open and he looked as if he were ready to shout. Gromm rushed Felta into the room as if she were an escaped hound. He gestured for the Scholar to leave them before shutting the door and locking it.

"Thane Leisa is wearing a band over her eye. Our Caser looks as if she wrestled with a ghete, and our previous Caser looks worse than either of you. Please. Entertain me."

Aerhee and Sheath looked at each other, but Aerhee took the lead. "Caser Zhil is guilty of treason. She worked with Thane Sorn to inspire local and neighboring riots against harvesting."

Gromm scowled. "How do you plan to verify your claim?"

"She confessed," responded Sheath. "Do you want to argue with a Feelman?"

Gromm sighed and muttered to himself. "We may need another to verify such a claim." He looked up, speaking with a normal volume. "What do you want me to do with her?"

"We wish for a Scholar's trial," said Aerhee.

"You believe it to be that dire of a matter? You of all people, Caser Kleeh, wish to invoke the judgment of the Patriarchy?" The corners of Gromm's lips hinted at a smile.

"Yes. Without attending to her wrongdoings, we invite even greater terrors. An example must be made of the guilty."

Gromm smirked. "It is funny that you say it so. During your absence, we Thanes of the nobility met to discuss the treatment of the rejectionists in the city center, but we can address that later." He turned to Sheath, "Thane Leisa, do you agree to Scholar's trial?"

His question tugged at Aerhee. *Does he question me even as I present him with evidence?*

"Yes, treason is not to be dismissed to the handling of the mere officers of the Canton of Veneration. She used her previous office as Caser to breed contention rather than bind the people together."

"Well then, Zhaeswomen, we will call a council to hear her plea and judge accordingly. Until then, let us take her to the central dungeons to be kept until she is called to trial."

"Thank you, Thane Gromm," responded Aerhee. "Have any other Cantons fallen victim to the mobs during our absence?"

"The organizations remain strong, but all the buildings themselves have been struck by vandals. Despite the damage, they remain standing. I advise caution in your travels throughout the city, it is not the utopia that we once enjoyed." Sheath nodded and handed Felta over to Thane Gromm.

They shared the Zhaes salute and left the Thane's chamber. "As I mentioned," called Gromm. They turned. "We have decided upon an offensive strategy for controlling the riots. I suggest you meet with Thane Belik to prepare."

Aerhee didn't reply. She did not feel so comfortable with Thane Belik or *Royss*, as he preferred to be called. He was a genial man, that was beyond doubt, but Aerhee could not dismiss the feeling that he forced politeness. The man always seemed to be plotting more than he shared.

◈

26 years ago, Court Zhaes, Kzhek
Year 306 in the Clerical Era (Cl. er. 306)

◈

"What is the Zhaes Ideal?" asked Faeth, pacing about the room as Aerhee watched.

"Whole is the Holy," recalled Aerhee.

"How do you live it?"

"Living by the law, neither word nor act dismissed."

"Whose law?"

"Our lord Laeih, the one true god."

"What does the *Tome of Measure* call you to do?"

"*Let Laeih dwell within thy spirit, becoming thy thought and deed among the wicked,*" quoted Aerhee, each response becoming less enthusiastic.

Faeth knelt at her side. "And who are you?"

"Aerhee Kleeh of Court Zhaes, daughter of Derlik the miner, and Faeth the priestess."

"*Oresmith*, Aerhee. Your father is an *oresmith*. Priessmen call them miners, but your father deserves more respect for his labor."

Aerhee stared at the floor.

"Aerhee." Faeth reached for her hands and lifted them to her chest. "We will work on this tomorrow, alright?"

Aerhee nodded and yawned. Though she knew her daughter wished to sleep, Faeth would make sure that Aerhee would endure the rest of the day.

They had traveled throughout Kzhek in search of supplemental religious materials for Faeth, who had been accepted into the Zhaes Priest Society. As a priestess, she was responsible for teaching children about Laeih's doctrine. She would be a poor parent if she failed to teach her own daughter.

They had been in Zhaes for just over three months. In an effort to fit in, they had lost their tan complexion from dwelling under overcast skies, but were still too dark for the average Zhaesman. Though it was costly, they were able to purchase a non-corrosive dye from a Kzhek alchemist that allowed them to change the color of their hair to match the ebony common to Zhaes.

"When are we going to eat?" asked Aerhee.

"Your father will be home past sunset again, so it will just be the two of us. Are you hungry?"

Aerhee nodded and searched the dining area for something to eat. "Can we invite the Kout family over?"

The Kout family was kind enough to have them for dinner a few weeks ago, but Faeth was not ready to return the favor. They could not afford to invite guests over to dine with them while they struggled to pay for their every meal. "I don't want to bother them at this hour, Aerhee." Her childhood was burdening enough and did not require additional financial worries. That fight was for her and Derlik to face. Faeth ate earlier in the day and could face a period of hunger. "I'm not hungry. Would you like to choose something from a market stand in the city?"

Aerhee perked at that suggestion.

Aerhee wandered the Kzhek streets, stopping to look into merchants' windows. Faeth was exhausted from teaching and could barely keep up. The girl would have already arrived in the center if her mother was not holding her back.

The sound of sizzling meat and the aroma of umami filled the wide street as vendors lined the sides with their dishes. The southern market sector of central Kzhek was a haven for unique meals at affordable prices. If food was prepared by immigrants from other Courts, she felt more inclined to pay well. Anyone who sought a new life in Zhaes deserved help from an ally. Aside from the critique of the general Zhaes population, it was one of the few places to get non-Zhaes food.

In other words, food with flavor.

Aerhee feigned indecision each time they came but had grown fixated on a Gruth vendor that prepared a wide variety of seafood. Specifically, she chose the garlic and honey-battered clamfish, though it was deemed "too flavorful" by Faeth's standards. She preferred the Chuss bread assortments and the colorful vegetable spreads.

"Aerhee," Faeth called as her daughter placed an order. "Order another for your father. We'll take it home for him." As requested, she placed a second order.

Aerhee returned to her mother's side with a smile. They sat at a street side table. The young Priesswoman, now Zhaeswoman, savored each bite bought with hours of her father's labor.

Immigrants filled the market, outnumbering the Zhaes-born consumers. She was far from her native home, but being surrounded by others in similar circumstances was comforting. Their hardships were shared; Kzhek was not a city that embraced diversity.

A large man of Gruth heritage pushed a cart filled with dough balls towards a humble bakery. His day of labor would yield him the equivalent of an hour of a nobleman's income, with the physical expenditure tenfold in comparison. Derlik was not making much more than the burly baker.

Still, those she saw around her seemed content. Whether they faced hardships at home or among the high classmen, it did not matter. This small share of Kzhek was their sanctuary.

"Done," said Aerhee, wiping the garlic glaze from her lips with her sleeve.

"*No, no, no.*" She pulled her daughter's stained sleeve away, dabbing at the corner of her mouth with a handkerchief. "*Zhaeswomen* do not clean their faces with their clothing."

Aerhee rolled her eyes and grinned.

※※※※ ※※※※

Faeth noticed Derlik's blackened boots on the doorstep. Light bled through the crack in their door.

"Mother?" asked Aerhee.

"Yes, little one?"

She pointed a finger. "Who is that?"

Faeth followed her daughter's finger to see a carriage parked beside their house. Each of the ghete rested on the ground, still in their bridle and reins. The carriage cabin was vacant. Adorned in white and bronze, it was much nicer than the one that had taken them from Priess to Zhaes.

"Go inside," Faeth directed her.

Three men stood in white robes and emotionless faces. Derlik sat between them and was bound at the wrists.

"Derlik?" Faeth asked. "What is this?"

"Allow me to speak for your husband," the rightmost intruder said. He was as bald and gaunt as a decomposing corpse. Stepping forward, he left Derlik in the grasp of the other two. "There is no need to be alarmed. We are no intruders."

"What do you want with my husband?"

"We are here to see him on behalf of the Patriarchy of Scholars."

❧ ⚬ ☙

The Present
Cl. er. 332

❧ ⚬ ☙

A day had passed since Felta was handed to the Patriarchy. *Laeih be with her on that road.* She was destined for the under realms after being caught as a traitor.

Lettre. How could I forget about Lettre? As the man had requested her help to search for the Sleff Endowed, she owed Thane Lettre a visit to explain her findings. With the commotion in the city, she could not confidently say that she would find him in his Canton, but it was worth a visit.

She hoped to avoid any disruptions or harassment in the city by spending another night in the Canton of Diplomacy. She was grateful for Sheath. It seemed to be the most fruitful of her friendships.

Zeir. He would be fine in her absence.

She was not neglecting Zeir. To turn her attention to him over the courtly manners would cause harm to the Court. Her duty was more important than her domestic affairs. Still, something festered at the back of her mind, telling her she should do more for her marriage.

❧ ⚬ ☙

After following a trail of advisors, she found that Lettre was to lead a council session at the Krall's palace. He was not meeting with the Krall himself, but the location signified that he had important business to conduct; yet, what business was not important to a nobleman?

She walked through the palace's halls and found Lettre speaking to another Zhaesman. She was relieved to find him outside of a meeting.

"... I would say that I am opposed to the reformation, although—"

"Thane Lettre, I have..." Aerhee glared at the man, hoping he would leave to let her speak with Lettre.

"Aerhee, I've been hoping to see you." Thane Lettre dismissed the man with an apologetic nod. "Much has occurred since our previous meeting. I'm sure you would agree. Come, let us find a room to talk without being overheard."

She followed him to a secluded council room near the northern end of the building.

"I found the origin of the riots," she said as soon as he closed the door. "And the Chussmen are not responsible."

"I know," he replied.

"But, how?"

"I spoke with Thane Gromm this morning. Nevertheless, thank you."

"I see." She nodded with a sigh. "What have you accomplished?"

"Gromm, Royss, and I have laid out a strategy to combat the uprising."

A secretive cult member with a heart of stone and a deceitful braggart. What better allies could you ask for? Gromm did not seem persuaded of Felta's guilt. Now he rejoiced upon her findings?

"What does that entail?"

After Lettre told her about the plan to deal with the riots, she remained quiet.

She tried to process the idea of attacking people. Regardless of their intentions, they were still Zhaesmen. *Is this the best solution?*

She looked up to see him uncomfortable with the silence. He then told her about the two Gruthmen who had agreed to help the Zhaes Thanes.

"Have the Gruthmen returned to their home Court?" she asked.

"No, they are still among us and I would not wish for them to leave now. Royss took the girl to persuade the Krall. The boy was sent to work with the Beastlings to recruit kaesan."

"Kaesan? Royss wants those beasts to join our ranks? Why not go invite the Middlemen while you are at it? That will ensure we can dominate all the *perding* Courts!"

"Aerhee." He sighed.

"The man is eccentric and impulsive. A little too much for me." *Is Royss so desperate that he wishes to recruit the sin-purging nightmares? Kaesan are sure to bring death to all sides.*

"And we will not 'dominate' the Courts. If all goes well, we extinguish the flames of unsatisfied Courts and we can remain to harvest as we please."

"Yes, I understand, but what of the other Courts? What if your fear-mongering does not stop the Chussmen? I am sure they are still working out a dignified reaction to the assassination of their krall. And what of the Canton of Endowment? I heard that Meant Sorn perished when the building fell, but I doubt his underlings were present during the collapse. Could they not be the ones instigating the riots?"

"Do I believe they are raging with those dissenters in the city center? No. Those ruffians are crazed locals in search of attention. However, you raise a possibility. What has become of the members of the Canton of Endowment? With Caser Zhil on trial, they deserve a similar consequence." Lettre bit his lower lip. "Do you think it is possible that they could already be spreading their propaganda in other Courts? If Thane Sorn planned the collapse of his Canton in an attempt to conceal his rebellious intentions, maybe he sent the rest of his loyalists to rebel in the other Courts."

"Sleff was unquestionably affected by it, being the first to rise in protest. Have you heard of any occurrences in Priess? Perhaps Gruth? What did those Gruthmen tell you?"

"Little more than we already knew. They only faced unrest while passing through Sleff."

"How do we know that is true, Lettre?"

"Why would they lie? A Gruth Thane that is close with Royss sent them here for another reason."

Royss dealing with foreign dignitaries. Strangers arriving at a time of discord? Did Royss have a personal agenda above his own Court?

"With Thane Sorn going rogue," proposed Aerhee, "would it be radical to suggest that another could be on the same path?"

"Now *you* are telling tales. It seems you have caught the spirit of war. Do you believe that we will soon stand at spearpoint with those we used to call brothers and sisters? Aerhee, return to the present. I did not send you to search for conspiracy, but to find a useful asset for our people."

"Then what would you have of me? Do you want me to sit and observe the battle like a Krall? I want this to end, Lettre. Taking in a few prisoners will not prevent repercussions. Little has come from violence. Suffering breeds suffering. It is in its nature. I would like to speak with Royss about this."

"I will raise your concerns to the other Thanes, but you are only a Caser and this has already been settled. Our council did not agree upon some child's fantasy. We have given this consideration. You did not seem so opposed to all of this moments ago."

"Superiority is your defense, then? I thought *you* would have enough sense to avoid war, Lettre. *War!* Are we truly barbaric enough to resort to murder for dominance?"

"Aerhee," he called as she stalked towards the door. She turned, only to view him with her left eye. "Laeih bless your way." He left her with the Zhaes salute, but she did not return it.

She recalled only moments before being satisfied with their plans for seizing the city center, even deeming it in line with the law. What had changed in only a few spoken sentences? *One violent action is just if it is left at that, but it never is. That was it. Lettre did not suggest it would be kept to a single act. They would attack and inspire revenge until the land would be left desolate.*

Children fought with fists while adults should attend to matters with civil words. *That is what I will do.* She would not try to change the course of the Zhaes nobility. They were too stiffnecked in their conviction. *I should know, I am the same.* She was determined to find an alternate path. She could discuss peace with someone who might understand her. Could the call of a single figurehead sway armies? Yes, Kralls and Thanes rule the Courts. Single voices to represent the grand population. Wars, or what she had heard of them, were won in council rooms and not by the prowess of footmen.

Where should she go? Where *could* she go? Sheath had likely already spoken with the other Thanes. Aerhee loved her as a sister, but Sheath was rash enough to stand behind their raid. *Perd her. Where can one find a diplomat that does not blindly follow the nobility?*

What if she were to depart and lead her own mission to confront foreign dignitaries? If war would arise, the Court leaders would search for treaties to bind broken bonds. Finding an ally amongst the dissenters or the Courts opposed to harvesting could prevent strife before it turned into a Facet-wide war.

Sleff? Perhaps they would be a fine target for persuasion. They had not yet converted to the side of the anti-harvesters.

Chuss? Whom could I approach?

Tchoyas? Yes, Tchoyas. The masked loyalists of Tchoyas seek to bind their people through harmony.

Aerhee had little on her. She would return to the Canton of Diplomacy to retrieve her necessities, but Zeir would have to wait a little longer before her return. Sheath's words concerning her marriage still cut at her.

With clothing and some food for travel, she had sufficient coins to rent a ghete. *Actually*, she had enough for two, but would need more for a carriage and coachman.

By the end of the day, Aerhee and her young scribe Fheo would be on their way to the capital of Court Tchoyas.

CHAPTER EIGHTEEN

AN ABRIDGED COURSE IN BEASTCALLING

The Serbic Wilds were only an hour's journey outside of Kzhek on foot. Yetrik did not expect lush green forests to be so close to the Court's capital. Rustling leaves caused him to search for shadows, though no beasts were visible. Gray bears were said to be scattered throughout, but Runith, the Beastling company's leader, said that they rarely saw any at this time of year.

Royss had sent three Beastlings, Yetrik, and a non-Endowed alchemist named Horrah to care for any wounds the company received. Despite the initial awkwardness, the company seemed quite amiable.

Yetrik walked alongside Runith. He was larger than most Zhaesmen and wore a collection of direwolf pelts. His appearance matched that of any hunter. He had the large build of a Gruthman, but his gray skin solidified his heritage as a Zhaesman. Long black hair with silver highlights, though well kept, hung past his ears and touched the high points of his matching beard. The other Beastlings fashioned a similar style.

"Runith?"

"Yes, Gruthman? What can I do for you?"

"How much longer do we have until…?"

"Oh, yes, another anxious one." He looked down at Yetrik with a grin. "Don't worry, I've had men older than you soil themselves on a bear hunt. I would guess that we are two-thirds of the way. Think you can handle that?"

"Yes, I hope so." Yetrik forced out a nervous chuckle.

"More questions?" asked Runith

"What?"

"People on their first hunt with Beastlings always have questions. What is beastcalling like? What's the largest thing we've called? Why do we do it? Do we have tails growing out of our asses?"

Yetrik looked at him with awe.

"No, lad, we do not. That would be a real trick for the taverns, though, wouldn't it?"

"Well then, if you don't mind me asking, what *do* you do?"

"Some farmers like having a tamed or 'stilled' bear or wolf to scare away pests. In the case of a ghete shortage, we are paid well to travel and tame steeds. Aside from that, many enjoy the sport of joining us on a hunt, if you can call what we do 'hunting.' Quelling a bear is easy money for us and a story for bragging to a gullible nobleman. You, my friend, are given the finest of experiences. I should ask for your firstborn for the worth of this one."

Yetrik offered an uneasy grin

"Say, why did Royss send you with us? I wouldn't say that we will be in *unsafe* circumstances, but this trip is a little more… intense than our typical assignments."

Yetrik shrugged. "I think he just wants to give me some experience."

Royss chuckled. "That would do you no harm, lad. You could put on some muscle to look more like a true Gruthman. If you had lighter skin, I might mistake you for one of our people. Who am I to judge? You probably think the same thing about me. I always wondered if my father visited a Gruth brothel without my mother knowing."

"Have you ever tamed kaesan?"

"Once, but it was not for military purposes. Using them will be like working with fire. It can destroy its user just as well as the opponent.""
Are you not going to control them in combat?"

"Is that what Royss wants from us? I can't blame the man, we are *quite* useful. I will have to speak with him again about payment... anyway, after we tame them, kaesan can be a threat. Have you ever seen one, besides on Zhaes banners?"

Yetrik shook his head. "I thought they were made up to scare children into obedience? Do they really—"

"—possess you with their demonic cry? Remove your soul with a glare? Feed on the sinners of the disobedient? No, but I would not doubt that they come from the under realms themself."

"How does it work?"

Runith raised an eyebrow.

"Beastcalling. How do you do it?"

"Speaking to the beasts of the wild is as simple as speaking a language you were born with. Sometimes it's easier to talk to a hog than to a human. Each animal is unique. Learning is neither difficult nor long, but it requires effort. Come to think of it, that is why we captured the first Kaesan. I rarely come across anything new anymore, and that is why we went for the kaesan. Derr and Jhael," he pointed to the other two Beastlings in their party, "were among the ten who spoke with the beast."

"Ten? But there are only three of you this time!"

Runith chuckled and shrugged.

Yetrik stared at him with eyes open wide. "Then you just... talk to it, as you would any human?"

"Not quite. Most animals are dimwits, incapable of constructing sentences. Bears rarely think beyond their immediate needs, 'food, home, sleep,' nothing worthy of a conversation. However, I recall having a pleasant conversation with a duck once. We usually learn to mimic their noises. I think we have a little bit of Shiftling in us, our throats produce such a wide variety of noises. My body should never be capable of mimicking a heron's call so well. Thank Laeih for such a gift. I mean no offense. I am sure your god has done well for the people of Gruth."

"I respect any god who produces such honorable people. There is truth in all beliefs. If people believe in a god other than mine, they must have grown that belief from some original truth. No one decides 'let me believe that there is a man above us' for pleasure. Faith is a difficult thing."

"Are you a priest in your homeland? A Scholar? You don't fit the look of a brother of the Patriarchy."

"I was, I mean, am a financial advisor to the Thane of Utilities."

"Well, advisor, you will be the only one of your kind to help tame a kaesan."

"Tame?" Yetrik gasped as if Runith had spoken in error. He had not expected to observe the taming behind a distant tree, but never actualized that he might assist them.

"If Royss called you to join us, you must be worth something. Don't worry, you won't be the bait. Derr will take care of that if we are fortunate enough to find a deer within the next stretch of forest."

"Then what should I do?"

"Kaesan need a spirit to catch their attention. We Zhaesmen believe that our soul is bound to the body, especially to the blood. Animal spirits exist, but their souls are of lesser value. When our blood is exposed, some of our soul is released. Kaesan crave that spirit. They eat not for physical hunger, but for *spiritual* hunger. They crave the souls of humans more than animals. We will use a deer to distract it, but we need the blood of a human to ensure that we catch its attention. We need you to open a small wound to rub it on the deer's antlers. The kaesan will pick up its scent and hunt. You follow?"

"Why can't you do it?"

"Don't worry, you're not here as a sacrificial lamb," he clapped Yetrik on the shoulder. "Simply stated, if we were to use the blood of one of us Beastlings, it would target us. If you provide the blood, we can communicate with it without being seen as food."

"Then why not Horrah? "

"If anyone gets injured, she's there to heal them. Do not worry, we'll keep you away from the beast. You are here to gain experience, not lose your life. Maybe Royss is just preparing you to be the next Beastling."

Yetrik forced a laugh. *What if Runith's ramblings were more than just jests? Could I become an Endowed?*

"Enough about me, Runith. Tell me about you."

"Nothing much to my story. I was a commanding guard for the Canton of Agriculture, though I had some time with Utilities and Endowment. A couple of years of work earned me a graft. I still think they got the wrong guy. Some sorry kulf is probably stuck in standing guard to the central riots while I am off beastcalling for the perding Krall."

"I would say you have quite a life." Runith spoke quickly and without looking at Yetrik. He knew there was more to the Zhaesman's tale, but felt it best not to pry. "You mentioned some caverns ahead?"

"Yes, there is a small 'mountain', as some refer to it, in the inner parts of the Serbic Wilds. In truth, it is more of a large rock that reaches only as high as the Krall's palace. Kaesan dwell deep within the rocks. At least, that is where we found one last time."

"Only one?"

"Yes. As far as we know, they are reclusive creatures. We would be lucky to find two before heading back today. Even one is well worth its price."

He turned to Yetrik. "You know, people tend to ask a lot of questions when they are worried. Are you ready, Gruthman?"

"Why? Are we close?"

Runith nodded. "Keep your distance and do what I tell you."

No promise of safety. Yetrik's mind would often grasp onto a single worry, keeping it captive until replaced by another uncertainty. He liked structure and clarity in his life. During the past few years, he had learned to become more accustomed to change and living outside of his preferred routine, yet he still abhorred uncertainty.

⋙ ⋘

The forest darkened as more trees covered the misty sky. Fewer birds chirped and the rustle of bushes seemed more ominous. Enormous stone walls were made vivid in the distance, as if they were approaching a dilapidated city. The fog had lowered to the forest floor, encapsulating the party like the smokestacks from the Kzhek bronze refineries.

"Is this it?" Yetrik asked.

"Not quite, but we are close," said Runith. "We still need some bait."

"Does it have to be a deer? I think I saw a lynx in the trees not too far back."

"Has to be a deer," Runith said. "Kaesan see the antlers of a deer and mistake it for one of their young." He turned to Derr, who had cupped his right ear and listened. The four other party members halted until Derr signaled forward.

Derr stretched his neck like an awakening tortoise and let out a painful screech. *An injured deer.*

They waited, to no avail. Runith beckoned the party to hide among the trail-side brush. Once comfortably hidden, Derr let out another cry. Yetrik's heart raced with anticipation and fear.

Branches rustled. A large buck sniffed along the trail with its charcoal nose in search of an injured youngling. It had four prongs on each side, and its hide bore no imperfections.

Derr took a delicate step closer. The buck perked up with wide, startled eyes, on the cusp of fleeing.

One deep breath. Derr called to the deer and revealed himself on the trail and the animal approached like he was an old friend. Derr and the buck spoke to each other with a mix of snorts and whines.

"We're ready," said Derr as the deer approached Jhael. Runith pointed to the right, leading them off the trail and into brush that reached their knees.

"Do you have to trick it into becoming bait?" Yetrik asked.

Runith shook his head. "We are not entertainers who speak to animals. Though they retain some agency, the animals are submissive to our voices."

They continued, clearing the brush and entering a dirt plane with scattered large rocks sticking up from the ground. The rocks were porous, leaving the observer wondering what kinds of creatures inhabited them.

"Keep your eyes out for opening along the rock face," instructed Runith. "Horrah, do you have the torches?"

"Yes, just a moment." The party stopped to watch her. She crouched in the mud and removed four wooden poles from her bag, each bound with a pale fabric.

"And the light?"

She nodded and continued fishing in her bag. She held a small steel rod and a palm-sized stone.

"Keep it on hand. We'll light it as we enter." Runith pointed with two fingers. "Keep close to the middle of the path. It's drier there."

Each step was harder than the last as the mud gripped Yetrik's boots. He wished Royss would have warned him to wear work clothes rather than the ones used in courtly meetings.

"Yetrik," Runith called with a harsh whisper.

"What?"

Runith signaled for him to come closer. He crept to stand beside Runith and saw a black, cavernous opening. Removing a hunting knife from a leather sheath, Runith handed it to Yetrik, who looked at the blade and back at him. Worry filled his eyes.

Runith directed Derr to call the deer to Yetrik. With shaky palms, he caressed the neck of the beautiful creature, upset that it would soon become prey. Runith motioned across his palm, showing Yetrik where to cut. He then held his forefinger and thumb close; Yetrik did not need to cut deep.

Yetrik opened his hand and sliced his palm with the knife. Pain lit his nerves as blood swelled. He winced but held firm, not shirking his responsibility.

He held out his wrist to Runith, who then pointed toward the deer's antlers. Yetrik reached towards the white prongs, checked Runith for affirmation, and received a nod. The creature lowered its head and permitted Yetrik to run a hand along its antlers, decorating them with a crimson shimmer.

Horrah poured clean water on Yetrik's hands from a leather canteen. She dabbed his wound like a protective mother and then wrapped his wrist three times with a thick cloth, tucking the end into the folds. It stung with each touch, but the binding helped him to feel comfortable.

She took the flint and steel and generated a few sparks to light a dead leaf-covered branch. With the end burning, she touched each torch. Runith led the party into the cavern. Yetrik and Horrah followed in the back of their line.

An orange glow slid across the walls. Water dripped in the distance, but nothing stirred. Anticipation was worse than fear itself. Yetrik could see no end to the tunnel. Darkness stared back at him like a distant stranger unsheathing a blade.

Runith halted, stopping his followers. Derr spoke with the deer and sent it forward with delicate steps. Yetrik clenched his fists, holding his breath in failed relaxation. They turned around and left the cave as the deer ran deeper into the black.

Runith motioned for them to head and hide among the foliage.

"Why did we have to go into the cave?" Yetrik whispered. He adjusted the branches before him to peer between their waxy leaves.

"I don't know why you came in, but I admire the confidence," Runith replied.

"Wait, I didn't *have* to go in?"

Runith shook his head. "We only entered to see if the cave could be a den. Many of these caverns are short enough that you could reach the end within a few paces."

"Will the deer not be eaten? Should Derr call it back?"

"Settle down, lad. We still have some time before the kaesan comes out. This tunnel looked like a den and kaesan avoid daylight, even in this pitiful excuse for sunlight. That being said, they never dwell near the entrance during the day."

"You seem to know a lot about them, having only had a few encounters."

"I was just as frightened of them as you on my first kaesan taming. Rather than worry, I learned as much as I could, hoping it would keep me safe. Don't know if it did anything, but I'm still here, am I not?"

Runith seemed to be less afraid of speaking at this distance. Yetrik listened as Derr spoke to Runith with hisses that sounded like rustling leaves. *Are they speaking in some snake language?*

After a few minutes of silence, a clatter echoed from the cavern, calling their attention back to the entrance. The deer pranced through the thick fog.

"Empty," he declared as he watched the deer. "Onto the next one."

"Hold, Runith." Jhael watched the deer.

The animal turned to reveal a large tear on its underside and down its back limb, dripping blood.

Runith hissed another command in the viper's tongue. Jhael and Derr took their positions, broadswords in their grip. Runith unsheathed a shortsword and grabbed his shield as crept closer to the cave. "Horrah, Yetrik, hide until it's over."

Yetrik scrambled away, drawing Runith's attention as he crushed dead leaves in his retreat. Horrah removed a bottle of a clear yellow liquid from a hefty leather bag and tossed a handful of herbs inside, preparing an emergency remedy. Yetrik held his breath and clenched his teeth, worrying that the bag's weight would drag her down.

An eerie call, similar to that of Derr's injured deer, emanated from the cave. Something scraped along the rocky walls, moving closer by the second.

It screeched, causing Yetrik's ears to ring. A giant demonic imp erupted from the cavern, breaking stones and smashing the entrance in a frenzy. It turned its head to reveal its fangs the size of human fingers. Each paw had four claws, with a fifth coming from the back side. It looked as if it wore a large brown pelt that had shorn to reveal pale arms and legs. Any deer would envy the majesty of its antlers with too many prongs to be counted. Black eyes the size of fists stared at the company with hatred and hunger.

The kaesan pranced forward, searching for the deer. Its nose crinkled like a hound's as it searched for the animal's musk.

Runith stepped forward, quickly drawing the kaesan's attention as it stood on its hind legs. He breathed deep and stretched his neck, replicating the screeches of the kaesan.

Aaaaaeeeeeiiiiiii

The kaesan stepped back and squinted, shaking its head.

"The mightier the beast, the sturdier its will. A Beastling must break its target's will before successfully taming it," Horrah said.

Derr mimicked the creature's call. It returned to all fours and charged at Runith. He rolled away before the beast would have impaled him with its antlers.

Jhael called for the deer to return to her. The buck sprinted through the bushes and ran to her.

With a sniff and whimper, Jhael asked the deer to make an ultimate sacrifice.

The kaesan grasped the buck with its nightmarish claws. The deer opened its mouth to let out one last cry, but was soon silenced as the kaesan bit into its neck. Its head toppled to the ground; lifeless eyes staring at the sky. The three Beastlings spread out around the kaesan while it finished devouring the deer, bones and hooves included.

"Gluttony and lustful pleasure break will," said Horrah. "At least, that is the theory. If a beast becomes too focused on food, it's easier to control."

The Beastlings let out the most forceful kaesan call yet, like a choir of insidious screams. The kaesan charged and swung its claws at Jhael, knocking her back.

It crawled towards Jhael as she withered on the wet turf, her side dripping red. Runith and Derr screeched again. The beast clasped its arms, or front legs, over its head as it hunched downward with a painful wail.

A moment later, the kaesan stood on its hind legs, docile and silent.

Horrah ran from her hiding place to Jhael. Derr already knelt at her side. Seeing that the beast had surrendered, Yetrik followed.

"Did its claws cause demons to possess you?" Derr asked with a smile.

"Must have. All I see is the most perding ugly demon before me," Jhael responded. "At least we never had to use our swords on the fat kulf."

Horrah touched the wound on Jhael's side from the kaesan's attack. "Your hunter's mail did not prevent all wounds, but it may have saved you an organ." Horrah pulled her rucksack to her side and dug through her collection of colorful vials.

"Clean the wound," said Jhael, hissing as Horrah touched it. "Have any ale? I could use a drink to take away the sting."

Horrah ignored her. She poured a sky-blue liquid onto her wound to disinfect the laceration. Yetrik cringed, touching the bandages on his wounded hand.

"Gah! Why didn't you warn me it would sting?"

"I feel like 'this might sting' has become a joke. Of course it will sting."

Yetrik stood to let Horrah deal with Jhael's wound while Runith spoke to the kaesan.

"Come meet our new ally," Runith called as Yetrik stood behind a thick tangle of brush. "His will is ours. Once we break past their initial instincts and make a connection, they can't go back without our command."

Yetrik reached out his uninjured palm to stroke the beast's matted brown fur.

"What are you doing?" Runith asked.

"I'm touching it."

"You might as well try to pet Derr. He's more of an animal than this one." Runith could not hold his laughter back. "I wish you could speak his language. I can already tell that Tooreith is quick-witted. If we didn't get too many looks, I would take him to the tavern this evening. I have no doubts he would out-drink me."

"Tooreith? *His*?"

"All creatures have names. And yes, this kaesan is a male, though I would not recommend checking. If you think his appearance is a nightmare, then his shaft is the high commander of the under realms."

Yetrik winced as Runith chuckled. "Well then, what next? Back to Kzhek?"

"Horrah will finish patching Jhael up. Then..." He smiled.

"What?"

"We go for the *second* kaesan of the day."

CHAPTER NINETEEN

SPIRIT OF THE SERVAL

Cheric, let this boy live. Do not abandon me. I have given thee my all. Where is thy hidden hand?

Voln's health declined a bit more with each hour. It was already late into the night. Voln still jested and complained, but words were drawn from him like blood. He had been sent with injuries to attract wild wolves to take the body of the scout who had died away for the journeyman's burial. Phenmir already regretted asking that much from him.

"Just a little more, Voln." Phenmir cradled the boy against his chest. The streets were nearly empty. Not knowing what to expect, they had sent one of the remaining scouts back on a ghete to inform the Allegiant in Tchoyas of their condition.

"There." Phenmir pointed to an imposing building on their left, its bronze edging shimmered in the foggy moonlight. "We will try the back first. Port, watch over Kaela."

They approached a dark stone wall and hid behind it while Phenmir studied the Canton grounds. He flicked his fingers and guided them around the side of the building. All the windows and doors remained dark. A few guards likely remained on the grounds, though fewer than during the day. No one ever needed to steal medical supplies, except in this very instance.

"Guard ahead," whispered Phenmir as he peered around the corner. The patrolman was less armored than those of the palace guards, made visible by the torchlight shimmering from their left hand. They wore a brimmed metal cap and short-cut robes that allowed for mobility. "Kaela, can you replicate Voln's direwolf?"

"I've never been a direwolf. They always seemed too mean to me, but I can try."

Phenmir encouraged her with a smile.

Hair tufts grew across her body. She fell to her paws as her hind legs became thinner. A vicious snout grew, filled with fangs.

Phenmir hid his discomfort. Watching a human become a beast is not a pleasant sight, perhaps that is why he abhorred war. He knelt aside the direwolf. "I need you to catch the patrolman's attention and have them chase you to the far side of the building, out of view. Once they are gone, meet us at the arch over there." He pointed to a staircase that descended below the floor level and led to basement access. "Can you do that?"

Kaela nodded and ran off to lead the patrolman astray.

"Once the patrolman is out of sight, follow me to the door. We should be able to make it inside without trouble."

The guard jumped at the sight of the direwolf, letting out a scream before deciding to chase her. Kaela ran past the far corner of the building. The patrolman drew their shortsword, but Kaela outpaced the guard with ease.

Phenmir adjusted Voln in his arms and sprinted across the yard. Port kept with his pace while the other Sleff Scout, Stenn, stumbled behind them.

Phenmir worked his free hand into his pocket and removed a set of keys, passing them through his fingers to find the right one. A cold shock froze his heart as he missed a step on the stone staircase, but quickly caught himself and tightened his grip on Voln.

His hands trembled, and he struggled to place the Canton key in the lock. One key failed to fit. Second key. Turf rustled in the field. Third key, failure. Why did these kulfs decide to make each key identical? Bounding steps from behind drew closer to the staircase. Fourth key. The metal clicked and slid with ease. Phenmir could breathe again. He forced the door open and glanced over his shoulder. Paws and fangs shifted into childish palms, pushing the rest of the group inside.

"There should be a candle..." he began, feeling the walls for a candle mount. Most of the sublevel chambers were built the same way, with candle mounts near head height. He did not yet know which room they occupied, but felt confident that he could locate the medicinal supplies without trouble. "Does anyone have a flame?"

His arms began to shake with the weight of the boy. Only adrenaline held them up. "A few more moments, Voln."

"Here," croaked Voln as he moved in Phenmir's arms.

"What is it?" inquired Phenmir.

"Pocket flint and steel. I always have a set."

Boys were little arsonists. Phenmir pulled the rock and rod free, then handed them to Port. "Strike this, will you?" He guided Port's hand with his to locate the candle mount.

Port removed the candle from the stand and attempted to strike the wick. The end caught flame after three attempts and was almost blown out by his relieved sigh. The familiar orange glow of candlelight filled the chamber enough for ample visibility. They had entered an armory.

Phenmir pointed, leading Port into the lower corridors of the Canton. "Left," he instructed, and they followed without question. The maze of corridors continued as his memory of the building gradually pieced itself together. With a sigh of relief, he found a room with a sign reading "Harvest 5," his old room of operations. He inserted a key into the door and rushed the group in. Without delay, he lit two candles on each of the walls, illuminating the room with a familiar orange glow. The lighting was less than optimal without his harvesting lanterns. It would be enough for two smaller operations.

"Stenn," Phenmir called the other Sleff scout. "Can you wait for me to tend to Voln's wounds?" he asked as he lay the boy on the cold metal surface in the center of the room. "Of course, sir."

"Grand. Take Kaela out while we care for her friend."

***

The stitches and wound care were less than ideal without broad access to medicines. Despite that, Phenmir was able to finish each procedure with minimal blood loss. Stenn took half as much time to treat as Voln, but had screamed more than any man his age could justify. Phenmir finally left the chamber with extinguished candles after cleaning enough not to cause suspicion.

"How is your hand?" asked Port.

Stenn held his bandaged wrist close to his chest as before. "It throbs but feels better." He turned to Phenmir. "Thank you, Thane Stolk."

Phenmir nodded and locked the operation room door. "Out the same way we came."

Though they met some dead ends, they eventually reached the armory. Phenmir's arms were exhausted from carrying Voln, so Port offered to help carry him until they were out of the city.

"Halt trespassers!" A Zhaeswoman called as they opened the door to leave.

"Wolfling," Phenmir called to Kaela, "pounce but do not kill."

"Stand down!" The patrolwoman commanded, removing a short-sword from her hip. She stepped down the stairs and neared the doorway.

Kaela jumped at the woman's sword arm and twisted an elongated neck like a serpent to avoid the blade. Kaela bit the woman's arm, causing her to drop the sword with a scream. With the patrolwoman disarmed, Kaela targeted her ankle and bit through her tendon.

The group rushed past the door, but Phenmir ripped a strip of cloth from his tunic and tied a gag around the guard's mouth. He waved for the party to continue up the stairs and shoved the women into the Canton, shutting her inside, and locked the door. She would survive.

Phenmir stared at his hands, red as if he had performed a harvest, then followed the others.

Port ran ahead of the group and waved for them to follow. Phenmir ran behind the others and checked to see if anyone was following.

"Thank Cheric," Phenmir whispered as they ran away from the Canton with no Zhaesmen following.

"Well done, Kaela," panted Phenmir. She ran beside him, still in wolf form.

The Canton of Haleness was further from the city center than most of the city's Cantons, granting an easier escape. Cottages of pale wood replaced towers of marbled gray; running a few more blocks would secure their safety.

Hazed moonlight provided little light, but enough for them to see where they were running. Kaela stopped ahead of the group and returned to her natural form. Phenmir ran ahead and waved for the group to join him for a rest under a willow. The nearby buildings were no longer the giants of the city center, but small cottages with large yards in between. Port took a deep breath, arching his back after he set Voln down. Voln shuffled over to sit beside Kaela, his head resting on her shoulder.

"Can you mold your body as baker's dough?" asked Port. "Forgive me if it is an inappropriate time to ask, but my mind has been so, excuse my language, perding fixated on that since you altered your body to dodge the patrolwoman's blade."

"Not quite like dough," said Voln.

"Our skeletons change, but remain intact," said Kaela. "Too much stretching can cause an injury."

"One of the lads back home tried to grow his arm into a bear's paw. The dumb kulf ended up tearing the skin and separating his wrist bones when he went back to his natural form." Voln laughed.

"Kenry is likely too far along the path back to Fayis to catch at this point. What do you advise, sir?" asked Port.

"Who?" Phenmir asked.

"The scout we sent back after our dispute at the inn. You know, to tell the others in Fayis what happened?"

Phenmir nodded. *Right. The other Sleff scout.* "It is unlikely that we will find allies by searching, like we've been doing. Our best chance is to seize the center of Kzhek and hope to gain allies by joining the rioters. Though we are returning to Fayis without allies, we at least have a clear idea of the situation in Kzhek. Voln may think that he is fine now, but we need to take him back to Fayis before we try anything here. "

"Sir Voln," the boy said with a pained smile

"I will give you that title if you can make it back to your home with no more injuries." Voln's smile turned bright.

Phenmir turned to the others. "I'm not comfortable spending the night here. We are still too close to the city center. Let's walk for an hour more. We will have to veer east to find our trail back to Fayis, but we are not far off."

They stood with gradual moans. The initial pace onward was no quicker than a slime imp, but they eventually caught on to a forceful pace.

Once they distanced themselves from the city, Phenmir found a branch alongside the road and picked it up. He reached into his rucksack and took some fabric and cleaning alcohol. He soaked the fabric in alcohol and wrapped it around the branch, lighting it with Voln's flint and steel. It wasn't the largest torch, but it provided enough light for the time.

Kaela brushed up beside him. "Voln will be alright. He'll get even better when we arrive," he said.

"It's not that." she sniffed and wiped her eyes.

"What is it?"

"The patrolwoman. I hurt her real bad. I've never hurt anybody before, except when I punched Voln, and maybe some of the other Endowers, but that was just to be funny. Will she die? I saw a lot of blood."

"She will be fine. I made sure when I locked her in the Canton." No, you didn't, you lying kulf. Unless she was found minutes after, she lost too much blood.

She nodded and continued to sniff and wipe. "Will the Zhaesmen come after me? Are they going to kill me? I don't want to be put in a dungeon."

"No one will be taken to any dungeon besides Voln and only because he smells like an actual direwolf." She laughed.

Voln walked on his own, paces ahead of the group on the straight muddy roadway.

"Feeling well, I see," said Phenmir as he neared the Endowers.

"Better than you. I have a long life ahead of me."

Phenmir smirked. "With a tongue like that, I am willing to gamble."

"I ache a little. How much longer until we reach Fayis? My people need me in battle."

"Voln, you need to rest when we return. Your wounds need time to heal."

"I am a Shiftling. I'll be healed to perfection by the time we return."

"Really?"

"No, but I can hope. Shiftlings aren't Eurythrins, but we heal a lot quicker than you kulfs." Voln turned back and Phenmir followed his gaze. Kaela was talking with Port.

"Thanks for helping Kaela." Voln whispered. "I don't think she was born to be a fighter, but that's okay. Right?"

"No child should see combat."

"I'm not a child."

"I shouldn't have used either of you the way I did."

"It's not your fault. It's ours. Endowers are the cause of this fighting. If we had never been born, Facet would be peaceful."

"Voln, you have—"

"Save your preaching for the other Chussmen. Let me fight my own fight."

He wanted to convince the boy to think otherwise, but Phenmir was too like-minded. Stubborn, failing to follow what he preached, even though he knew it to be true.

After days of monotonous travel on misty Zhaes paths, they crossed the border into Court Tchoyas. The glimpse of the Tchoyas capital on the horizon felt like a thirst quenched.

Fayis was alive with the sounds of swords clashing as Allegiant soldiers practiced for what was yet to come. Townspeople helped load carriages and wagons with food and supplies.

"It's beginning," said Port.

If riots had not yet awakened Phenmir to the imminent battles, seeing an army did. He pointed at the Krall's palace. "Focus, we need to see the Krall."

Voln shouting and raising his hands to punch the sky, soon dropping them to his side to clench his wounds. Legends of knights and lords seemed to jump off pages as captains shouted drill commands, causing legions of Allegiant warriors to practice spear and sword stances.

Groups of soldiers marched in unison with spears and blades held at the ready. Where did they find all these weapons? Phenmir was surprised that Court Tchoyas had an abundant stock of seemingly useless objects in an age previously absent of warfare. Was I mistaken to believe that no Court prepared for and feared the possibility of war?

"We could have used some of that on our journey," said Stenn as he pointed to the blacksmiths.

"Armor is much too cumbersome for my liking, even a layer of chain mail is a tedious load," noted Port

"When have you worn it?"

"Look at their wares. There is no way in the under realms that much metal can be as comfortable as my tunic. As a boy, I was somewhat of a miscreant, stealing fruit from the markets. No guard could ever catch my nimble legs while they tried to run in those layers of steel."

Nearly everyone Phenmir saw seemed keen to prepare for the fight. Not only were Tchoyasmen preparing, but Sleffman and even a few Chussmen had arrived to join the ranks. Little time had passed since Phenmir had joined the Allegiant, but they were able to gather a sizable army.

No one appeared happier with this than the merchants. Tchoyas was wealthy enough to provide for this army, but what of Court Chuss and Court Sleff? Who would pay for war?

Everyone would, with their lives.

The group entered the Krall's palace, finding it empty aside from the usual staff members. Most of the city's residents were likely preparing to march to Kzhek or helping those who would.

"Your Grace, it is a pleasure to return to your presence," exclaimed Phenmir as they entered Krall Trhet's throne room. His Thanes surrounded him with an unfamiliar guest who stood tall and with black hair.

"We are likewise pleased about your return, Thane Stolk."

"We have much to inform you about."

"We will attend to that soon. First, we have received a messenger from Kzhek." Krall Trhet gestured to the woman at his left side. "This is Caser Aerhee Kleeh of Court Zhaes. She would like a word with the Harmony Allegiant."

CHAPTER TWENTY

SOUND PRIDE IN HUMBLE PATHS

26 YEARS AGO, COURT ZHAES, KZHEK, YEAR 306 IN THE CLERICAL ERA (CL. ER. 306)

P ain flared in Derlik's face as if it was forced against a crucible. It tortured him to see his wife and daughter so distraught. They knew nothing of his crime. Disappointment would break their hearts.

Each pale-skinned Scholar wore white robes, with the frontmost wearing a gray Scholar's cap to signify his position as the leader of their troop.

"Father?" Aerhee uttered through her tears.

"Please," Faeth took a deep breath. "Explain why you have bound my husband."

"Priesswoman, there is no need to—"

"We are Zhaesmen and will be addressed as much." Faeth countered.

"According to your husband, you are illegal immigrants," said the capped Scholar. "He paid your immigration tariffs with counterfeit coins, nullifying the documentation and making him a criminal."

"Derlik?" Faeth trembled as she spoke. "Is it true?"

"Yes," he replied. Guilt tore him from the inside. "My wife and daughter knew nothing of it. It was my sole misdemeanor."

"No!" cried Faeth.

"Yes, Faeth," he said, reluctant to look his wife in the eyes for fear of being overcome.

"She and the child will be brought to trial as well. We will not allow any crime to go unpunished."

Former Scholars? Dissenters from their creed? He did not know of any connection between his coins and some supposed opponent of the Patriarchy. "I am sorry, Faeth, Aerhee. Please forgive me."

"No, Derlik, we are not allowing you to be taken for serving our family."

The rightmost Scholar stepped in between Derlik and Faeth. "You will see him again when he stands trial. Until then, your husband is a prisoner of the Patriarchy of Scholars. Resist and you will be charged."

"Let me be, Faeth." Derlik said. "We will see justice in due time. Don't make this any worse."

"Justice will be served," remarked the capped Scholar.

Derlik turned to Faeth and Aerhee, a painful attempt at a smile barely remaining on his lips.

"The Patriarchy will inform you of the trial date soon," said the Scholar as he watched the other two lead Derlik through the front door. "Failure to attend will result in a seizure of your property and possessions."

The door closed, and she heard the carriage tearing through the wet soil of the street.

Faeth stared at the door as though waiting for Derlik's return. Her eyes were bloodshot but had not yet given in to tears. She was left to the torture of hopeless anticipation.

"Mother?"

"I think it is time to sleep, Aerhee. Go to your room. I will be there in a moment."

Faeth appeared a moment later, holding a wet rag. "We can talk tomorrow, little one. Now, get to sleep." Aerhee nodded and pulled her covers up to her shoulders. Faeth blew out the chamber's candle and shut the door to walk to her own room.

Faeth collapsed to her knees at the foot of her bed and seized the pillow, sobbing into it. Sorrow and fear pained her, but she was relieved that she held herself together in front of Aerhee. Her nails dug into her palms, almost drawing blood. She wanted to sleep, to forget it all. She wanted to forget herself and the pain.

Life had felt like a dream in Kzhek. They had enough money, though they could use more. She had grown her faith as a Priestess and Aerhee understood their deity. Had the dream come to an end? What of Aerhee? Would she grow to hate this new land?

She pressed her face further into the damp pillow and yelled to Laeih for justice.

***

The Present, Court Tchoyas
Cl. er. 332

***

Entering the city had awoken her to the reality of war. She expect-ed rebellion, but not that an alliance had already formed between the anti-harvesting Courts.

Fheo had a different reaction to the commotion. He was a law-abiding Zhaesman to his soul, but boyish excitement overtook him at the sight of pristine blades and suits of armor.

Not only were Sleffmen and Chussmen involved, but they had filled the Krall's throne room.

A Chussman with dreadlocks and worn travel garb approached the Krall.

"Caser Kleeh, this is Phenmir Stolk," said Krall Trhet. "He is the recently appointed Chuss Thane of Harmony."

Phenmir looked at Aerhee. His gaze reminded her of Sheath when she was trying to read a mind.

"Thane of Harmony?" Aerhee asked. "Do Chussman create new titles as it suits you?"

Phenmir took a deep breath. "New circumstances call for new respon-sibilities. If you have questions, you may speak to Colrig. Now, allow me to address the Krall."

Colrig. She recalled Krall Trhet mentioning the name a few moments ago.

"Krall Trhet," began Phenmir, "has Kenry returned with our report?"

"Yes," replied the Krall.

"The inn and all the happenings there?"

"Yes."

"Very well. As you can see, Voln and Stenn are healing though they still need to recover." He glanced at Aerhee. "Shall we find a more secluded place to speak?"

The Krall shook his head. "Caser Kleeh wishes to discuss matters of peace. What better way to gain their sympathy than by speaking of our struggles and supposed oppression in Kzhek?"

"You wish to ally with us, Zhaeswoman?" asked Phenmir.

"By Laeih's sacred name, no!" she cursed. "Excuse me, but this is no surrender to your cause. I agree with the Chussman. May we host a more private council?"

"That would be wonderful. Where shall we go?" A boy worked himself into their circle.

"Voln, you need to find somewhere to rest." replied Phenmir.

"No need," replied Voln. "I'll bet you two petiir that you will need rest before me."

"As the leader of our Court' young Endowers, it would be appropriate that he represent their voice," said the Krall.

"And Colrig? I find it counterproductive to have a discussion without him," said Phenmir.

"He informed me that the efforts in northern Sleff required his assistance," replied the Krall. "He said he would meet you at the next stage."

Where is the next stage? Aerhee thought.

"Then Port will suffice. I trust he can represent Court Sleff," said Phenmir. "Port!"

"Yes, sir?" the man replied as he ran to Phenmir's side.

"How well do you know Colrig's motives and that of the Harmony Allegiant?" Phenmir asked.

"I cannot say how well I represent his ideals, but I have done my best to bind my heart to the pursuit of the Allegiant."

"Splendid. While Colrig is attending to other matters, you will represent the Allegiant in council with this Zhaes dignitary."

"Sir? I am no—"

"You will be more than sufficient." Phenmir interrupted, then turned to the Krall. "Our time in Kzhek has proven Port's worth."

"I trust your word, Thane Stolk."

"Fheo," Aerhee called. He turned and lifted his chin slightly to pay heed. "Remain here while we converse elsewhere." He nodded, though she knew he would be uncomfortable alone. He needed to learn how to function without the crutch of a superior.

⁕⁕⁕⁖⁖⁖ ⁕⁕⁕⁖⁖⁖

The council room was ostentatious, even compared to anything in the Zhaes Cantons. The council of five sat on the far end of the long table, near a stained glass portrait of a masked figure and a glowing being. Aerhee assumed it had some religious significance. It felt as if she had entered a dream. Nowhere else would she expect to meet with a child, the Krall of Tchoyas, a lowly Sleffman, and a Chuss medic.

"Caser Kleeh, you may state your concerns," said the Krall.

"I have come in hopes of starting a dialogue between our Courts. If both groups charge into this like headstrong boars, we will face catastrophe. I wish to prevent unnecessary suffering. I believe we can do this if you allow a bridge to be built between forces."

"Your proposition would not change the law on harvesting in your Court," said Phenmir.

"We would allow courts to practice or restrict harvesting under their individual jurisdiction."

Phenmir shook his head. "Colrig has given too much for all of us to surrender now."

"Krall Trhet, do you wish to send your people to war? Do wish for casualties?" Aerhee asked.

"No man ruler ever wishes for bloodshed," replied Krall Trhet. "But I do not want to debate the morality of this issue, only discuss peace. What would you ask of us?"

"I want you to stop preparing for war and foster a dialogue between both sides. We can avoid all of this before we begin."

"What about those who have been fighting harvesting in your city?" questioned Phenmir.

"Authorities will charge criminals for their behavior."

"And what of those who will take their place? Quelling a single protest does not prevent future riots. It only breeds more anger."

"Proper punishment prevents future crime. It is a law of nature. When a lamb partakes of a poisoned berry and dies with its delicacy, the herd will fear the same fate. If you stop now, you will save the lives of your people and the Zhaes rebels."

"Poison? 'Fear the same fate?' Those are not delicate words, Zhaeswoman. How are your Thanes planning to punish the rebels?"

"We have our means."

Phenmir scowled. "I doubt any that would include mercy. These people are only fighting for what they believe to be right. If you want to have a diplomatic conversation, we need to know what threats your Thanes are making."

Perd, he's prying. "Please heed my advice; prevent the inertia of war and call off your attack."

Phenmir's glare grew with contempt. "Voln?"

"Yes, sir?"

"Bring me one of your Feelmen Endowers. If Caser Kleeh will not disclose the Zhaes nobility's plans for dealing with the riots, we will use a Feelman to pry the information from her." Aerhee saw a grin of malice through the boy's mask as he fled the room.

Perd them all. She would have never expected a Feelman's reading in a Court opposed to harvesting. *You ignorant fool, how could you forget about the Endowers?* The child would read her before she could escape. *Would revealing the plans for controlling the mobs be so unfortunate? No. It will only anger them further.* The table was positioned such that the three men sat in front of the doorway and equally spaced to seize her with any maneuver she could attempt.

"You wish to rob me of my thoughts? I came to offer peace, yet you seek my blood."

"I regret to be inhospitable, but we cannot permit your departure, Caser." said the Krall. "As you have said, you have seen too much of our preparations to be released."

She stood, but Port and Phenmir blocked her path.

The shame of foolishness pained her ample mind. Even though she knew she risked much in coming to Tchoyas, it was the only plausible option of preventing war. She wanted to cry, having lost her final hopes of preventing war.

⋙⋙ ⋘⋘

The creaking doors caught Aerhee's attention. The wolf-masked Endower entered with a taller Endower girl beside him. Mahogany hair reached her jawline, with a few strands that draped across her lacquered mask of an open-mouthed mink.

"Here you are, Thane Phenmir," the wolf boy said. "This is Crowl, one of our Endower Feelmen."

"What can I do for..." the girl named Crowl turned to Phenmir.

I know that stare. She is reading him. They actually brought a perding Endower Feelman.

"Read the Zhaeswoman?" said Crowl. "Consider it done."

Aerhee had no way to retreat nor hide. The child would read her just as Sheath did.

"So," said Crowl as she turned to Phenmir.

"What did you find?"

"A bombing, or the use of explosives. The Zhaes nobility is going to kill half of their 'dissenters.' They will then pursue the fleeing survivors of the attack, locking them up in the city's dungeons for further punishment."

"When will this be?" Phenmir leaned forward.

Crowl turned to Aerhee. "She only knows that it will be soon, perhaps weeks, even days."

"You say we were the ones igniting war, but your actions will create martyrs!" Phenmir said with a frightened laugh to Aerhee. "You came to offer peace backed by a threat!" His voice escalated as he stood up and paced toward Aerhee with an accusatory finger.

"Thane Stolk!" called Krall.

"Forgive me, Your Grace, but it infuriates me to be condemned by one guilty of that very crime!"

"It was beyond my control," her voice trembled. "Why do you think I fled here to plead for peace, not knowing you were preparing for war? I had hoped that you could help prevent this attack on the rebels of my Court."

"What are we to do?" Phenmir said. His voice shook as hers.

The Krall looked at the Chussman. "Colrig recommended you as a man with a knowledge of combat strategy. What do you propose?"

"A little reading is not equivalent to experience, but I can offer some suggestions." Phenmir bit his lip. "We can head into Kzhek, hoping that their attack does not coincide with our entrance. We could wait while we remain in the marshlands and pursue control right after a period of detonation. Or we might seize the city swiftly enough and disarm their attack. I was quite surprised to see how many soldiers filled the city. We might be able to actually have a formidable force."

"Colrig has spent years gathering forces beneath the eyes of the nobility," said Port. "He told me that your Thanes, who pledged themselves to the Allegiant before you did, were working diligently on conscription. I can only assume it is the same with the Tchoyasmen. Aside from these, we have legions of Allegiant rebels on the way from Sleff."

Phenmir smirked. "Are the troops ready to march, Krall Trhet?"

"They can be called to march within a day. With sufficient warning, they should be available by dawn."

"We shall rally the troops and march in the morning directly to Kzhek. If we do not act, we will lose the lives of the Zhaes rebels. If we arrive before their attack, we can seize power before they have an opportunity to oppose our force. "

"I will see to it. May our gods be on our side," the Krall replied. "Voln?"

"Yes, Krall?"

"Speak with Thane Stolk about which Endowers will accompany the troops."

"Yes, Krall."

"What of her, Your Grace?" asked Port, gesturing at Aerhee.

"She will remain here. Perhaps she could provide bargaining power when we deal with the rest of the Zhaes nobility." The Krall looked down on Aerhee. "Your intent was a noble one, but we cannot comply with your wishes. My Thanes shall find a room for you that will suit your needs. You will be comfortable, but communication with your colleagues and superiors will be restricted."

"What about her scribe?" Voln asked.

"He will be kept likewise comfortable."

"A fine decision, Your Grace," replied Port.

The attendees left the room except for the Krall, who approached Aerhee once they were alone.

"I admire your valiance, Caser Kleeh. You have a spine firmer than most. Perhaps this war does not need to begin after a single engagement in Kzhek. We shall speak soon, Caser."

CHAPTER TWENTY-ONE

CRACKS IN THE FOUNDATION

No chains rattled, nor was there gnashing. Yetrik trusted the Beastlings' abilities, yet still wondered if it was wise to let two unbound kaesan follow them into the city. His anxiety kept him looking back at them, fearing the spell would lose its grip.

They had been in the wilds for a day, though he felt it had been much longer without the comfort of the city. He looked forward to working with the nobility again, where he felt valuable, especially to Royss. Had the Thane seen live kaesan before? Had the other Zhaesmen? Would their existence be as novel a spectacle to them as it was to him?

Yetrik wondered how their preparation for dealing with the mobs was progressing. Royss and Semi had likely secured the contribution of Gorgers and guards. *Semi. Has she missed me?. He* had missed her.

The sight of the Beastling trio was sufficient for the guards to open the gates and permit their entrance. It was midday, around the hour when most of the townsfolk would cook or head to the central markets to eat. Yetrik almost laughed at their group. A Gruthman walked beside Zhaesmen dressed as beast hunters, as a train of two towering beasts followed them with the demeanor of sheep.

The gate creaked open, showing an empty walkway into the city. Buildings loomed over each side of the street.

"I thought we left through a different gate?" Yetrik said.

"Yes, we did," replied Runith.

"Then why come through here?"

"We can't have the public in panic marching these two through the city, can we?"

"I suppose that makes sense. Then does this lead to a Canton? Some hidden dungeon?"

"Anywhere you want it to go is where it can take you." Runith shook his head. "You'll see what I mean. I pray Royss will tell us why we collected the perding beasts."

They continued as arches obscured the sunlight over them. Horrah lit a torch as they proceeded toward the stretching darkness. The welcome glow revealed a staircase downward that was wide enough to permit entry of the kaesan without issue.

"I suppose kaesan can see well in the dark," commented Yetrik. They made their way down the stairs and into another tunnel. Despite their initial hesitation, the kaesan descended the stairs with ease.

"They are not solely cave dwellers. They tend to be nocturnal, but are occasionally seen during the day. Superstition surrounding them leads to a lack of proper research. I think they dwell only in Zhaes, because of our overcast skies. I have no fear of marching them to Chuss, if they require it, but they would not be as tame under the burning desert sun."

"Only in Zhaes?"

"As far as I know, though, I assume the Tchoyas marshlands would not be fine for them. Maybe they have some seaside relatives in Gruth." He laughed.

As they descended further, the tunnel split into three paths. "You see it now?" Runith asked.

"A tunnel system?"

"Right. We can reach a number of destinations. Canton, the back of the market, the Cloven Gleff, *brothels*." He mentioned the latter destination with a nudge to Yetrik's shoulder. "I jest. I know you have your eyes out for the Gruthwoman who came with you. Royss told me so." Yetrik blushed. "Some say that the city's founders designed these tunnels. Royss says they were built when I was just a lad. The nobility allows access only to a select few."

The stone walls were wet with humidity. Petrichor remained the boldest scent. Distant echoes hit the floor ahead, likely the sounds of rodents. Thankfully, his boots reached high enough to protect him from any creatures eager to bite. Small puddles of accumulated water were spread throughout the floor, wetting his boots enough to feel a chill in his socks.

"Left," Runith called. It felt like they had been walking for the greater part of an hour. Long enough to pass through most of the city, as far as he could guess. Exhaustion pulled at Yetrik.

Kzhek was losing its novelty and charm. He enjoyed the forest more than he had expected. Searching for a mythical creature had reminded him of his childhood. He still held onto the idea that he was young enough to see himself as a child, though he could have had one of his own by now. The comments on his youthful face used to bother him, but he had grown to appreciate it as he approached his third decade.

"Up ahead!" Runith called. Yetrik was relieved to see that they had finally arrived at a staircase to escape the damp caverns. Runith led the group up the stairs and out of the tunnels into the open. With each step, he felt the weight of his journey. The small amount of sun that seeped through the clouds pained his eyes after the vice of darkness had gripped them for so long. The light did not seem to bother the kaesan, though they blinked more intensely for a few moments after reaching ground level.

They entered a wooden-walled chamber in what appeared to be a large barn, despite the absence of livestock. Runith strode to the monstrous doors without explaining where they were. How the man still had any strength remaining was a mystery as he lifted a large wooden latch the size of a tree from off of the door's lock. His arms flexed as he opened the doors to reveal a large jousting yard in the center of an arena. Beyond the arena's walls stood the Zhaes Canton of Agriculture, Royss' domain.

A bronze-bordered platform stood in the stadium's seats like a king among beggars. The rows were barren of observers, except for a lone figure on the high seat. Royss stood and clapped as he saw the hunting party.

"What beautiful creatures!" he exclaimed as they approached him. "How did our Gruthman fare, Runith?"

"He was nervous, but we made good use of him. We could use a man like him. Stay here long enough, Yetrik, and we'll make a fine Zhaesman out of you." Royss laughed.

"How did you know when we would arrive?" Yetrik asked.

"I sent scouts on ghete to assure that you left the wilds safely. Once they spotted your party, they returned to inform me that a rescue company would not be necessary." He stepped closer to look at the kaesan as if they were nothing more than statues. "You've all had a long walk and deserve some food. The Canton's cooks are preparing meals as we speak."

Royss stepped back from the kaesan to view the crew. "Any injuries?"

"Nothing that needs immediate attention," Runith responded.

"Splendid! Follow me. Let's get some meat in these kaesan' stomachs before they gain a craving for Zhaesmen."

Runith called to the beasts in their tongue and received a similar response as they stepped forward to follow Royss.

Royss paused to wave the group forward. He joined Yetrik as they walked through a gate into a different courtyard of the Canton. The plain stretched out wider than the jousting field and was spaced for varieties of livestock. Grass and willows replaced dirt and flagpoles. Yetrik had almost forgotten Royss was the Thane of Agriculture, though he would not deem kaesan akin to cattle or sheep to be used on his farm.

"Runith and the others will take the kaesan to a secluded area." Royss said. "Head into the Canton. I have food and drink waiting for you. After you've had enough, we have somewhere to go."

✥✥✥✥✥ ✥✥✥✥✥

A wave of fatigue flowed over Yetrik after his meal. The mutton was overcooked and unseasoned, as he had expected, but the abundance of root vegetables reminded him of home. If they would have added some strong cheese to the beets, he would have shed a tear for his father's cooking.

The Beastlings were led by one of Royss' underlings to an eastern wing under the Canton once the kaesan were satisfied by a meal of three goats each. Yetrik was glad he didn't have to witness their feeding. He could not stomach his own food if he had to watch a kaesan massacre its prey again.

A Canton guard waited for Yetrik in the dining hall and led him to Royss' study on the second floor.

The door opened to the Thane's bearded smile. "Thank you for joining me, Yetrik." Royss waved him forward and motioned to a padded seat beside a wide desk covered with a variety of scrolls and paperwork. "Tell me, how was your journey? Did Runith treat you well?"

"I would have never thought myself to be the type of man to accompany a hunting party, let alone for a kaesan, but I was pleasantly surprised by the excursion."

"I know who to turn to if we need any assistance."

Royss smiled. "Tell me, Yetrik, how are you truly feeling?"

"Why do you ask?"

"You and Semi arrived here as humble messengers, but somehow fell into a coalition set on removing the lawless from our land. What were you, a scribe? A Thane's apprentice?"

"Financial advisor to the Thane of Utilities."

"It seems we have thrust you into a much different role."

"It has been a rewarding experience. I feel confident enough under your command and the counsel of the other Thanes."

"Do not rely on us too much. We are more flawed than you would guess. Zhaesmen may profess to abide by the law, but that is just a fallacy of the self-righteous."

Yetrik thought for a moment. "I suppose it is quite surreal. All of this... talk of war. I feel like I want to take part in some heroic rescue of our society. My heart wants to fight, but something pulls me back." He looked at Royss like a confessing sinner.

Royss sighed. "Semi has been just as unsure as you."

"Did she leave you alone to speak with the Krall about the Gorgers?"

"No, she complied, but I noticed a shift in her demeanor over the past few days. I wanted to find some way to help reassure her, but I have known her for such a short period, which is why we are taking you to speak with her about why we must establish order."

"How am I going to help her if I have my own doubts?"

"Faith is gained by forcing through doubts. I brought you here to speak while we waited for a carriage to the Canton of Diplomacy, but I think we will go for a walk."

"But... the riots?"

"Exactly. I'm going to show you why we must stop them *now*. We have discussed them enough. Once you see what they are doing, you will no longer be as hesitant to advocate our cause."

Perhaps blind obedience was not such a poor option.

"Don't worry, Gruthman. I will have three of my guards accompany us. We do not need to engage with the rebels, but you will see their idea of a revolution."

Royss stood and opened the door to his study, waving for Yetrik to follow. "I'll meet you at the Canton's entrance."

A guard stood outside the study and led Yetrik down to the entrance chamber to await Royss.

Half an hour passed as he waited for the Thane near the Canton's entrance. Royss descended the chamber's large staircase with three armored Canton guards in behind him. "Out." He pointed to the entrance with a scowl.

Yetrik nodded and opened the door, then rushed to Royss' right side with a guard on his other side.

They walked onto the street and stood, waiting for Royss to direct them.

Yetrik could not hear any distinct shouts, but picked up on a clamor that sounded like the roar of the ocean. Smoke clouds rose up ahead.

"To the right." he said. "Stay close to us," he told Yetrik, his hand pressed against a large double-sided axe hanging from his belt. He recalled seeing the decorative weapon on the wall of Royss' study. *Are the rioters that hostile?*

"Royss," said Yetrik, "my doubts are not something to worry about. Honestly, I think they were just a few...you know, I think we would be just fine in the carriage. I really–"

"Towards the shouts," Royss commanded the two guards ahead of them.

Directly to the center? "I can already see it." Yetrik gestured to closed businesses, many with shattered windows. Small gatherings of Zhaesman glared at them as they passed, clutching blades at their sides.

"This is nothing. You will see them for what they truly are."

The few dissenters that they passed remained silent. The shouts of the mob ahead grew louder, echoing off of the lofty buildings.

Entering the central square made Yetrik's heart stop. The size of the square itself was three times as big as the center of Gruth's capital and was encircled by a wall of close-packed high-rise buildings. The mob was not a single congregation, but multiple groups scattered throughout the area like ants infesting a bakery. Some shouted while others fought amongst themselves and with others.

Fallen buildings and angry Zhaesmen were tame compared to the extremist displays. The Krall and other Thanes had sent guards to pacify the unrest, but their efforts only fed the violence. Dissenters had torn armor from the corpses of ten guards. Royss pulled Yetrik closer, forcing him to look at what had been done to the guards. In a mockery of harvesting, each of the guards in the line had their organs pulled out. Some entrails were placed in their dead hands, while others were shoved into their mouths like pigs for a feast.

"Please, Royss," Yetrik forced his eyes closed. The back of his throat burned, and he shook like a naked man in a blizzard. "Please, I've seen enough!"

"You will not have seen enough until we end this!" Royss shouted.

"Sir," one of the guards pulled Royss's shoulder back, "we should not be so loud."

"Get your hand off of me, you perding kulf! I am teaching this scared bastard a lesson! This is no longer an argument between Courts. This is murder! Anarchy!"

Royss kept a grip on Yetrik's forearm, his grip growing tighter with each shout. He turned away from the Thane back to the crowd. Despite the clamor of the riots, Royss still attracted attention.

A group of six Zhaesmen, the type that looked like they carried ore from the mines, moved towards them. Royss paid them no heed.

They left the central square and entered an alley no wider than a single building.

"Do you understand now, Gruthman?" asked Royss.

"Yes, sir, I–" Yetrik turned back. The six Zhaes rioters had followed. "Royss, look!"

"The noblemen have come back to try to punish us!" one of the rioters shouted.

"Leave!" one of the guards shouted.

"Perd you!" one of them shouted.

"I'll kill every Thane like you who tarnishes Laeih's name!" shouted another.

They charged, raising their weapons like enraged apes.

Royss turned to his guards and spoke as if he were discussing dinner. "Kill them."

The three guards ran into the fight while Royss followed. Each guard had slain a rioter by the time Royss reached them.

The final three rioters hesitated in their stances, nearly dropping their weapons with quivering hands.

Yetrik remained behind but heard Royss' shouts as clear as if the Thane stood beside him.

Royss pushed one of his guards out of the way and faced the largest of the remaining rioters. The other two met the guards and swung at them with cracked poles that only scratched the brass armor. One rioter fell, impaled through the chest. The other tried to hold blood from his slit throat.

Royss pulled the axe attached to his side and ducked to swing it at his pursuer's legs. The rioter fell, screaming at his broken and bleeding legs.

Royss knelt at the rioter's side and held him up by the throat.

The rioter looked into Royss' face and spat blood. "I will gladly die if it means that kulfs like you won't have the power of gods. You demons don't deserve th–"

Royss slapped him with his free hand. He stared into the rioter's dazed eyes. "Perding fools. What did you expect to accomplish by attacking us? Laeih damn you." He turned back to his guards. "Take this one back to the Canton. Make sure he survives."

Yetrik focused on the sound of his breath, heavy and shaking. He hoped they would only interrogate the rioter, but worried about what they would do to him. Regardless of the man's conviction, he didn't want to see more pain inflicted. He had witnessed guards killing rioters. Their actions were charged by more than a hope of defending themselves. Royss had not killed any of them himself, but he seemed more guilty than any of them. *Is he guilty if it is part of war?*

"We cannot stand down, Gruthman." Royss did not look at Yetrik as he spoke. "Enough violence for today. The Thane of Diplomacy is waiting."

※>>>>- -‹‹‹‹※

The Canton of Diplomacy was not far from the center. No column had fallen, but large stones were broken from the walls. Vandals left illegible words on entrance with what appeared to be mud or dark excrement. *May Laeih aid them in recovering from such defamation.* Yetrik did not pray to other gods, but felt the thought was appropriate for the afflicted party.

A group of Zhaesmen in pristine robes met Yetrik in the front corridor of the Canton.

"Take him to Sheath," commanded Royss.

They nodded and led the way.

"I'll leave you here," said Royss. "I have responsibilities waiting back in my Canton. Remember your Ideal, Gruthman. *'Firm is the Founda tion.'*"

"Firm is the Foundation." he muttered. He had never felt less firm in his life.

The guides opened two large wooden doors with bronze inlays and gestured for Yetrik to enter a capacious dining hall. Two large tables spanned the length of the room, with four candelabras placed on each table to supplement the lamps. People spoke quietly as they ate. The dichotomy was humorous when compared to a Gruth feast hall with half-chewed seafood falling out of mouths. Gruth feasts were a celebration of plentiful harvests and successful fishing trips.

A young woman of perhaps fourteen approached Yetrik after wiping the corners of her mouth with a silver kerchief.

"Greetings," she said with a polite bow. "You must be Semi's companion. Thane Leisa told me to expect a guest from Court Gruth."

"I do not know if I would refer to her as my companio–"

"Come dine with us."

"Is Semi here?"

The girl opened her mouth but was quickly interrupted by a voice from behind Yetrik.

"Are you that desperate to see me?" He turned to see Semi standing behind his chair with a drumstick in hand, eating in fierce Gruth fashion. "At least we will have another Gruthman to show these people how to hold a proper feast."

Her countenance was brighter than after the council of Thanes.

"How wa–" he swiped his hand through the air. "We can talk about it later. Is there a seat near you?" *I can't be alone with my thoughts now.*

"Not yet, but if I eat like a Gruthman, I am sure those around me will flee. Have you ever seen Thane Keff at a feast? I heard that he once ate a whole boar and wore its face as a mask for the rest of the night."

"Those Thanes of Agriculture sure have a type." he forced a laugh, though knew it sounded insincere. "Don't worry about a seat, I'll join you once a seat opens."

"Whatever makes you comfortable."

"Semi?" Yetrik asked. "Is Thane Leisa here?"

"Yes." She pointed to the head of the back table, at a woman with a white cloth covering one eye. "She would be delighted to speak with you. I've already told her about you." Semi returned to a seat near the Thane.

He stared at the Thane's dignified mannerisms and observed her as she spoke with a man at her side, likely her husband Her head turned to lock her remaining eye on him and smiled.

CHAPTER TWENTY-TWO

RALLY THE TROOPS

Sleep was unobtainable. After hearing of Court Zhaes' plot only hours before, Phenmir felt he would never rest again. Any bed without Meira was desolate and cold. No companion to console him. No son to inspire him.

The sun had not risen, yet he heard the rough whispers of waking infantry. In temporary barracks, Sleffmen and Tchoyasmen would be waking to march to Kzhek. He was offered a bed in a neighboring Canton, but felt any captain should live, and suffer, as his soldiers would. Commanding the Chuss legions still frightened him, though he would never show it.

He lifted his canteen to take a drink and stood. Phenmir thrust open the doors of the neighboring chamber.

"Heloath, Allegiant!" he shouted, waking anyone who was still sleeping. Groans and exaggerated yawns responded to his greeting.

Ghete were already strapped, fed, and rested. Carts were filled with food for the journey, though an army would require the spoils of war to feed their numbers. The armor had been fitted and repaired for the frontmost men. Cheric bless their souls in the fields ahead.

"I expect you to be ready for my call to advance within the hour! The Zhaes rebels need us," he said, looking over the faces of waking Chussmen. "I will head to the other barracks to see how many Endowers will join us." Neither Court Tchoyas nor any other Court, as far as he knew, harbored any true barracks. As the Allegiant conscripted members over the years, they were unable to build such structures without alerting the public. Merchants emptied food storage units for the traveling troops, freeing space in some buildings for the troops to spend the night. Other business owners had complied with the Allegiants' pleas, giving their buildings as well.

They had not informed Phenmir how many buildings were in use, but he knew where the Endowers had spent their night.

The Tchoyasmen, Sleffmen, and even the Chussmen who weren't with Phenmir were already donning their armor. The sun had lit the sky with a glacial blue in the heavy morning mist, but it had not yet climbed over the distant hills. Phenmir drew in a deep breath, inhaling the humidity like an airborne refreshment.

After asking for directions from some Tchoyasmen, he found his way to the Endower barracks. The doors were shut, but the walls were anything but silent. In the daylight, he could see the structure that served as their inn. It was a wide storage for ghete carriages, only a story high but sufficient for multiple people. Civil servants had moved the carriages behind the building, making it look like the aftermath of a royal festival.

The hinges on the doors had rusted, telling that this storage had been out of use for some time. Loud creaks disturbed those within like an out-of-tune horn, though their attention returned to a speaker. The sight was no surprise. Voln had built a small stage from wooden crates and stood a few heads taller than his audience. The Shiftling had encountered two brief instances of violence in Kzhek and claimed himself a veteran.

"The Zhaesmen are emotionless fiends who will bleed you like a fountain from which their hounds will drink! Embrace your gifts!" Phenmir smirked at the lad's resemblance to a zealous preacher. "We will claim victory as we hold the perding hearts of our enemies in our perding hands! To the under realms with those kulfs!"

"What a show." Phenmir chuckled as the boy's audience dispersed.

"Someone has to put the fight into them."

"How many of your Endowers are coming?" Phenmir asked.

"One-fourth of us." Responded Voln.

"I'm sure Krall Trhet has a reason for requiring so many."

"So many?" he responded with clenched fists. "One-fourth is too few! This fight is about *us*!"

"Be rational, Voln. This is only the beginning. There is no reason to burn a candle before nightfall."

Voln scratched the top of his head. "I guess we will be fine without some of them."

"We? You cannot tell me you are coming with us, Voln."

"I'm no broken child." Voln revealed the skin beneath his bandages, showing thick purple scars from his injuries while in Kzhek. "I think my mother did it well with an Eurythrin, if you catch what I am throwing." The boy winked through the eyehole of his mask.

The timeline and politics did not add up to give sense to his claim, but he allowed the boy the humor. "That may be so, but I still worry."

"I know," Voln responded.

"And Kaela? Is she here? Surely she will stay behind."

"She left with some of you Chussmen already. She hopes to organize a union of Chuss Endowers."

"That is marvelous! How did I not think of that before? Who called for it?"

"Colrig. Once he met us, he knew our value."

"I should have known," Phenmir said as he looked at the crowd of masked children. If only Hir could see this. "Are your troops prepared to march? I told the others to be at the gates by midday."

"I hope so. You saw me yelling. It's not my fault if they don't listen."

"Keep doing your job, young wolf. I will see you at the gates." Phenmir gave him the Chuss salute with circled hands over the center of his chest. Voln returned the gesture with the Tchoyas salute.

Phenmir ran through his list of responsibilities. Port should be gathering and preparing the Sleffmen, or at least helping to do so. Colrig was coming from Sleff with more reinforcements, or so he had been told, to meet them in Kzhek.

The energy in the city had become charged. Families embraced and bid soldiers farewell. Tchoyasmen, Chussmen, and Sleffmen chanted to inspire their allies.

He walked toward the Krall's palace. *The strongest bindings are revealed when they are tested,* he thought as he drew near his destination. The words filled him with guilt, as he could not remember the last time he had read the scripture. He had promised his wife that he would seek Cheric more diligently, yet he felt more distant from his god than ever. *Is this because I fail to live as I profess?* If there was a God, could not that being prevent the bloodshed of war? *Only fools blame suffering on the gods. This is our fault. Cheric forgive me. Cheric help me.*

Phenmir proceeded up the stone steps to the entrance and was let in without question. He passed by clusters of noblemen filling the main chamber, stepped past inquisitive glares, and sped to the Krall's chamber.

The guards opened the doors for him and he thanked them with the Tchoyas salute. The Krall sat on his throne in the spacious chamber. Blue light shone in through cyan stained glass windows. The ceiling was higher than any room he had been in, reaching up several stories with clear windows peeking into the rooms of the upper levels. Lines of people filled the space hoping to speak with the Krall. It appeared as if half the city chose to wish the army farewell while the others sought the counsel of the Krall.

Phenmir pressed forward, pushing Tchoyasmen to the side to reach the throne.

The Krall lifted his gaze from a pleading Tchoyasman at the bottom of the steps. Krall Trhet sat hunched as he waited for Phenmir to wade through the sea of Tchoyasmen.

"Away," Krall Trhet commanded the man. "Thane Stolk, I assumed that you would be preparing to march to Kzhek."

"We are," Phenmir stared into the eyeholes of the Krall's mask. "Who is leading your troops to Kzhek?"

"I delegated the military command to my Thane of Endowment, Kollra Holmn."

The name sounded familiar, but he could not remember which one she was. He had met too many Thanes as of late to remember them all.

"Where is she? Has she mustered the troops?"

"She set a base in the financial sector of the city."

"Thank you, Your Grace. May your god be with you during our absence."

The Krall nodded and beckoned the next citizen forward. The monarch was compliant, yet Phenmir felt that the old Krall held something back, some inner inhibition that Phenmir could not identify. His directness left no room for conversation, as if the march to Kzhek was a distant event beyond his concerns.

Phenmir was relieved to find armed Tchoyasmen filling the western district. Many stood at attention, while the others sharpened blades and adjusted their armament before joining their allies. Several sparred with one another while they waited.

He glanced beyond the lines of troops and noticed the blue Tchoyas banner bearing the insignia of the amphibious putle, hanging on the left side of a worn building of ash-gray stone and chipped brick. If this was not the base of their operations, he would be lost searching for a second option.

He walked through the battered door.

Numerous sheets and fashioned cloth piles for pillows were scattered throughout the room to serve as a barrack similar to the one in which he had spent the night. Four individuals sat around a triangular table, engaged in discussion.

A scribe held a wet quill. The other three people were recognizable as Thanes, upon further inspection of their mask designs. Each Thane wore a mark of nobility by having some part of their mask made into silver.

The elderly man on the left wore the face of a bearded goat with silver horns, while the woman in the middle bore a mask with arched eyebrows and silver, smiling lips. The final Thane was a stout woman. Fiery eyes stared at Phenmir through the eye slits of a beast's face. Her mask bore sharp silver teeth through an open mouth, though hers remained closed.

"The Chuss commander, if I'm not mistaken," said the woman in the middle. Her voice was delicate and smooth.

"Correct," Phenmir said as he approached. "I came to speak with Thane Holmn of the Canton of Endowment."

"That would be me," said the beast-faced Thane. *She was the one in our first meeting that Colrig identified as an early member of the Harmony Allegiant.* He felt reassured to be with someone with deep Allegiant ties.

"Do you have a moment to discuss the march to Kzhek?"

"We were discussing that very subject." She motioned to an open seat.

Phenmir sat, nodding to her and the other Thanes.

"The gentleman is Thane Lehket of the Canton of Veneration." Thane Holmn pointed to the goat masked Thane. "We could all use a moral guide in the coming days, right Chussman?" She turned to the Thane with silver lips. "This is Thane Trhet. I suppose you recognize her surname. She is the Krall's eldest granddaughter and presides over the Canton of Progress, helping us navigate through an ever-evolving political climate."

"Pleasure to make your acquaintance." Phenmir shifted. "Tell me about the Tchoyas militia. Will they be ready in time?"

"Yes. Didn't you see them outside? These soldiers have been training for over a year."

"A year?"

"Yes, haven't your soldiers been doing the same?"

"Colrig and had many Chussmen trained."

"And he has handed his trainees to you for command?"

"Yes."

She took a moment to reply. "You will do great things, Chussman. The gods are on our side."

Phenmir nodded. "Will I see you on the front then, Thane Holmn?"

"Is that it, Chussman? A greeting?"

"I have to make my soldiers look as prepared as yours," he said.

***

Phenmir took a moment to catch his breath after jogging to the Chuss barracks.

Side by side, Chussmen, Sleffmen, and Tchoyasmen prepared to march upon his command. Melancholy brushed through him. He wanted to appreciate the unity, but the cause of their gathering soured the kinship of it.

He brushed through the crowd to reach the front lines as they faced an iron gate three streets wide on the city's edge. Once beyond, they would be en route to war.

"Commander Port! What stunning armor!" Port turned and held an iron helm in the pit of his right arm, complimented by the mail beneath his yellow tunic.

Port cringed at the title of 'commander.' Without Colrig, someone had to take the mantle. "Likewise, Thane Stolk." Port studied Phenmir's garb. "Where is your heavy armor? Do you mean to view the battle from afar? I don't mean to judge. That is a wise strategy. Conserve the commander!"

"I will not cower while the people of my Court offer their lives. I will be among the ranks."

"As I expected." Port waved for him to follow to an armorer's stand.

The armorer handed Phenmir his chain mail. He placed it over his head and turned to the troops as he reached for the next piece.

Each soldier wore leather armor.

"What is this? Where is their protection? These men will fall to any strike."

"The leather is quite formidable. Did you not see your men donning their leathers in your camp?" Port said.

"I haven't seen my troops since before sunrise. I had one of my officers gather them while I checked on the Sleffmen and Tchoyasmen."

"They saved the tougher armor for high officers and noblemen such as yourself, Thane Stolk."

"If I deserve greater protection, then the troops are that much more entitled to finer materials."

"We had neither time nor resources for so many," said the armorer. "Sit while I secure your boots." Phenmir complied. "Do you expect us to smith hundreds of full suits of armor with a few days' notice? Your Sleff-man leader may have spent years training and recruiting, but he should have thought of stockpiling armor beforehand. We were fortunate to have enough weapons, though many of them were left with woodmen's axes and farming equipment."

Phenmir noticed garden forks and tree knives among the weaponry of the back lines.

"Have you finished reading *The Strategist's Dilemma*?" asked Port.

Where did I put that book? "Most of it, but I've had little time for study since our arrival in Fayis. Why... how did you know I was reading it?"

"Colrig wanted us to read it. Near the end, he writes of battle positions and the role of the commanders. A trooper's goal is to pursue victory in conflict, a strategist's is to win the war. Frontmen will perish. That is the price to pay for our means to an end. If we send you deep among the troops, you could fall and forfeit your preparation and knowledge. Coals burn to fuel the fire. It is the reality of warfare. "

"What of Lord Detti's statements of equality between commander and trooper?" Phenmir replied, trying to avoid an argument while still resolving his concerns.

"There is no right or wrong in war, only the least destructive option. There is value in all soldiers. A captain must understand that and act accordingly to share the same spirit as his troops. Now, this does not mean he shares the same responsibilities. A captain is entrusted with the role of logical warfare, while the physical portion is left to the trooper. Adjusting their roles by placing a captain on the vanguard risks the entire plot, should he fall to a sword, turning it all to senseless violence."

"Port, I appreciate you more by the minute," replied Phenmir. The Sleffman was wise, yet Phenmir could not help but feel underprepared. He was the high Chuss advisor, Thane of the Allegiant. Colrig did not yet expect him to be a general. *This is only the beginning.*

"How are we going to enter the city?" asked Port. "Do you have a formation in mind?"

"Colrig told me to lead a lunar crest formation. Without him here, it remains our tentative plan. He wants us to meet the protesting crowd and draw them outward and away from the presumed area of destruction. This is no siege, nor is it a use of blunt force. If violence is kept out of the confrontation, all the better for both parties, though I doubt it will end so peacefully. Once inside, we can work outward to reach the Zhaes nobility."

The armorer adjusted the Port's mail as it fell across his shoulders. Phemir looked over the crowd. Some avoided his gaze, but many smiled confidently in his direction. *Will they continue to view me positively after they take their first loss? Their second?*

A horn sounded.

Atop the tower gates stood a heavily armored woman; the sun shining from the silver teeth of her mask.

"Sleffmen! Clussmen! Tchoyasmen! Let us join our allies in the harvesting capital of Facet to liberate them from the vice of harvesting!" A rambunctious choir of chants erupted from the militia. "Up with the gates!"

Aged steel cogs turned to raise the gate like titans of old.

"To Kzhek!"

CHAPTER TWENTY-THREE

WISHES OF THE OWL

"I would argue that we are safer here, Caser," remarked Fheo as Aerhee searched their chamber for means of escape. The Krall provided an accommodating space for them, but Aerhee refused to be held while conflict ravaged her homeland.

"Safety is not my concern. Kzhek is."

"Do you think that we will be emancipated once this conflict ends?"

"Is that what besets you, Fheo? Your comfort and freedom? An army composed of three Courts is heading to our city to be met with combustibles, Gorgers, and Zhaes troops. People will die on both sides. Each lost life is a waste because of a dam of pride."

"You came here and gave it your best. Is that not enough? Excuse me, Caser, but what else did you think you could do?"

Aerhee spun toward him, breath catching. "I have failed our Court. I left to mend a tearing seam and only aggravated the conflict."

"They were going to charge into the city regardless of your intervention." He approached the table and set his palms out on the surface across from her. "Self-deprecation will lead you nowhere."

"Just because you are a Zhaeswoman does not mean that you need to be perfect in every moment. Isn't that what we live for? To improve? Keep complaining if you want, but you sound as prideful as a Priesswoman. Remember which Court you represent. We may have lost this battle, but don't lose yourself. If you can't take care of yourself, things will only become worse."

"Now you sound like your Ideal is more aligned with a Chussman's." She smiled at him.

"Care beats pride," he returned.

"Thank you, Fheo." She sighed. "I need to speak with Krall Trhet."

A boy, not any man, had guided her rationality. Would Fheo gain appreciation from this exchange, or would he let the success of his persuasion inflate his ego?

⁂

Hours, though she didn't know how many, had passed since their last meal, and the light from the window had gradually faded to a darker blue.

A knock rattled their door and Aerhee set down the notes she'd been working on.

"Stand back," commanded a voice from the other side. From the voice's resonance, she figured that the door was fashioned from a frail wood, like those used in most modern designs. One of humankind's greatest weaknesses is substituting reliability for comfort. Breaking it would solve little, for she knew that at least one guard always stood to watch on the other side. If she escaped, it would be another way.

A Tchoyas guard opened the door and was followed by another in identical armament, as well as a woman with their evening meal.

"Excess seasoning has been withheld as requested to suit your Zhaes customs." She set the dishes on their table. One guard placed a pitcher of water in the center of the table near their long-emptied glasses. The woman turned to exit without addressing the prisoners further.

"Pardon me, Tchoyaswoman," said Aerhee.

"Step back, Zhaeswoman," said the guard to the woman's left.

"I have a request," Aerhee said.

"Speak," uttered the woman.

"Might I speak with Krall Trhet?"

"Unlikely."

"I just want to speak with him. With his soldiers marching to my Court, he might be interested in what I have to say."

"I'll relay the message." The Tchoyaswoman waved for the guards to leave. She followed behind and shut the door, locking the two bolts.

"Surely you do not wish to sell the Zhaes secrets to the Tchoyasmen?" plead Fheo. "You said enough to be banished from your office within the Kzhek heights!"

"I will tell him nothing of the sort. I know how to control a conversation. If our Court is to survive, we must recognize that deception is the key to victory."

❦

The familiar knock of a guard rattled the door in its frame. A day had passed since her request to speak with the Krall. The door swung open and the old owl stood on the other side.

"Thank you, Your Grace, for coming," Aerhee said.

"What did you wish to say, Caser Kleeh?" Krall Trhet stood just beyond the doorway, not showing any intention of staying and to talk.

"You told me the other day that you wanted to speak with me. You told me 'Perhaps this war does not need to begin after a single engagement in Kzhek.' Am I mistaken?"

Krall Trhet dismissed his two guards to rest near the doorway, though did not send them away. "You are correct."

Aerhee pulled a chair from the table. "What were you alluding to?"

"You are wise, Caser." The Krall sat with a nod. "You know that this attack will only inspire further violence."

"Are you suggesting that you do not agree with the Sleffmen and Chussmen?"

He tilted his head like an owl. "This is about more than just agreeing or disagreeing. I believe there is a way to diffuse this unrest."

"And what might that be?"

"I believe in the basis of their cause, however, Facet is not *yet* prepared to eliminate harvesting. True, that would please me, but I do not wish for your Court to collapse because of your reliance upon the Endowed. Harvesting could be dissolved, but that would take time. We need to approach this conflict through other means."

"Why are you saying this now? Why didn't you say this before the others left?"

"My Thanes think little of me. Sometimes I feel like I am no more than a figurehead. All they see is an old man that cannot raise a voice as loud as theirs. Between you and me, I think we can approach this in a new way."

"I am glad to see that neither of us wants to resort to violence."

"Are you sure your Thanes feel the same way?"

"I tried to persuade them to hold back," she grumbled. "Why do you think I ran to your Court in hopes of another solution?"

"My Thanes are souring hopes of peace alongside the Sleffmen and Chussmen, but *I* would be willing to speak to your Thanes to discuss another approach to peace. Without some of my Thanes away at war, my voice will have more sway."

"You want to reestablish your authority by meeting with the Thanes of my Court."

"Perhaps that is a promising start."

"So you want to side with the Zhaesmen?"she asked.

"I would not say that. It seems like you do not wish to side with them. Why else would you have come here? There are more than two sides to this conflict. Even the rebels do not all share the same goal. Some strive for liberation, while others fight for revenge."

"Why didn't you stop them before they left? Just look at all the resources *your* Court has spent in this fight."

"As I said, I did not have the power to stop them. Their momentum was building for years. I did not know this revolution was rising until the Sleffmen messengers came. I would have never suspected that some of my Thanes had pledged their allegiance to something other than our Court."

Aerhee stared through the eye slits of the owl's face. Krall Trhet was an enigma. His intentions were vague and suggestive, yet they did not reveal enough for her to grasp. He could not tell if he was trying to manipulate her or if he was speaking sincerely. "Then use me to help reestablish your control before Facet destroys itself."

"How would you hope to accomplish that?"

"Send an emissary to Zhaes. If you declare that *you* do not condone the acts of the Allegiant, the Zhaes Thanes will be less likely to seek retribution to your Court because of a few destructive extremists. Tell them that you want to discuss alternative means of peace."

"Caser, I may have my disagreements with the Allegiant, but I cannot free you. Your offer is enticing, but I cannot trust you."

"Of course. I do not expect freedom, nor that you would grant it after the conflict ends. All I ask is that you send my scribe Fheo to tell the Zhaes Thanes of your willingness to cooperate."

⠿⠿⠿⠿⠿ ⠿⠿⠿⠿⠿

26 years ago, Court Zhaes, Kzhek (Cl. er. 306)
Year 306 in the Clerical Era

⠿⠿⠿⠿⠿ ⠿⠿⠿⠿⠿

"... In three days," read Faeth from the Patriarchy's message. She had spent days waiting for a messenger. Each passing moment cut deeper. She had given her all to live in Zhaes. No close-minded government or sect of Scholars would deprive her of that.

"Aerhee!" she called.

"Has it arrived?" Aerhee said as she ran in from outside.

"Please close the door when you're out there. The insects here are worse than any in Priess." Faeth's eyes returned to the parchment. Sweat had already creased the side margins. "It will be in three days."

"That is not much longer."

"No, but three weeks without him has been long. How can they treat a family like this? Three weeks without Derlik in the house. I'm surprised we still have enough money to keep ourselves alive."

"It will be alright, Mother."

"You are probably right." Faeth nodded. "Would you like to go into the city?"

"Where? Can we see some ghete? Or to the foreigner's square? The Gruthman there told me he would have another kind of fish for me to try next time!"

Solace Square was the district's official name, but it had adopted the moniker of foreigner's square. It was an area where immigrants gathered to embrace their cultures, free from Zhaes dominance. All of them tried to live as Zhaesmen, but needed a place where they could feel welcome beside others in similar circumstances.

Faeth laughed and blinked away her tears. "You still protest the Zhaes food?" Aerhee nodded with a furrowed brow. "I have been meaning to speak with Thenta. She should still be around the market."

Aerhee ran to retrieve her shoes. "Wear a proper dress, Aerhee!"

Aerhee had adapted well enough to the Zhaes culture, but Faeth still found more acceptance among the foreigners. Thenta and her husband were also Priess-born.

"Why? The foreigners care less than any Zhaesman about how we dress." Aerhee ran out of her room with the right shoe still untied.

"I need to visit the chapel on the way."

"I know."

Faeth fastened her shoes and noticed that her daughter was already waiting at the door.

"Are you coming or do I have to tell the market that you despise their food so much that you would rather eat your own?"

"I do not despise their food. I am only trying to adopt the Zhaes taste."

Aehree shook her head. "If I have to eat like them, I don't think I'll ever be a Zhaeswoman."

The chapel was only a fifteen-minute walk from their home, an easy commute for Faeth. High steeples caught her eyes, but the building itself reached thrice as high as its surrounding structures. It was no monument in comparison to the Cantons, yet it struck viewers with reverence.

Aerhee pulled Faeth's hand forward, trying to run into the chapel.

"Aerhee," whispered Faeth, "please calm yourself. Laeih desires solemnity, regardless of their age."

"At least I'm not as loud as a baby. Laeih should cast all of them to the under realms for how much they cry in the chapel." Faeth suppressed a laugh.

"They will grow out of it soon enough. You too are still a child, Aerhee, but that is your advantage."

"But I know what I'm doing in life and don't cry as much."

"There is nothing wrong with being young. Children are wiser than the most educated scholar."

Aerhee scowled. "How?"

"They know how to live life joyfully and treat others well, never knowing prejudice. Children are pure and the gods can only work through pure people. Children are the most desirable crop in the plains of the gods."

Aerhee stared ahead.

Two robed figures stood at the chapel doors with bronze hems on their gray robes. Each one reached out the doors with acquiescence. Faeth was a priestess and was beginning to build a reputation in the more religious circles in Zhaes.

As they entered, Aerhee looked up at the bronze statue in the center of the chapel. Faeth realized Aerhee had never seen a depiction of Laeih. She led Aerhee to her first glimpse of their god.

The effigy was cast in Zhaes bronze with veins of crystal whose shade was reminiscent of storm clouds. The figure stood with the posture of a Zhaes nobleman, shoulders back and chin lifted upward, and wore similar robes to the priests in front of the chapel. His head was adorned with a helm like those in knights' tales, but it had a large cone on the apex that extended and lifted the hood of his robes an additional head's length. Elbows were raised slightly outward from the body, leading to a large tome tucked into the left arm and an orb upraised in the left palm.

Aerhee pulled on her elbow, but Faeth shook her head with pursed lips.

Faeth then retrieved a copy of *The Tome of Measure*. She had taken her to worship in smaller chapels, ones that permitted speaking and conversing as it pleased the guests, but this one was revered more as a temple.

Faeth ascended a short staircase up to a dark podium on the statue's right side. She whispered for Aerhee to wait with the crowd. Reluctant to join them, Aerhee spaced herself behind the people and leaned against a bare section of the gray wall.

The congregation collected themselves near the podium. Faeth opened the book and began her sermon, hoping that Aerhee could now see that Zhaes culture was more than culinary styles. Zhaes culture was piety. Zhaes culture was servitude and obedience.

❧❧❧❧❧ ❦❦❦❦❦

The Present
Cl. er. 332

❧❧❧❧❧ ❦❦❦❦❦

"Me? An emissary? I am a mere scribe, not some political messenger!" said Fheo after the Krall left. "You want me to go back to Kzhek while an army of anti-harvesting zealots marches there to attack?"

"Do you have a better suggestion? I would gladly leave, but the Krall refuses anything of the sort. You are more capable than you believe."

"That may be true, but I doubt Thane Gromm likes me."

"That perding kulf does not admire a thing aside from his texts."

"Your language, Caser!"

"I would say that to his face if given the opportunity." She paused. "You know me beyond a Caser, Fheo, and should treat me as a friend."

He looked up with shy hope. "Thank you... Aerhee."

"Thank you for doing more than any other scribe, Fheo."

"Are you complimenting me? Aerhee Kleeh, the Caser with the reputation of a Zhaeswoman harder than the stones of the Gleff?"

"Know how to control your pride. Do not run to join Court Priess now that you have received some appraisal. I would never give you reassurance if you did not deserve it. Perd, now I sound like a Chusswoman. Are you willing to return to Kzhek? I will sign the documents to name you my surrogate during my absence."

"I... I will."

"Look up and tell me with the dignity of a nobleman."

Confidence filled his eyes. "I will."

INTERLUDE III

"Will he be given a trial by the Patriarchy?" asked Yellin.

Bashin stared out the carriage windows, too tired to pay any attention to the fool. He almost laughed as they talked about the Proctor, as if he did not sit bound next to them.

"No," replied Deim. "The case is too simple for a trial. It was treason and murder. If this man is not executed, I will move east and become a Priessman." He turned to Bashin, receiving a nod of confirmation.

At least one of them understands the justice system. There was no reason to question the Proctor's motives. He was a murderer and propagated anti-harvesting motives.

The carriage slowed as they arrived at the Caton of Veneration. Though the Caton was the Court's head of religious practice, law and justice fell under its jurisdiction. For a Zhaesman, there was no difference between holy and temporal laws.

Bashin waved his associates out of the carriage, delegating the prisoner to their care once again. They forced the Proctor out and held him from behind as they approached the Canton.

Bashin shook his head. Now that they were back near the center, the clamor of the rights gave him another headache. The deputies seemed not to think anything of it.

The unrest was aggravating, yet it caught Bashin's curiosity. He had not yet seen the heart of their gathering in the center of the city. *How large can a mob be to withstand the city's attempts at controlling them?*

"Take him in." Bashin shouted. "I will follow soon."

Yellin nodded, but did not look back.

Laeih protect me from my own foolishness. Bashin turned away from the Canton of Veneration and walked towards the tumult of restless dissenters.

Bashin knew that his deputies would not follow him. They had tried to invade his privacy in the past and soon learned the consequences of angering someone who could read minds. Bashin avoided reading them intentionally, but was prone to slipping. He had learned more by reading them than in any conversation. Deim was as sanctimonious as a Zhaes priest and as condescending as a Priessman. Yellin was too dull to understand what those words meant.

The shouts were clearer. He was close.

"Child-eaters!"

"Sick kulfs!"

Endless shouts came from otherwise pious Zhaes rioters. When emotions stir the minds of the weak, their inner beasts take control.

Bashin stepped closer, though remained in the shadows.

He almost forgot to breathe as he beheld the dilapidated central square. The Canton of Endowment was a pile of collapsed walls and pillars. Other surrounding buildings had shattered windows and bricks falling from their corners. The rioters were maggots feasting upon a festering wound.

"Get out of here, lawman!"

Bashin turned to his side to see a group approaching him.

"Perd you–" a woman placed her hand on the shouting rioter's shoulder.

"Stop." she told him. "You'll only make things worse.

"They should have learned the consequences of trying to control us by now," said the rioter. "Look how he's dressed! He must be a Feelman inquisitor!"

"Child eater!" a rioter beside him shouted.

"Back off," the woman said. She stepped towards Bashin, but remained close to the other. "Just leave. You're going to get yourself hurt."

Some of them seem to have motives other than violence. "What if I want to stay?"

The group of rioters snickered.

"This isn't for you," said the woman.

"Why not?" asked Bashin.

"You want to join?"

Bashin shrugged. "What do you want to accomplish here? How do you expect to change Court law by throwing a fit?"

"What do *you* wish to gain here?" one of the rioters asked. "Are you hoping to feed some sick desire of yours by patronizing us?"

What am I doing? Is there any harm in hearing what they have to say? I am a part of the harvesting machine. I see how it functions."

The rioter continued. "Give it a couple of years and the Chussmen and Tchoyasmen will have adult Endowers. By then, you will see how obsolete harvesting is. It is nothing else besides a bureaucratic excuse for placing people in power even higher. Impatient and selfish. The Court worships you now, but you will be just as worthless as any of us."

His arguments were simple, mere repetitions of every rioter's claim. Still, the words stirred his thoughts, agitating doubts that he had hidden for so long.

Bashin nodded. "I respect your conviction."

"No argument?" one of the other rioters said.

The head of their group ignored him and stepped forward to offer Bashin the Zhaes salute.

"Whole is the Holy, Zhaesman." He returned the salute. "May Laeih help us all find a light to guide us forward."

⁕⁕⁕⁕⁕ ⁕⁕⁕⁕⁕

"Where have you been?" Yellin stood from the steps of the staircase on the main floor of the Canton of Veneration as Bashin entered.

"Where is the Proctor?"

"In a cell, we will deal with him tomorrow," replied Yellin. "Thane Lettre left hours ago. The Proctor will face his final judgment in the morning."

"Which is only a couple of hours away!" complained Deim. "I fell asleep while we waited for you."

"You should have left. I'm not not your mother. I suppose we have finished our work."

Yellin shook his head as he passed Bashin, waving for Deim to follow.

Bashin turned to sit on the staircase. Footsteps echoed in the distance, but there was no one in sight. He hung his head, taking in a deep breath, then laying back on the stairs. The stone ridges were uncomfortable, but not unbearable. It was still a relief to take a moment of release.

If dissenters are victorious, what would become of me? Would I be punished for the dictates of the Court to make me an infallible interrogator? Am I forced to plead the cause of harvesting because of my Court? Because of what I have been told? Because of what I am?

The Canton remained silent while the city grew with sonorous terror and a city of bronze falling to discord.

CHAPTER TWENTY-FOUR

POLITICAL INTIMACY

"The most popular Gruthman in Zhaes," said Thane Leisa.

Yetrik and Semi sat down on a gray divan across from the desk in her study.

Yetrik laughed. "I don't think I have captured that much attention."

"Say what you will, but Royss has taken a liking to you, as I am sure others have. Semi and I had some time to get to know each other while you were helping Royss. What a remarkable girl. I would advise you to note that." She winked at him. His cheeks grew warm.

"She has been formidable." He knew his word choice was wrong the moment he spoke.

"She told me about your journey." Yetrik and Semi shared a glance. "I understand that she is uneasy, considering the action that we must take to dissolve these rebellions." Thane Leisa brushed her finger alongside a quill on her desk, twirling it in the inkwell.

"I am sure we can resolve our–her concerns alone, though I wish no disrespect, Thane Leisa." Yetrik said as Thane Leisa raised an eyebrow.

"No offense taken," said Thane Leiss. "I must have confused you. I do not want to impede, only to offer comfort during your stay. As a Thane of Diplomacy, I am inclined to treat our foreign guests with the best possible care, regardless of the turmoil."

"Thank you for the offer." He rubbed the hem of his shirt between his fingers. "I don't want to sound ungrateful, but why are you doing this for us?"

Thane Leisa smirked. "If you want me to be blunt, we need your Court to commit to our cause."

"But neither of us are Thanes," said Yetrik.

"I've spoken with the other Thanes about you. Why do you think Royss would send you two to me, the Thane of Diplomacy? We need two to persuade Court Gruth to pledge loyalty to preserve the state of our Courts."

"Surely a carrier raven's letter would be sufficient, if notarized by a Canton."

"Do you wish to explain this all in a letter? What if they believe that Zhaes has already been overtaken by dissenters? What if the raven was intercepted? There are too many risks. You two have been in our Court during the worst of this insurrection. You two can make a much better argument than any of us."

But what about our doubts? Yetrik thought, but feigned confidence. "So you want us to return to Gruth to try to convince our nobility to commit to your cause? You really think we have that much influence?"

"You have proved your worth here, but we only need one of you to return. Royss has plans for you here in Kzhek. Semi may have questions, but those will be resolved if she works with her people. It is difficult to fight a war away from your closest allies. She is going to help us fight by serving as a diplomat back in her home Court."